D0283841

THE
FALL OF
JERUSALEM

Omega Books
100 N. Peachtree Pkwy.
Peachtree City, GA 30269
487-3977

Other Books in the Series
The Dawning
The Exiles

BOOK III
THE PEOPLE OF THE COVENANT

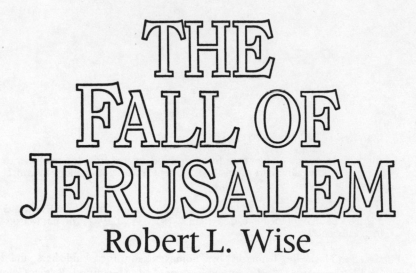

THE FALL OF JERUSALEM

Robert L. Wise

A JANET THOMA BOOK

THOMAS NELSON PUBLISHERS
Nashville • Atlanta • London • Vancouver

To
the memory
of my mother,
a woman
of the covenant

Copyright © 1994 by Robert L. Wise

All rights reserved. Written permission must be secured from the publisher to use or reproduce any part of this book, except for brief quotations in critical reviews or articles.

Unless otherwise noted, all Scripture quotations are from the NEW KING JAMES VERSION of the Bible. Copyright © 1979, 1980, 1982, Thomas Nelson, Inc., Publishers.

Published in Nashville, Tennessee, by Thomas Nelson, Inc., Publishers, and distributed in Canada by Word Communications, Ltd., Richmond, British Columbia, and in the United Kingdom by Word (UK), Ltd., Milton Keynes, England.

Library of Congress Cataloging-in-Publication Data

Wise, Robert L.
    The fall of Jerusalem / by Robert L. Wise.
        p.   cm.—(The People of the covenant ; bk. 3)
    ISBN 0-8407-3161-2
    1. Church history—Primitive and early church, ca. 30–600—Fiction.
I. Title.   II. Series: Wise, Robert L. People of the covenant ; bk. 3.
PS3573.I797R4   1994
813'.54—dc20   93–30653
                                                        CIP

Printed in the United States of America

1 2 3 4 5 6 — 99 98 97 96 95 94

Contents

PART ONE
1

PART TWO
95

PART THREE
159

Acknowledgments

THE FIRST two books in the *The People of the Covenant* series, *The Dawning* and *The Exiles*, contain many Hebrew names and phrases to reflect the provincial setting of the early decades of the first century. However, by the time of the destruction of the Temple, the process of gentilization had deeply affected life in Israel. Consequently, this book uses fewer Hebrew proper names and idioms to convey the changing situation.

The only fundamental sources recounting the final days of the Holy City and the nation of Israel are *The Antiquities of the Jews* and *Wars of the Jews*, Flavius Josephus's great contribution to the history of the ancient world. His personal story, the siege and fall of Jotapata, and the story of Simon Ben Giora are taken from these pages.

Because Josephus chronicled the fall of the Temple on the tenth of Av, that date has been used throughout the book.

The account of Yochanon Ben Zakkai's escape from the dying city and his start of Rabbinic Judaism in Yevnah is corroborated by Paul Johnson's *A History of the Jews* and Chaim Potok's *Wanderings*.

The story of the Ben Aaron family is fictitious, but is inspired by the account of the healing of the daughter of Jarius. However, as is true of the first two books of *The People of the Covenant* series, historic details are accurate and faithful to the period.

With Gratitude

As has been true of the entire series, I am grateful for the support, comment, and editing of my friend and colleague Janet Thoma. Her wisdom remains the editor's finest tool.

I thank my secretary Kristin Jacobs for her work on this volume, as well as on the two preceding works in the series. She burned the midnight oil in order to produce this manuscript.

Finally, I thank the staff and publishers of Thomas Nelson for their confidence in me and this project. Their conviction that fiction can tell the truest story is a credit to their industry.

Robert L. Wise
PENTECOST 1993

PART ONE

A.D. 67

"For nation will rise against nation,
and kingdom against kingdom.
And there will be famines, pestilences,
and earthquakes in various places.
All these are the beginning of sorrows."

Matthew 24:7-8

I

JUDEA, WINTER A.D. 67

Even the bright light of morning did not dispel the shadows from the bends of the winding streets and the corners of the alleys of the Holy City. The street of the gold merchants was unusually wide for the lower city, but the high walls and sheer sides of the two- and three-story dwellings shut out the sunlight in many places. Shadowy shapes lurked in the black recesses of the steep stairwells that disappeared in the opaque unknown far above. A stranger did well to approach each blind turn in Jerusalem with considerable caution

Walking into one of the narrows, the unsuspecting Greek found he could avoid the irritating sting of the pungent smell that burned his nostrils and eyes only by covering his face. The scent of acid eating away the dross around gold and other metals lingered and settled beneath the dark overhangs. Even the momentary blurring of his vision added to his nervousness. The lanky visitor already felt conspicuous and somewhat disoriented by the unfamiliarity of the back streets of Jerusalem. The stranger blinked his eyes and peered down the stone-paved street. Through a break in the walls he could see the high south wall that separated the lower and upper parts of the Holy City. The street abruptly ended there.

The sojourner walked faster until he was again in a broader, well-lit section of the street, which was lined with jewelry shops and the workshops of the artisans.

3

He stopped and looked for some reassuring sign. Immediately merchants emerged from everywhere offering their wares. Some vendors pushed gold bracelets and chains toward his face; others dangled long necklaces before him. Forced to stop, the lone traveler fully heard the intrusive cries of the peddlers for the first time. Trays filled with gold and silver trinkets were thrust in his face. The stranger clutched at his leather money pouch while the swarm pressed forward like bees around a honeycomb. His finely woven tunic clearly separated him from the average Jewish citizens, thus marking him as a potential customer. The clear distinction was an unfortunate disadvantage in his desire for anonymity.

"Gold coins," an old man in a long, black silk robe called out to the tall stranger. "Each imprint marks our victory and overthrow of the Roman oppressors. Your children's children will treasure such a gift!"

The Greek did not acknowledge the vendor. A sudden cold blast caught his white tunic, beating it against the side of the narrow, wooden case he carried at his side. Walking with decisive intent, the stranger didn't give the merchant so much as a glance.

"Our soldiers accomplished what you Greeks couldn't!" The salesman sneered at the silent rebuff, then spit on the street. "You still kiss the feet of the Roman pigs. We're free!"

The narrowing street forced the wayfarer to walk close to the low, single-story stucco shops that crowded the street and claimed every bit of space. The dull brown and gray walls were accented by occasional red and green tents. The awning-covered pavilions filled the empty spaces between the shops. Traffic became congested as people formed a bottle-neck in the passageway. The press of the crowd caused apprehension. People withdrew from each other as if they feared any form of contact. Suspicion and irritation hung in the air, but these did not deter the sojourner's progress.

When the street opened again, the stranger moved quickly, carefully reading the few signs above the doors. The street of the jewelry merchants was well known. Pilgrims who came to make sacrifices at the Temple always found their way through the Tyropoeon Valley to search for the special gold and silver creations that could only be found in this part of the Holy City.

About seven hundred feet ahead he saw the high wall and knew he was running out of options.

"The finest topaz in the entire jewelry market." A small, dark man in an expensive linen robe stepped out of the shadows and blocked the traveler's path. "Buy now. The prices rise as our people prosper with their new freedom." He held a ring up, letting it sparkle in the afternoon sunlight. "Come in and warm yourself by our fire."

"I seek a certain family," the Greek spoke firmly. "The family Ben Aaron."

"Hmph!" The merchant shrugged. "Our workmanship is as good as theirs. Why go further?"

"I understand they are the best in Jerusalem," the man pressed.

"All in the eye of the beholder." The merchant lowered the ring and studied his potential customer carefully. A small leather headband held the traveler's closely cropped, graying hair to his head, and his white tunic was worn in the draped style of the Athenians. Appearing to be around the age of forty, he had the demeanor of a world traveler with intelligent and unrelenting eyes. Not an easy sale. "A special price today for a Greek," the vendor suggested.

The slight shake of the stranger's head ended any further discussion.

"Over there." The merchant pointed to the end of the street. "The last shop. Just beneath the wall. But my prices are better!"

"Thank you," the Greek said pressing on without

looking back. The wooden case swung easily at his side. His short hair was combed forward on his forehead, framing clean-cut, defined features. The man's strong, square jaw and his flawless olive skin added to his rugged handsomeness. Creases and wrinkles had started their work around his eyes and cheeks. His arms had the well-defined muscles of an athlete, but his hands and fingers were long, delicate, and slender.

At the end of the street he saw the old one-story building sitting alone in the shadow of the great wall. Little distinguished the brown stucco jewelry shop except the Hebrew sign that read *Family Ben Aaron*. Broad canvas flaps comprised a front door covering. A mazusseh, a religious ornament containing a Scripture verse, was attached near the top of the door post. Even though the sun shined overhead, the small front window was boarded shut from the inside.

The stranger could see the entry was similarly boarded shut from within. He stood and frowned at the situation before knocking on the barricade behind the faded canvas strips. Only after he began pounding did someone respond.

"We're closed," a gruff voice barked. The boarded window cracked open slightly.

"I'm not a customer," the traveler spoke loudly in Greek. "I seek the Ben Aaron family."

Wood scraped against stucco as the window covering dropped further. "We're not making any special orders," the unseen man answered in bad Greek. "There are others . . . down the street . . . who can help you."

The stranger peered into the opening but could see nothing. "I don't—"

"Closed!" The head of a swarthy Arab popped up in the window. His skin was so dark it looked as if it had been baked in the desert heat too long. Even though his face was deeply wrinkled, there was not one gray strand in the Arab's mass of uncombed, untamed black hair. "Good-bye!"

"No," the Greek stuck his hand in the opening to keep the window from being closed. "My business is personal," he answered in Hebrew. "I seek Mariam Ben Aaron."

"Who?" The Arab squinted one eye until it was nearly closed while turning the other suspiciously toward the stranger. He leaned forward, straining to get as far out the window as possible. "What do you know of Mariam?"

"I've come a very long way," the stranger spoke harshly, "and I'll not be turned aside. I'm prepared to beat on this door until it falls down."

The Arab nearly had his head and shoulders through the opening, as he glared at the persistent intruder. "You're a Believer? What's your name?"

"My name is Luke," the Greek stood erect and proud. "Yes, I am a Believer, a Christianios. I came from Antioch in Syria."

"You trade in gems, gold?" The Arab sounded skeptical and unimpressed.

"No, I am a physician." Luke held up the wooden case he carried at his side.

"Doctor!" the Arab gasped. "A healer!"

"Such is my trade."

"I will make you a deal," the Arab spoke slowly and cautiously. "Trade your services for information. Maybe I'll tell you about Mariam Ben Aaron's whereabouts if you're good at what you do."

"My services?" Luke chuckled. "Freely have I received; freely do I give. Of course, I help any sick person. Offer accepted. Your name?"

Instantly the head disappeared from the window and the wooden barrier at the door began to shake. "Ishmael," he called from within. "I'm Ishmael." Timber bars dropped and the wooden planks fell away, letting light seep into the room.

"Luke, you say?" Ishmael reached out and pulled the Greek past the flaps. "A real student of Hippocrates?" The doctor stood head and shoulders above him. He stealthily felt Luke's expensive and finely woven white tunic.

Luke blinked and peered into the dark, musty room with faded cloth strips hanging from the walls. There was no fire and the place was cold. A rancid, nauseating odor rushed up his nose and he coughed. Years before the fabric decorations might have provided cheerful color, but time and sunlight had bleached the hangings into dingy rags. A large wooden display table immediately in front of the doctor was empty. A small table and several chairs in the corner looked dusty. As his eyes adjusted to the darkness, Luke recognized the shape of a man covered by a blanket, lying motionless on a cot in the farthest corner.

"How do you know the Ben Aarons?" the Arab circled Luke.

"The man?" Luke pointed to the blanket. "He is your concern?"

The Arab nodded his head vigorously. "He's hurt bad. He's dying."

"Who are you?" Luke suddenly took control of the situation. "Why are you here?"

"Ishmael," he repeated again but added no further definition. "The man is my best friend. He's dying."

"Who is he?"

"Yochanan Ben Zakkai." Ishmael uncovered the man's head.

Luke walked quickly to the cot and turned the blankets back. "I see." The doctor put his hand on the man's forehead and set the wooden case by the side of the bed. "He's burning up!"

"Very bad," Ishmael shook his head and wrung his hands.

Luke turned Yochanan Ben Zakkai over on his back. A large black patch covered one eye and a nasty scar ran down his pale, sunken cheek. His white hair and beard were matted and tangled. Tied over his chest was a large, blood-soaked bandage that Luke carefully peeled away. A sickening smell rushed into his nose. Underneath, two gaping holes split the man's chest open. The jagged wounds were fiery red and festering.

"He's been stabbed!"

"Twice," the Arab replied.

Luke immediately opened the wooden box and found a long metal probe. "I always carry my case with me."

"Ben Zakkai was recovering from an attack several months ago and was nearly well when the Zealots caught us outside this building last week. I pulled him in here and haven't moved him since."

"I must have hot water for compresses," Luke spoke rapidly. "Make all haste. Then I want you to go to the market and buy herbs. I will tell you the variety later, but get the fire going now."

The Arab said nothing as he immediately began throwing wood in the corner fireplace. He lugged a large clay jug over to a metal rod that was hanging over the hearth. Once the flames leaped up, he poured water into the jug.

"How did you escape?" Luke suddenly broke the silence. "He's been stabbed twice and you're not scratched. Interesting."

"I am a worthless dog of the desert," Ishmael spoke flatly. "Yochanan Ben Zakkai is a very important man. He sits on the Great Sanhedrin and is a respected teacher. Yochanan is a man of power. And besides," the Arab said as an afterthought, "I killed all the attackers."

"All?"

"All five." Ishmael did not look up as he put more wood on the fire.

Luke quietly continued to probe the wounds, squeezing and cleaning them, and then poured a dark bronze-colored liquid over the wounds. "Quickly," he called to Ishmael. "Bring me a cloth! I have found the problem."

As the Arab rushed across the room, Luke stuck two fingers in Ben Zakkai's chest. The old man's body stiffened and he groaned deeply. Luke jerked straight up, pulling out a long metal sliver. Blood went in every direction, but he grabbed the cloth from Ishmael and plunged it in the wound.

"Get to the market," Luke commanded. "Buy oil of eucalyptus and salt. Bring me a vase full of camphor and root of ginger. Get ginseng for a hot drink, if possible. You must also find saffron ointment. Run quickly! And if you know how, pray!"

The doctor pushed the cloth deeper by pressing his palm inward, but the unceasing flow of blood soon drenched the cloth and ran over the physician's fingers. The old man's lips began turning white and his face lost any lingering color. His fingernails also started losing their color.

Luke bit his lip and pressed harder. Sweat began to gather on his forehead as the whole side of his own white tunic turned crimson. He dropped his head and closed his eyes. "O Lord, I can do nothing. I need *your* hands to touch this poor man." Luke's words became inaudible as he kept praying the same sentence over and over. "Please touch this man."

The sun had long since disappeared when Ishmael lit the olive oil lamps around the jewelry shop. The smell of spices boiling over the fireplace dispelled the stale aroma of the long-closed building. A cold, invigorating breeze drifted in the little window, clearing any smoke escaping the chimney. Yochanan Ben Zakkai breathed much easier, and the clean compresses were only slightly stained with blood.

"You saved him." Ishmael held up his clasped hands. The Arab sat down at the little table across from the doctor. "I didn't think such was possible." Ishmael pushed a plate of fruit toward Luke. "You have more than kept your part of the bargain."

"No." The physician shook his head. "I did nothing but remove a piece of a knife. Only the hand of God accomplished what happened in the last few hours."

The Arab squinted and cocked his head sideways, taking full measure of the stranger. "You have healing hands," he concluded. "Like Mariam."

"Mariam Ben Aaron?" The doctor brightened. "Yes, so I hear, but who is Yochanan Ben Zakkai?" Luke began eating an orange.

"The best man I ever knew," the Arab relaxed and reached for a piece of fruit. "The smartest, too."

"You've known him long?"

"Many years." Ishmael rolled his eyes and smiled wickedly. "We've traveled the trade routes and worked the gem sellers for decades. He saved my life in the deserts of Saudi Arabia. In a world of thieves and liars, he's the most honest and righteous man I'll ever know." Ishmael leaned across the table. "We're half-brothers through our father Abraham. He's a son of Isaac and I come from the first Ishmael.

"A Believer? A Christianios?"

"Oh no!" The Arab shook his head vigorously. "Never! Ben Zakkai is a true son of Abraham. He would never forsake the Temple or the ancient ways. He is one of the most respected Pharisees in the city. Everyone on the Great Sanhedrin seeks the opinion of Yochanan Ben Zakkai."

"Why is he here in the jewelry store of the Ben Aarons?"

"Oh," the Arab quickly looked away and sounded suddenly distant, "they have been in business together for years. When the rest of the family went to Rome, Yochanan managed the place. He is a master craftsman himself."

"And you know when the family will return?" Luke pressed. Ishmael leaned back into the shadows and his eyes disappeared in the blackness.

"Brother Jarius will never come back," the Arab looked soberly at the table. "Nor will Mariam's husband, Philip, come again. Romans killed them. Very recently we received a communique telling us of their fate. Mariam and her youngest son, Zeda, are on their way back."

"How soon?" the doctor asked quickly.

"Only the Almighty can say." Ishmael threw up his hands. "Winter is not a good time to travel. We can only watch the horizon."

Silence, like the darkness, fell between the two men as they ate. Finally the doctor asked, "Why do you continue to stay here?"

"The fools in the markets celebrate and dance about their so-called liberation from Rome but nothing, no one, no place is safe in this land," the Arab clipped in rapid fire. "We are at war with Rome and these crazy Jews are killing each other in the streets! The Zealots would gladly kill my friend if they got the chance again. No one can know how seriously he is injured or his political enemies would seize the moment." The Arab looked at Luke out of the corner of his eye. "We must stay in this shop tonight."

"I have just come from Greece and do not know anyone here," the doctor spoke slowly. "Yes, I would be glad for a place to stay. I know little of what has happened in recent days. Have the Jews really overthrown the Romans?''

"Only for the moment," Ishmael shook his finger in the physician's face. "When they return with many legions, the streets will flow with blood. The Romans will never allow the Jews to get away with the humiliation they caused them."

"Humiliation?" Luke sat back in his chair. "How so?"

"Gessius Florus was the fool who started it." Ishmael hovered over the table, his voice filling with intense emotion. "Florus, Nero's idiotic new procurator, paid no attention to the reason for the riots in Caesarea. Instead of pacifying the people, he came down here and staged a raid on the Temple to force an illegal collection he claimed the Jews owed him. The city exploded! People counterattacked the Romans!"

Ishmael whipped a knife from under the table, stabbing the dagger in the tabletop in front of Luke's hand. The blade quivered ominously as its thud echoed off the walls. "Suddenly Florus attacked Upper Jerusalem!" Ishmael's eyes widened, looking as if they would pop out of his head. "Everywhere swords were swung at the Romans! Even children threw rocks from the roofs. Zealots went crazy killing soldiers and every sympathizer they caught. Finally the high priest's house was burned to the ground and all the records of public indebtedness were destroyed!"

"The Romans lost?" Luke asked incredulously.

Ishmael clapped his hands and shook them in the air. "Gloriously! When Florus tried to escape, his soldiers were cut to pieces. The Zealots stormed Agrippa's Palace as well as the Antonia Fortress. They burned the citadel and humiliated the procurator. More than 3,600 were killed and Florus was lucky to escape alive."

"And so the war began," Luke observed soberly.

"Some devil named Manahem attacked the fortress at Masada and killed every Roman in sight. He redistributed the Romans' weapons to the people and the whole countryside revolted." Ishmael sat back and crossed his arms over his chest, smiling a wicked twisted grin. "Romans bleed just as red as everyone else!"

"So you are free now?"

"No," the Arab said flatly. "And neither are you, Greek. The Sicarii, the worst of the Zealots, assassinate people and roam the streets, killing with no provocation. The political divisions in this land are so great that no one can restore order. Outsiders, like Arabs and Greeks, make excellent targets for the murderers who slide out of the dark corners like adders from their dens. The knife's bite is just as deadly as the fang.'

Luke blinked several times and stared at the Arab. The doctor shook his head as if not quite sure what to say.

"Yes," Ishmael grinned cunningly, "I would suggest you spend the night with us. If not for the sake of your patient, then for your own health."

II

Yosef Ben Mathias walked quickly through the tall columns lining the cloisters that separated the Temple proper from the Antonia Fortress before crossing the large courtyard surrounding the Temple itself. The cold winter winds whistled about him, but the gold-covered buildings still glowed with yellow splendor in the late afternoon sunlight. He turned and shielded his eyes from the dazzling reflections. The smell of incense and burning sacrifices rolled over him. Yosef looked up at the guard posts in the high towers of the Antonia. He smiled knowing that Jews, not Romans, now looked out across the Holy City and down on the place of holy sacrifices.

Yosef was tall and commanding. His face, like a marble statue, was solid and perfectly proportioned; yet dignity, not his unusual handsomeness, was the primary impression always left with people. The gray around his temples blended into his long, black hair, which was reverently covered by his tallith, a prayer shawl worn by the Jewish men. Although a Levite and a priest, Yosef had broad shoulders and a massive back that better fit a warrior. Even Yosef's long, flowing silk robe did not conceal his big, strong arms.

Yosef walked to the back entrance of a compound that was on one side of the Temple. The door was covered entirely with white gold. He banged the knocker several times and a servant opened the door to the high priest's

15

quarters. Inside a dozen men stood around a large table. Yosef nodded reverently to the priests. At the center of the table sat Elezar Ben Simon, who became high priest after his predecessor was slain by the Sicarii. The high priest's ceremonial breastplate with a jewel for each of the twelve tribes was set to one side on a small table beside the white, dome-shaped hat the high priest usually wore.

"Ah, Yosef is here," the high priest spoke over the noise of the group. "We can begin at once. Let us consider the map of Judea." Unusually young for this high office, Elezar spoke with bold authority.

Immediately the rest of the men sat down around the magnificent inlaid mahogany table. The large parchment map was divided into seven sections by heavy dark lines. Elezar pushed the sleeves of his white linen robe up to his elbows. He leaned over the map and pointed with a long, thin stick at Caesarea-by-the-Sea.

"We now have a full report," Elezar spoke confidently. "We know that Nero has dispatched General T. Flavius Vespasian with at least three legions and they will soon land on the coast. Cestus and Florus continue to blame each other for the debacle when they marched on Jerusalem during the Feast of Tabernacles. Their disastrous defeat at Bethoron shocked Rome. The news of five thousand six hundred dead soldiers terrified Nero. Gentlemen, the real war is about to begin!"

"Hurray!" the priests shouted and beat on the table. "Death to the invaders!" echoed across the room.

"We must prepare quickly," a white-haired sage in a brown robe broke in. "Repairs must be made on the walls and the city gates. Time is precious."

"Of course," a younger man in priestly robes agreed. "But I am more concerned that the Zealots are brought under control. I hear terrible rumors about the intentions of this Simon Ben Giora character who is rampaging through the countryside even as we speak."

"Yes, yes." Elezar held up his hand to silence the discussion. "Let us pursue one matter at a time. We must know more about our enemy. I have asked Yosef Ben Mathias to give us a full report on the new Roman general we face. No one is the student of these matters as is Yosef."

Yosef stood slowly, silently collecting his thoughts. His dignified and eloquent manner always added weight to whatever he said, but his demeanor had taken on a ponderous look as if the world rested on his shoulders. "T. Flavius Vespasian and his son, Titus, have been dispatched by Nero himself. Vespasian will soon land at Caesarea with at least three legions. He is Rome's finest general and a man of great courage. He defeated the German tribes. During the reign of Claudius, Vespasian fought more than thirty battles against the tribes of Britannia and returned that island to Roman control. Like an old bulldog, he controlled the western frontiers with brutal force. Vespasian has called his son from Achaia to join him. He brings the fifth and tenth legions with him. Titus is about twenty-nine! He will pass over the Hellespont and travel through Syria. Father and son will rendezvous on the coast, where they will gather auxiliary forces from some of the neighboring kingdoms who have been our enemies. Arabs . . . Agrippa's men will join them."

"How do you know such things?" a white-bearded old man interrupted. He hunched over the table. "This city is abounding with such rumors!"

"Yosef does not deal in gossip, father," Elezar snapped. "His word is impeccable."

"The Romans know me as Flavius Josephus," Yosef spoke directly to his detractor. "I have had a strong foothold in their world. My friends are numerous within the highest circles of Rome itself. Do you question me further?" Yosef stared insolently around the table.

"No, no," rumbled across the group. The old man looked away.

"As I was saying," Yosef began again, "we will face the finest soldiers Rome can throw at us. I believe they will start in Galilee and work their way down to Jerusalem. If we can stop them in the north, the war will be over. We must have our best generals in Galilee."

"Exactly!" the high priest turned to the assembly. "We must have a single front poised to face the onslaught. The people must become a united force."

"And therein lies the flaw," a deep bass voice growled from the opposite side. "As sure as my name is Ananias Ben Masmatheus, we are hopelessly divided!" He rose slowly. Ananias was dark-haired with black eyes that were nearly hidden beneath thick eyebrows. "One faction hates Herod Agrippa while another spies for the old fox. Many of the Pharisees hate us with a passion while our own Sadducees act as if there is no crisis that we can't bribe our way through. Everyone is terrified of the Zealots, yet the war among themselves makes the Romans appear civilized. Our divisions and conflicts will murder us!" Ananias slammed his fist on the table.

"Indeed!" declared a man dressed in the dark street robe of a rich Sadducee. "We should fear Simon Ben Giora as much as any Roman. He and his Zealots kill with the slightest provocation! They are the force to be reckoned with."

"And the crowd that hates us is not small!" the old man with the white beard shouted again. "When Albinas was high priest his arrogance had no bounds. I warned him that we should not kill James the Bishop of this new sect of Believers. Albinas wouldn't listen!"

"Gentlemen, gentlemen," Elezar pleaded. "Please. We sound like the confused rabble in the streets. Unity must begin at this table."

"Unity!" Ananias Ben Masmatheus exploded. "When have the Jews ever been unified? Not since the days of Judas Maccabees have we even pretended to have a single cause. Now we don't even have one religion. The Pharisees quote the Torah and the Essenes run to the desert. The Pious Ones seek reform and this new sect attacks the Temple! Look at us! Sadducees! We hold the priesthood and yet everyone hates us. And this is to say nothing of the suspicions that the country people have about citizens of the city."

"What do you say Yosef Ben Mathias?" Elezar cut off the conversation. "We need your opinion . . . without interruption."

Yosef stood stoically until several moments of complete quiet settled. "We have the capacity to defeat the Romans," he spoke in slow measured tones. "As surely as the Maccabees overthrew Antiochus Epiphanes we have the resources to do so. Our men are more courageous and fierce than anything the Romans have ever seen. However . . ." he stopped and looked hard at each face in front of him. "Two facts will determine the future. First, unless we unite to form a solid front, we will fall. Second, should Galilee be lost, our doom is ensured. I am willing to stake my life on that assessment."

Deafening silence fell over the room.

"What do you propose?" Elezar finally asked.

"Send representatives—and spies—into the camp of the Zealots," Yosef answered. "Contact should be made with Simon Ben Giora. Everything possible must be done to create a unified front. At the same time we must prepare Galilee for battle. In addition to fortifying this city for attack, we need to consolidate with the Pharisees and even this new group many call the Christianios. We need everyone if we are to prevail."

Elezar's white-haired father stared at the floor with a nasty scowl on his face. Ananias Ben Masmatheus pulled at the ends of his beard but said nothing.

"You are exactly right," Elezar broke the hush. "For these reasons I have already divided the country into seven districts." The high priest pushed the map forward. "I am going to appoint commanders and administrators to coordinate and develop each area. Some of you will be asked to take a command. Others will make the contacts Yosef has designated."

Each of the elders of Israel nodded in solemn approval.

"Most importantly, I am appointing you, Yosef, as commander in charge of Galilee. No one is your equal. I believe the future rides on what happens there. Are you prepared for the assignment?"

Yosef sighed deeply and furrowed his brow. "The Holy One must bless," he concluded, "or no man can endure. I can only offer my life."

"Excellent!" the high priest smiled. "The people will be encouraged by your acceptance. Now, our next task is to gain a consensus throughout the city. The Great Sanhedrin must be fully behind us. We need someone who can pull that quarrelsome lot together and only one man can do that job. We must confer with Yochanan Ben Zakkai."

"I've not seen him for at least a week," Ananias stated. "No one has heard from him. He's usually in the portico of the Temple arguing with someone, but even his followers haven't gathered lately."

"Find him immediately and make sure Ben Giora's soldiers don't do him in," Elezar concluded. "He's too important. I think you should talk with him, Yosef. You've always been friends."

"When I leave here I will go to his business."

Elezar nodded his approval. "Now we must access the treasury and count our reserves. Our loss of the financial records and accounts of indebtedness has cost us greatly. Tell us how much we have, Father."

The white-bearded old man hobbled over to a desk and picked up a large scroll. He returned and pushed the map toward Yosef, spreading the scroll over the table. "First, I will tell you of the revenue that we are currently receiving from Temple offerings."

As his dull voice droned on, Yosef pulled the map of

Judea closer to him. He put his finger on Sepphorius and then Gamala, tracing a line from Joppa to Tiberius. For a long time he tapped his finger on the place named Jotapata.

Ishmael sat looking out the window watching for any sign of trouble while Luke carefully observed his patient. "Well, well." Luke sat back in his chair in front of Ben Zakkai's bed. "Late afternoon and my patient finally awakes."

Yochanan turned uncomfortably and blinked. The sinking sunlight fell across his face and directly into his good eye. He tried to block out the glare but the movement made him groan. Ishmael left his lookout at the window to check on Ben Zakkai's condition.

"I trust the last nine days of my instructions and care have not been wasted." Luke folded his arms across his chest and smiled.

"When does it stop hurting?" Yochanan grumbled.

"Consider the alternative." Luke grinned. "You should be glad to feel anything."

The old man rolled over to his side. The black patch over his eye no longer hid the empty socket. A wicked scar ran from just above the eye down the side of his face. His deeply wrinkled face sagged. The grinding wheel of time had etched and pitted his skin. "I seem to have a propensity for knives," he moaned. His cheeks were sunken and pale.

"A little something to drink?" Ishmael asked.

"Thank you, my friend." Ben Zakkai carefully pushed himself up on his elbow. "I would prefer a little water."

"I believe you are much stronger than you were yesterday." Luke studied his patient's color as he talked. "Before long you will be ready to exercise. Then the rest of your recovery will come quickly."

The one-eyed man sat up on the edge of the cot and took a slow sip from the cup Ishmael gave him. His white hair stuck out in all directions. "I am indebted to you," he spoke to Luke. "Yes! I would have died if you had not come. The Holy One of Israel used you to save me for another day. Where are you from?"

"I was born in Antioch in Syria. I studied medicine there."

"Now tell me *why* you came here."

"I am seeking Mariam Ben Aaron." Luke leaned forward in his chair. "She assisted a man named Matthew in writing a scroll that I must read."

"Mariam?" Ben Zakkai raised his eyebrows. "Oh, yes, I know of this writing," his voice betrayed a hint of disgust.

"I wish to talk with her."

"Where did you hear of the scroll?" Yochanan spoke slowly.

"I once traveled with a Jew named Saul from Tarsus. His name in Greek is Paul."

"Saul!" Yochanan exploded and fell on his back. "Not him!"

"You know him?" Luke's eyes widened.

Yochanan shook his head in disbelief. "Do not speak of the man," Yochanan said contemptuously.

"I knew that Paul made many enemies when he called himself Saul," Luke said apologetically. "I thought all those fences had been mended."

"I am not a Believer," Ben Zakkai said forcefully. "I have no sympathy with this unfortunate movement and less for that man who leaves pain in his footprints."

"But how can you be in business with the Ben Aaron family if . . ."

"I am the brother that—" Yochanan stopped abruptly. "I mean, I am bothered by everything these people profess," he said sharply.

"I would not mislead or deceive you," Luke answered.

"I am a Gentile Believer. In fact, I have given my life to understanding this faith."

"Oh no!" Yochanan turned away. "What Mariam and her family do with this new religion is their business," he said sourly. "It has surely cost them dearly enough. I am *not* one who believes that our messiah has come."

Luke studied his patient, searching for the right response. "Your messiah has not come?" the doctor repeated.

"Three things grow here," the one-eyed man scoffed. "Rocks, grapes, and messiahs. We eat grapes for strength to throw rocks at the Romans. But nothing protects us from the new messiahs who appear weekly. They will be the death of us!"

"Of course." Luke smiled mischievously. "There could only be one true messiah."

"And he hasn't come yet!" the old man hissed and sat up again.

"How do you know?" Luke shot back.

"Listen," Ben Zakkai's voice took on a condescending professorial tone. "The true Messiah would defeat the Romans and secure our borders. Like David, he would once again make us invincible. When he truly appears, the world will turn to Israel and come to us seeking our knowledge of God. None of this has happened! Instead a rebellious rabbi came down from the north attacking our leaders and calling for the destruction of the Temple. Save your breath, physician. I've seen too many dead Jews hanging on crosses to believe that one misguided teacher's death could redeem our nation."

"To cross oral swords with Ben Zakkai is verbal suicide." Ishmael snickered. "Stay with your medicines, Doctor. You are arguing with the master of the Torah."

Someone abruptly knocked on the wooden barrier behind the canvas flap. Ishmael pulled out a dagger and dashed to the window. Yochanan's hand automatically covered the wound in his chest and he fell back on his bed.

"Who is it?" the Arab called out crouching beneath the window ledge.

"Yosef," a voice answered, "Yosef Ben Mathias."

"Ah!" Yochanan relaxed. "Let him in quickly."

Ishmael dropped the bar from the door and pulled the barrier back, letting the priest slip through. Immediately the Arab put the barrier back in place.

"Good heavens!" the visitor stopped abruptly. "What has happened?"

"Sicarii attacked me." Ben Zakkai beckoned his friend forward. "I would have died but this Greek physician saved me."

"Thank the Holy One!" Yosef slipped down by the cot. "You are too valuable to leave us yet. We have many battles to fight now."

"I am Luke." The physician offered his hand.

"You may speak freely in front of our friend." Ben Zakkai beckoned with his thumb. "He comes from Antioch. Unfortunately, he is one of these followers of Yeshua Ben Yosef, but he is no lover of the Romans. I learned that the first day."

"You should leave," Yosef said sharply. "A great war is about to swallow the land. No safe havens will be left . . . anywhere!"

Yochanan shook his head in despair. "We cannot win, Yosef. I have seen Rome itself. I know what the Romans can do. They will stop at nothing. How can they let our rebellion succeed? Their empire would start to unravel."

Ishmael pushed an empty chair near the cot for Yosef. "We have no choice," Ben Mathias responded. "The conflict has begun. When the agitators attacked and took the fortress at Masada, the course was set. The day that Elezar persuaded the rest of the priests to stop making sacrifices for Caesar, the war started."

"A rash but bold act from our young governor of the

Temple," Yochanan answered. "I am glad he has become the high priest, even at his age."

"Yochanan, we must believe that we can win! If we fail, it will be because God has abandoned us."

"The cost in human life will be enormous!" Ben Zakkai lifted his hands despairingly. "I have already lost more family than I could stand in ten lifetimes. I do not want any more death!"

"Then you must help us unify the city," Yosef pressed. "Our only chance is to become one people. Yochanan, you can persuade the Great Sanhedrin to support the high priest and the temple officials. You are the most respected man in Jerusalem today."

"Flattery!" Yochanan grinned. "You charm the sandals off the Romans and now you come to woo the Pharisees." The old man smiled cunningly at his friend. "No, Yosef, *you* are the most valuable man left in the country. We are surrounded by fools and opportunists who will do anything to gain power. Even I am a marked man."

"I will immediately send a contingent of soldiers to be your bodyguards. I will arrange for you to return to your house and see that you have ample food. And this doctor will not go unrewarded, regardless of his strange beliefs."

"Ah, Yosef, you are a true friend as well as a clever politician," Yochanan answered. "If only all Sadducees were as you! You know I would support anything you do."

"Good." Yosef stood. "I am to be the general of our forces in Galilee. I must leave immediately but I will make sure all provisions are made for you." He turned to Luke. "Doctor, get this man back on his feet. He must speak to the Sanhedrin and teach again in the porticoes of the Temple as quickly as possible. If anything more is required, I will provide. Simply tell them that Yosefus has need and it will be yours."

III

Workmen shouted short, loud commands back and forth as they pushed the blocks of granite into place in the city wall. Grinding sounds of the large stones grating over each other rumbled down the steep banks of the Hinnom Valley. Yochanan Ben Zakkai listened as he looked down from the Jerusalem city wall above the Gate of Potsherds, watching the masons busily repairing the cracks along the side of the entryway. Five stout young bodyguards surrounded him.

"This is only the second time in a week that you've been on your feet," Ishmael cautioned. "You are walking too much."

"The city will be ready for war." Yochanan waved his Arab friend away. "No one is wasting any time." Ben Zakkai walked to the other side to look down into the city.

The high sides of the Temple Mount loomed up in the background and the tall, far away towers of Phasael, Hippicus, and Mariamme seemed to pierce the gray winter sky. The weather was still unseasonably cold. To his left Ben Zakkai could see that the Pool of Siloam and the other large reservoir, called the Lower Pool, were full.

"Good water reserves," Ishmael mused.

"Does the physician ask you many questions?" Yochanan abruptly turned to his Arab friend.

26

"All the time!" Ishmael threw up his hands. "He inquires too much."

Ben Zakkai nodded and leaned over the granite wall. "He constantly writes in his scrolls. He talks, asks questions, writes."

"Could he be a spy after all?" The Arab narrowed his eyes and scooted closer to the master of the Torah.

"No, no." Yochanan watched a group of young men training rigorously just below him. "He is infected with messianic madness. His interest is in *Jesus,* as he calls the rabbi—not the Romans. I'm sure he will leave quickly after Mariam returns."

"Where is the doctor now?"

"He's gone to find a cousin of this messiah named Simon . . . the one who replaced James as the new head of the sect here in Jerusalem. He seems to want every piece of information possible about what happened thirty-five years ago."

"Has he found Mariam's scroll?"

Ishmael nodded his head vigorously. "Oh, yes! He sniffed out that heretical *Gospel According to the Hebrews,* like a rat after grain."

"He already knew Mariam wrote the propaganda. Now he knows Leah has a copy of the manuscript?"

"Indeed!" The Arab tossed his head. "The doctor attended some of the meetings of the Christian sect and found out Leah was Mariam's daughter. Even now he visits her house to study the scroll."

"Just as I suspected." Ben Zakkai turned away and watched the white columns of smoke rising up from the blacksmiths' shops. "There's no end to the spears that will be needed."

"Should we keep helping him?" the Arab probed. "You have recovered now."

"He saved my life," Ben Zakkai mumbled. "Amazing what he did. I owe him a debt, but I still won't give any help to the sect."

"Your niece, Leah, has not been around in a long time," the Arab tried to sound disinterested.

Ben Zakkai looked at him out of the corner of his eye. "You know we don't care much for each other. She's too fanatical, abrasive."

The shouts of young soldiers drilling in mock combat were swept up by a sudden gust of winter wind that sent Yochanan and Ishmael's long woolen robes flying. "They will die quickly," Yochanan said cynically. He pointed at juveniles lunging at each other with swords and shields. "War is tragic foolishness. Boys get caught up in the rhetoric and are too young to recognize death when it stares them in the face."

"You have heard nothing of the family of Zeda's betrothed?"

The old sage shook his head and sighed. "It is as if the Ben Ephraim family has disappeared off the face of the earth. I asked Yosef Ben Mathias to inquire, and I put the word out over the entire city. The best I can tell is that Florus took the entire Ben Ephraim clan captive in his retreat. There are some reports of Jewish prisoners at Ptolemais. Who knows? We can only hope."

"I hear of increased slave trading at Caesarea-by-the-Sea." The Arab kept looking straight ahead.

Yochanan said nothing more but turned back to watching the young men march in formation. "So much tragedy," he mumbled. "So much death."

"Surely Mariam will return shortly," Ishmael concluded. "But I do not think that young Zeda will give up the search. I can see nothing but disaster if he pursues the Ben Ephraims."

"Unfortunately," Yochanan looked him full in the face with his good eye, "the Ben Aarons are a persistent lot. We hold our opinions and commitments with deadly tenacity."

Suddenly someone began shouting. Yochanan and Ishmael scurried to the other side. A small group of people hurried up the narrow road that followed the wall toward the Gate of the Potsherds. The workmen stopped and rushed out to help the battered and bloody travelers.

Ben Zakkai called down, "Romans attack you?"

"No!" a young man yelled up. "We were peacefully minding our own business in Bethany when Simon Ben Giora's soldiers attacked and plundered our town. They ravaged the countryside and headed south for the wilderness."

"Why?" Ben Zakkai called back.

The young man shook his fist as he shouted. "Simon said they are raising money to fight the Romans, but they're nothing but thieves and liars. The Romans are better than those dogs!"

"Ben Giora!" Yochanan straightened up. "And Yosef Ben Mathias thought he could quickly unite the country! We have only begun to see anarchy sprouting up like the first weeds of spring."

Far to the south the late afternoon shadows helped conceal Simon Ben Giora as he crouched behind a tree. His hand was poised in the air waiting for the perfect moment to signal attack. His troops hovered behind the wilderness rocks along the steep bank of the En-gedi springs, waiting to drop on the Roman troops that were silently marching beneath them. Fatigued after the long ride from Bethany, Ben Giora's mercenaries were ready for a fight.

Simon was built like a bull. The line of his neck started at his ears and expanded outward until it merged into his massive shoulders. A tightly wound, sand-colored turban concealed his jet-black hair. His similarly colored tunic made him blend into the terrain. The back end of the tunic was pulled up between his legs and bound at his waist with a heavy leather belt that held a large sword. A small dagger was strapped on the inside of his right thigh.

"They're a scouting party," his lieutenant whispered. "Going to Masada to check our fortifications."

Ben Giora displayed an evil smirk. All his teeth were gone on the left side of his mouth, leaving a black gaping space in his face. His eyes twinkled with devilish delight. "Let us spare them the long walk." He suddenly dropped his hand.

Immediately the thieves and robbers hurled spears and darts down on the Romans. Others farther down the cliffs hurled large rocks at the startled legionnaires. Wildly screaming, Ben Giora's men charged down the slopes. The Romans fell back toward the Dead Sea, trying to regroup. Dropping to their knees, the front line of the Roman defense braced their shields together to block the deadly spears. Before they could firmly entrench, the first wave of Jews crashed into the metal wall, knocking many of the Romans backward.

Simon roared down the hill, swinging his sword over his head. "Death to all sons of Romans!" he screamed at the top of his voice. "Taste the steel of Israel." When he reached the bottom, he charged straight into the center of the fighting.

At that moment, a smaller contingent of Simon's men, located behind the boulders at the edge of the salty sea, began shooting darts and arrows at the Romans' backs. Because of the noise of the battle, the soldiers did not detect the sounds coming from behind them. One by one the Romans fell forward. Only as they retreated backward did they realize the deadly trap set on all sides.

Simon was swinging his sword with reckless abandon. The highly disciplined Romans were confused by the Jew's complete disregard for his own life.

"Stop him," a commander in the center pointed his sword at Ben Giora. "Surround that maniac!"

Three men with shields rushed toward Simon. The

Jew crouched with his sword at his side as if welcoming the death descending upon him. The solid front of shields made an impregnable protection that left Simon completely vulnerable to the vengeance of the attackers.

"Come on, you Roman pigs!" Simon taunted his pursuers. "I may go down but I'll take every one of you with me!"

When the soldiers were almost in front of Simon, they began circling and stalking their prey. Simon watched indifferently. Suddenly a Roman in the middle tumbled forward, an arrow in the back of his neck. Before the other soldiers could move, another shower of arrows came from behind the Romans. With groans of agony, the men sank to the ground.

Simon roared triumphantly until a stray arrow sank into his massive thigh. The chieftain's shouts dwindled into a gasp of pain as he buckled in a heap. The fall snapped the arrow's shaft, leaving the metal tip buried in his leg. Simon rolled sideways, back onto one knee. Instantly, he began struggling with his sword, but no one seemed to notice his plight. By the time he hobbled to his feet, the battle was nearly finished. Everywhere he looked the ground was covered with Roman bodies. Simon picked up a spear to use as a walking stick and slowly shuffled forward.

"We captured their leader," a Jew called from the center of the battlefield.

"Save him!" Simon shouted. "Kill all but the ones in charge!"

The skirmish ended as quickly as it had begun. Ben Giora's men quickly pulled the breastplates and helmets off their victims. Any gold coins in the leather pouches became booty, and the Roman swords and shields were piled together in the center of the battlefield.

"Only two survived," a man called to Simon. "We've got 'em over here."

The bull hobbled past several bodies to a cluster of

men pointing their swords at two captives pinned against the rocks. Simon parted the group. "Well, what do we have here? The master and his slave."

The legionnaire held his side where an arrow stuck out of the leather breastplate. The soldier's left arm was so badly slashed that his hand hung motionless. Next to him a terrified young boy huddled on the grass.

"I heard them call him centurion," a bandit told Simon. "He was shouting commands to the troops."

The Roman officer looked stoically over the Dead Sea. The tight, bulging muscles in his jaw betrayed the severity of his pain, but he made no sound.

"Ah!" Simon ran his sword gently back and forth across the Roman's neck. "A tough old bird, indeed." With a quick flick of the wrist Simon nicked the man's throat, letting a trickle of blood run down his neck. The Roman flinched but made no response. "And who might you be, my fine young man?" Simon turned to the boy.

The teenager dug his fingers in the dirt and shook his head, unable to speak.

"Come now," Simon smiled benevolently. "We would not hurt an innocent bystander. Why are you here?"

"I' . . . m . . . m an a . . . a . . . arms . . . bearer," the boy barely spoke.

"Oh!" Simon rolled his eyes and laughed. "You have better sense than our mighty general here. Your tongue will work long after his has left his head. Where have you come from?"

"Pt . . . Pt . . . Ptolemais." The boy shook. "The fortress by the sea."

"Indeed!" Simon squatted down on a rock, sticking his wounded leg straight out. "You are a long way from the north. I bet you came down here to do a little spying on the fortress at Masada."

The boy's head moved mechanically up and down.

"Shut up!" the centurion snapped. "Death is more

honorable than collaboration. Keep your mouth closed."

Without a word Ben Giora reached over, pushing the arrow in the soldier's leather breastplate inward. The Roman screamed in agony.

"He's not so tough." Simon smiled at the terrified boy. "As you were saying about your expedition. You came to spy on us. Right?"

A puddle began creeping out from under the boy's legs. He could only nod his head vigorously.

"Easy, easy." Simon smiled even more broadly. "We are very good to our friends. What is your name?"

"S . . . Sh . . . a . . . mir," he barely whispered. "I am a Phoenician conscript from T . . . Tzidon."

"You were kept at Ptolemais long?" Simon asked.

"Long." Shamir's head bobbed up and down.

"H . . . m . . . m . . . m," Simon pursed his lips. "What's at Ptolemais?"

"M . . . man . . . y s . . . s . . . oldiers. Defending the fort . . . the prisoners."

"The prisoners?" Simon scratched his head. "What prisoners?"

"Shut up," the centurion groaned.

Without even looking, Simon wildly swung his sword, nearly severing the Roman's head from his body with one blow. "As you were saying," he smiled wickedly at the boy as the centurion's body slumped silently in the dirt.

"Th . . . Th . . . The people they took from Jerusalem," the words exploded from his mouth. "Wh . . . Wh . . . When Florus retreated."

"Prisoners?" Simon leaned back and stuck his sword in the sand. "So the rumors are true. How many?" he snapped at Shamir.

"I . . . I . . . I don't kn . . . kn . . . now," he kept shaking. "Lots."

"Do you know where these people are?"

"In . . . side. Down in the c . . . c . . . aves be . . . beneath the fortress."

"Caves? How interesting! Ah, Shamir!" Ben Giora patted the boy on the back. "You have earned yourself a place of honor among us. We will feed you well." He smiled at the lad.

"I . . . I . . . I ca . . . can live?"

"Oh, much more!" Simon patted him again. "We have plans for you." Simon beckoned one of his men. "Take our friend down to the sea and help him tidy up a bit. He has a problem with his tunic."

The men roared.

"Take very good care of Shamir." Simon extended his hand to have someone pull him to his feet. "He's going to be quite a gold mine for us."

Ben Giora slowly hobbled back to the center of the battle. He began shouting to the men around him. "Don't bury them! Leave their standard sticking in the ground so the whole world will know of the slaughter. Let the wind carry their stench back to Rome itself!"

The familiar sight of Ben Zakkai and his troop of five protectors tromping to and fro from the little shop beneath the Great Wall became routine for the merchants doing business along the main boulevard of the Lower City. Yochanan's recovery was nearly complete. The company of bodyguards that traveled with him prevented any more surprise attacks and diminished the possibility of a need for future services of the Greek physician.

In late February, Yochanan called a meeting of his fellow Pharisees at the Sanhedrin for the end of the sixth hour.* Leaving Ishmael behind, he and his bodyguards

*Noon to 3:00 P.M.

made the journey to the upper city. The Sanhedrin met in a large building not far from the Temple Mount. Huge pillars surrounded the imposing entrance. The capitals of the towering granite columns were sculptured with the ornate symbols of Israel. A large Star of David was surrounded by vines and grapes. Even five-point Stars of Solomon enhanced the stone border.

The enormous mahogany door opened to the large assembly room where the scribes, Pharisees, and Sadducees debated, screamed, and threatened each other. Because the Sanhedrin was the legal center of Jewish life, the debates were always intense. Every synagogue had its own Sanhedrin to decide local matters, but the Great Sanhedrin concerned itself with problems of national importance. The members sat behind desks that faced a platform in the center of the room. Five large, elaborately carved chairs were on the stage area and faced the assembly. The entire room was illuminated from little, narrow windows near the high ceilings.

When Haman the caretaker opened the door for Yochanan Ben Zakkai, twenty men were already standing around the room talking. The shafts of mid-afternoon sunlight brightened the usual gloom of the dark-paneled room. Each man's attention was immediately drawn to the flood of light that poured in through the entryway as Ben Zakkai entered.

"Friends," Yochanan waved for the men to circle around him. "Let us immediately get down to business." The master of the Torah briskly walked down the side aisle collecting the Pharisees as he marched toward the center platform. "We must consult immediately, for the days move swiftly."

Ben Zakkai plopped down in the largest of the chairs on the platform. His friends snickered as they watched him position himself comfortably in the high priest's chair. "Fits me well!" he winked at the group.

"What has happened in the north?" an old man named Zorah immediately asked.

"Yosef Ben Mathias is doing well!" Ben Zakkai announced. "Ah, if all Sadducees were as that man, then Israel would have no troubles!" Yochanan shook his fist in the air to enforce his point. "If anyone can pull the village people together, he can do it. In fact," he looked slowly and carefully around the room as he lowered his voice, "that is why I have called this meeting."

The group gathered more tightly around Ben Zakkai, trying to catch each word. He spoke softly so that no one lurking behind a closed door might hear.

"Are you sure you can trust this Ben Mathias?" a young man named Malchor grumbled. "After all he is a Sadducee. He has a reputation for cavorting with the Romans—even calls himself Josephus half the time. I don't like any of it!"

"Absolutely!" Aristeus, the scribe of the Sanhedrin shook his finger at Yochanan. "How can we dare trust any of those hypocrites?"

"I agree," Perez, a younger leader, pushed forward. "My feeling is—"

"Have you come to explain reality to me," Ben Zakkai snapped, "or to listen to what I have discovered?"

Immediately the group become silent and Perez stepped back.

"We are about to be invaded by three legions." Ben Zakkai settled into the chair. "They will be fierce, but we have a good chance of defeating them if we can unify the people in the North. They must be stopped in Galilee if we are to prevent an attack on our city."

"Is such a defense truly possible?" Aristeus probed.

"If we are *unified*," Yochanan said sternly. "But if we cannot hold the North, then the Romans will descend on us like wild locusts destroying the fields. Should that be the case, I fear they will not even spare the Temple."

The men stroked their beards and murmured.

"Pharisees must seize this moment!" old Zorah exclaimed. "We can trust no one but ourselves. Pharisees must lead. We must take charge!"

"Don't be fools!" Ben Zakkai's voice was icy. "Did you not hear what I said? Unless we unite with the Sadducees, Zealots, and even this new sect called Believers, we cannot prevail!"

"The fanatics who believe the Messiah has come?" Zorah recoiled. "They are crazy! Heretics! Worthy of death!"

"Yes!" the group mumbled.

"I don't even associate with the Nazarenes!" Perez interjected.

"If we insist on being exclusive," Ben Zakkai scoffed, "then we must prepare for death. Unless we stand together, the Romans will cut us in a thousand parts."

"I would rather die than jeopardize our purity," Perez said as he again stepped into the center of the group. "The Holy One expects us to be set apart regardless of the cost!"

"I stand ready to die for our principles." Zorah beat his fist in his palm.

"Anyone can die any day of the week," Ben Zakkai shouted in their faces. "Dying proves nothing! Do you want to have our Holy City reduced to ashes? Do you think the Romans will be singing praises to God for your holiness as they slit your throats?" Ben Zakkai stood up. "Let me say it again. ANY FOOL CAN DIE! Men of courage will choose to live in order to be of service to their God on the other days He has need of them."

Once more the group ceased their arguing and looked silently at each other. Finally Perez reluctantly nodded his head in agreement.

Zorah held up his hands in frustration. "Who else can we turn to but you, master of the Torah?"

"All right." Yochanan leaned back in the chair. "Listen

without interruption. First, we must attempt to bring the Great Sanhedrin behind the leadership of the Temple."

No one made a sound.

"But I have other options that must be explored." Ben Zakkai lowered his voice further. "Even now we must prepare for the possibility that the Romans cannot be stopped. Gentlemen, the worst may come, and we may be the only ones with enough sense to prepare for the final disaster."

"Final disaster?" Perez scratched his head. "I would think working with this new sect of Believers would be the final disaster."

Ben Zakkai suddenly grabbed Perez's robe and yanked him forward, holding the young man's face just inches from his own. "Isn't the idea of having the streets filled with the bodies of your children and women more important than your personal purity? Doesn't the total destruction of this city and the possible burning of the Temple seem slightly more significant to you than rubbing elbows with a few people whose beliefs differ from yours? My friend, we are running out of time!"

IV

Spring days in Galilee brought dazzling fruit trees exploding with blossoms of new promise. The problems of Jerusalem seemed to evaporate in the warm breeze. Almond trees swayed gently in the warm and invigorating Galilean gusts from the landlocked sea. March brought the vineyards that covered the hillsides back to life, and the farmers worked the fields on the fertile plains. Life was simple and good around the magnificent Lake Galilee.

Yosef Ben Mathias thought about how different Galilee was from city life. As he prepared for his planning meeting with aides and captains, Yosef reflected on the simplicity of the Galileans. He liked their straightforward, unsophisticated manner. As he pondered the morning assembly, he spent a long time looking out his window at the great lake.

Gentle, rolling hillsides slid into the sparkling azure waters that emptied into the Jordan River. Quaint villages like Capernaum, Bethsaida, and Magdala dotted the Galilean coastline. Sea gulls circled above the sparkling sea, and dove into the abundant schools of fish. Fishermen sometimes walked along the shoreline casting their nets by hand, while the more affluent ones crossed the lake daily in boats that sought the larger catches of the greater depths.

Lake Galilee could suddenly be covered with terrible

storms, sending the sailors rushing for the harbor. Then, just as abruptly, become a tranquil sheet of glass. The usually placid sea invited children to play among the reeds and on the beaches, and it offered families green carpet for their Sabbath walks.

Galileans were generally scorned by the aristocracy of Jerusalem since education in the North was considered inferior and never orthodox enough. Because of inter-marriage, the northerner's Jewishness was always suspected. Rabbi Nathan had once charged, "Galilee, Galilee, you hate the Torah. Before long you will have common cause with the tax gatherers!" The epitaph stuck, and it became a painful cliché that no one of value came out of the northern country.

The incessant political bickering and religious wars that raged in the Holy City were foreign to the simple village people who were far more apt to live and let live. While the Romans were certainly hated, they weren't much more of an irritant than were the politicians to the south.

Yosef Ben Mathias had reasoned through all the matters thoroughly before making Tiberius the center of his administration. Positioned in the center of the Galilee, the city was the end of the trunk road that ran from Caesarea-by-the-Sea through the Megido Pass, giving the military complete access to the plain of Jezreel. Vespasian would certainly use this route as had all the invaders who preceded him. Tiberius also had an easy connection to Beth Yerah and the crucial pass into the high country of the Jaulan.

Herod Antipas created Tiberius only forty-one years earlier, naming his new capital after the Roman emperor. The warm springs and therapeutic hot bath of Hamath Gader created an inviting setting. Because Antipas built over a cemetery, law-abiding Jews shunned the city, forcing the king to import citizens from other quarters. Eventually new Jews settled in. Yosef could make good use of the diversity.

The Tetrarch of Galilee erected a new palace as the showpiece of his private city. Beneath the fortress, Herod had imprisoned a prophet named John the Baptizer for condemning his scandalous marriage to his brother's wife Herodias. On a cool, summer evening, the leading notables of Galilee had been invited to a sumptuous birthday feast for the old fox. During his step-daughter's tempestuous dance, Herod's desires for Salome had led to a foolish promise that resulted in the execution of John. When the story spread throughout the region that the holy man's head had been served on a platter, Herod's harvest of hate and contempt exceeded the combined produce of all the vineyards.

While Herod was intensely despised by pious Jews, he did spawn a circle of admirers labeled Herodians. A Sadducee like Yosef Ben Mathias could expect the support of these political opportunists. Rather than court officials or a political party, the Herodians attempted to provide improved public relations for Antipas. They had a vested interest in preserving the status quo, and bent wherever the wind was blowing. Yosef had no misgivings about their trustworthiness; yet the Herodians might be of some value in solidifying Upper Galilee if they believed the Romans could lose power.

Yosef quickly realized that the southern trade route running down the King's Highway must also be kept open. When he walked into the assembly of his captains, Yosef knew vengeance was once more about to descend on the crucial little town.

Yosef carefully studied each of the seven men standing before him in the assembly room of what had once been Herod's prize palace and fortress. "Shalom! Address me as you wish," Yosef began factually. "I care not whether you call me Ben Mathias or Flavius Josephus. The people will soon learn I am neither an opportunist nor a tyrant." He turned and looked out the window. "The citizens care nothing for titles. Galileans are pragmatic and want the war to pass quickly. The sooner life returns to normal, the better they will like it."

"Ah! But you are respected and feared!" a man in a plain brown robe of thick wool spoke in a northern accent. "We are ready to comply with your wishes, General."

"You amaze us." Yoel, a young lieutenant, shook his head enthusiastically. "Yosef Ben Mathias! A high priest has become the master of the Galilee with nothing more at his disposal than sheer cunning and intelligence!"

Yosef looked beyond Tiberius's fortress over the crystal blue waters. "I was surprised myself," he said quietly. "I really didn't think it would be so easy." He looked down at the harbor packed with boats.

Tabor laughed. The old man had lived in the city from the beginning and always sensed where the political tides flowed. "One of our people, Ciltus, was the ringleader of the revolt. He wanted to keep Tiberius for the Romans, and he persuaded the senate to stand against you, Yosef."

"But when they saw your fleet of ships strung across the lake, Ciltus was terrified!" Yoel continued. "There must have been two hundred and fifty boats out there! It looked like the whole fleet of Vespasian had sailed up the Jordan River. All we could see were the boats bobbing up and down on the horizon. Everyone thought you had the whole southern army with you."

Yosef smiled cunningly as he continued scanning the city.

"No one would have guessed you only had four sailors on each boat!" Tabor threw his hands up in the air. "And only seven bodyguards! Absolutely brilliant!"

"Tiberius's control is now ours." Yosef walked away from the window. "All that really matters is that we are consolidating our command over all of Galilee. Now I also rule Sepphorius, Gamala, and Gischala. We are making excellent progress." Yosef sat down at a large table in the center of the room. "The time has come to plan the rest of our campaign."

The seven gathered around a scroll Yosef unrolled. Before them was a detailed map of the area.

"A stroke of genius!" Tabor thumped on the map. "First you took Gischala and let your men plunder the city. Then you gave all their money back the next day. No wonder they are delighted to follow you. You have a way of explaining politics they understand."

Yosef began reading from another parchment. "We now have generals assigned across the country. Yeshua Ben Sapphias is in Idumea. He is a high priest and will join Niger in governing the Idumeans. Yosef Ben Simon is our general in Jericho, and Manasseh will oversee Perea. Yochanan the Essene has been sent to Thamna where he will also be responsible for Lydda, Joppa, and Emmaus. Yochanan Ben Mathias is the governor of Gophnitica and Acrabattene. I have great confidence in each of these men."

The lieutenant put his finger in the center of the map. "But who is the general in Jerusalem? Who governs the holy city?"

"Elezar, the son of Ananias, is the high priest." Yosef folded his arms and looked down at the table. "As the head of the Temple, he should be able to lead the people."

"You did not call him a general," the lieutenant persisted.

"Must you be so persistent?" Ben Mathias said wearily. "No, in truth there is no one completely in charge of the city. The factions still battle each other, but unless they set their bickering aside and listen to Elezar, there will not be a single voice for the people to heed."

Tabor pointed on the map. "A capital city without a leader? How can a divided house stand?"

"We must not fail," Yosef snapped. "We must hold the north and the outlying areas! There is no alternative. The future rises or falls with what we do here." Yosef suddenly pushed the map forward. "Look," he pointed to the area around Lake Galilee.

The men pressed in closely and stared where the general directed. "I am appointing each of you to an area. There will be seven judicial districts in this region."

"Exactly as Moses divided and judged," one of the Galilean men observed.

Yosef smiled at his awareness. "Indeed! All matters are to be administered exactly as prescribed in the Torah. We will administer justice and distribute food and materials in accordance with the Law. The people must know that they will be dealt with justly and honorably. I want all duplicity and mendacity to stop. There can be no unity unless we offer a better way of life than what they have seen under Herod."

"I stand with you!" Jonah, a Galilean, answered enthusiastically. "We have longed for a man of integrity to lead us. You will have the affection of the people."

"And that is exactly what we must count on!" Yosef shook his fist. "If we have favor with the multitudes, we can execute our command. Let us show the people that we are trustworthy. We must identify seventy prudent elders to be judges. I want seven judges in every city to hear complaints. The people need to see immediately that we will care for them."

"We are prepared to start building fortifications," the lieutenant interjected. "Where do we begin?"

"Japhia and at Mount Tabor!" Yosef pointed again on the map. "Put walls near the caves in lower Galilee. Tell the people at Sepphorius to rebuild their own wall. They are rich enough."

"At once!" the young man snapped to attention.

Yosef tapped firmly on the place named Jotapata. "No expense is too great to make sure this city and its walls are secured. Gentlemen, our fate rests with the people of Jotapata and the future swings on the gate posts of their town."

"I suggest we also send a spy to Caesarea to observe the landing of the boats," Jonah said. "We must know at once when the Romans land. Information may drift in, but we should have a spy at Ptolemais also. I offer my son Jesse. He is a stout lad and travels quickly. Jesse will only need to walk among the landings listening to the sailors and send us reports. My boy knows the coastal area."

"Excellent," Yosef answered. "Send Jesse at once!"

The men returned to the map, dividing up responsibilities and planning the next step. Jonah slipped away to find his young son.

More than a week passed before Jesse Ben Jonah completed his journey through the narrow passageway at Megido. He descended down to the coastal plains and on to Caesarea, leaving Ptolemais for last. Once he left the strategic checkpoint on the hilltop at Megido, Jesse was in Roman-held territory. Soldiers patrolled the roads and subservience was clearly expected. At night, Jesse made contacts along the way to ensure quick communication when he needed to pass his discoveries on to other military leaders throughout the region.

His twenty-four years had been spent in Tiberius and around the great sea. His father, Jonah, originally came from Bethsaida, which literally meant "the house of nets." Jonah purchased the family fishing business of a man named Simon Peter who left the area to follow the rabbi Yeshua Ben Yosef, now called Jesus by the Greeks and Romans. Eventually, Jonah expanded the business and moved his headquarters from the west side of the lake to Tiberius.

Toiling on the rolling lake and drawing in heavy nets had given Jesse a strong back and made his body as hard as a rock. Long days on the waters had developed considerable endurance, so he was able to make the lengthy journey to the Mediterranean quickly.

Once Jesse reached the sandy coastal beaches, he slipped easily into the city limits of Caesarea. Years earlier Pontius Pilate had enlarged the amphitheater that overlooked the city. Caesarea had been the fortress where Cestus and Florus retreated when the great revolt began. Because the harbor was an excellent landing, the city was a natural dock of Roman vessels.

For two days Jesse watched the harbor, but he saw little unusual activity. On the morning of the third day he found that the tides brought significant change.

Jesse walked slowly among the sand dunes as he surveyed the anchored ships in the harbor in the early morning. A number of huge Alexandrian corn ships were being unloaded at the docks. Many of the smaller Phoenician trade vessels were tied to the buoys. Of course, small fishing boats were everywhere. At the end of the longest pier was precisely what Jesse hoped to find. One of the large Roman Mediterranean galleys had just docked. Men were carrying cargo down the gangplanks and passengers were beginning to come ashore. The ship looked like it would carry at least several hundred passengers. Both soldiers and civilians were leaving.

''Excellent!'' Jesse said to himself. *What fortune!* He thought as he hurried to the dock. *I got here just in time. If I can simply mingle with the passengers, I know I'll hear something. Maybe I'll recognize somebody.*

Representatives of the cursus publicus, the Roman courier that took mail from station to station, stood on the pier waiting for the delivery. Behind them were men with horses for transportation to other places. The cursus velox was the fast service that also provided guards to protect travelers from highwaymen. The slower carts of the cursus clabularis were usually pulled by oxen and took the heavy baggage and other goods to their destination. Jesse wound his way through the crowd of observers and walked slowly toward the galley.

Roman soldiers and dignitaries were the first ones off the boat. They walked quickly toward the area on the shore that was secured by a large contingent of soldiers. Security was obviously high. Jesse watched the nobility pass and waited for more friendly faces. He turned quickly at the sound of hobnailed sandals pounding on the pier. Only the Roman soldiers who were prepared for battle wore cleated soles.

"Hail, centurion," one of the men called out.

Five men in ceremonial breastplates with red capes hanging from their shoulders fell into single line formation. Each man wore a plumed helmet. As they snapped to attention, each soldier struck his chest with the closed fist.

"Welcome to you, Marcus Quintus Cunctator!" the man on the end called out. "The legion is honored to receive the new primus pilus. We are here to escort you to Ptolemais."

An unusually tall soldier walked briskly past Jesse. At his side was an aide carrying the soldier's helmet and other equipment. The tall soldier returned the salute of the group.

"Your reputation for valor precedes you," Marcus Quintus Cunctator spoke briskly. "I welcome the opportunity to fight with you, gentlemen. We will serve the Emperor well." After saluting again, the primus pilus extended his hand and the men immediately responded.

Jesse watched intensely as the six men joined a larger company of soldiers who waited on the shore with horses. The troops quickly saddled up and rode off.

Eventually Semitic faces appeared among the debarking passengers as they hurried toward land. Jesse inched his way toward the gangplank. A young man started to help an older woman down the walkway when a soldier suddenly darted off the ship and pushed the man aside.

"Out of my way, Jew," the Roman scowled as he shoved the traveler aside. "I'm in a hurry!"

In three long strides the soldier was down the gangplank but the young man tottered frantically on the edge of the boards, swinging his arms wildly, trying to regain his balance. The soldier didn't look back.

Instantly Jesse charged up the walkway and lunged for the man's robe. Clutching Jesse's shoulders, the stranger finally regained his footing.

"Thank you, thank you," the young man sputtered. "I nearly fell in."

"You're all right?" Jesse held his tunic tightly.

"Yes, yes. I think so. Mother, were you hurt?"

A small Jewish woman around forty-five shook her head. Her black eyes flashed with indignation.

"Let me help you down." Jesse reached for a bundle the little woman was carrying. "Romans are pigs," he said more loudly than was prudent.

The mother and son walked beside their new friend who helped carry their belongings to the end of the pier. Nothing was said as they passed a group of soldiers, joking alongside the dock. The Roman who had pushed his way off the boat spat as they passed.

"Matters are very tense here," Jesse began explaining. "Perhaps you are not aware that we have revolted against the Romans. You must be careful of these swine."

"Is travel dangerous?" the young man asked.

"All depends," Jesse explained. "I came down from Tiberius without much difficulty."

"Tiberius!" the mother smiled. "I have wonderful memories of Galilee. Your family lives there?"

"Originally my father was in a fishing business in Bethsaida before we moved across the lake."

"Ah," the woman acknowledged, "I had a good friend

who fished at Bethsaida, but that was many years ago and he is gone now."

"Where are you headed?" Jesse asked.

"We are from Jerusalem and are returning," the stranger explained.

"And you have come from Rome?"

"Yes," the mother answered. "I have been there for a number of years, but my son came to help me return."

"We hear there are many legions on their way," Jesse probed. "Have you seen any signs of their fleet?"

"Indeed!" the young man spoke softly. "Even at this hour they are winding their way from port to port picking up men and supplies. Vespasian's fleet will soon cover the horizon."

"His son Titus was sent from Achaia to Alexandria to bring the fifth and tenth legions with him," the woman added.

"Ah!" Jesse exclaimed. "This is news indeed! We have not heard of Titus bringing these two legions."

"We?" the young man asked very slowly.

"I am with the commander of Galilee," Jesse whispered proudly. "Yosef Ben Mathias."

"Yosef, the high priest?" the young man asked skeptically. "My family is acquainted with him but he lives in Jerusalem."

"Much has obviously changed in your absence," Jesse explained quietly. "Yosef is now the commanding general in the north."

"Very interesting," the young man mused. "I am sure my uncle can explain the details when we get home."

"I just saw a dignitary arrive," Jesse pressed. "Called him Quintus Cunctator, I think. Tell me, what is a primus pilus?"

"Ah," the young man smiled. "You speak of Marcus Quintus Cunctator. We made his acquaintance on the ship. He is going to Ptolemais. The primus pilus is the senior ranking centurion who answers only to the legion's commander himself. He will be preparing the way for the landing of Vespasian."

"What you have told me today will be of great value to our people," Jesse spoke with quiet intensity. "I will leave shortly for the Roman fortress in Ptolemais and then return to Tiberius. My name is Jesse Ben Jonah. Possibly one day I can return the favor. Please call on me. And may I have the honor of knowing your names?"

"We can always be found at the end of the jewelry market just beneath the south wall in the Lower City. Our family is well-known for our artistry. Just ask for the family Ben Aaron. This is my mother, Mariam, and I am Zeda Ben Aaron."

V

———

Just before the end of the third hour,* Leah's personal servant burst into the jewelry shop beneath the south wall. "Please come as soon as possible," was all the servant said or seemed to know. He left as suddenly as he came.

"I think it would be best for you to go alone and find out what this business is all about," Ben Zakkai said thoughtfully. "I will not have bodyguards available until this afternoon."

Without question or reply, Ishmael simply put his work aside, threw a cloak over his shoulder and hurried out. The Arab took the narrow path that ran along the edge of the high wall rather than the usual broad boulevard that ran through the center of the jewelry market.

The morning was almost gone and the sun reflecting off the huge gray stones warmed the Arab. The stony path was higher than most of the shops that bordered the wall so Ishmael could see merchants transacting business. The smell of bread frying filled his nostrils as he hurried down the trail.

When Ishmael reached the main gate, he turned north into the Upper City taking the familiar street that ended at the Palace of the Hasmonean. If he turned to the right, he would eventually cross the great Krytus Bridge, which spanned the Tyropoeon Valley and ended up in

———

*9:00 A.M. to noon

the Temple. Instead, he chose to turn left to go toward the neighborhood where Leah's family lived. Soon, Ishmael passed the sprawling food market filled with grain and vegetable vendors. On all sides people jockeyed for the best buys. Carcasses of lamb and baskets of fish were on display. The smell of meat, spices, and grains took the fresh morning air captive.

Ishmael could hear Ben Zakkai's voice ringing in his mind when he crossed the market plaza where Yochanan's brother had been killed decades before. Every time they came to this exact place, Ben Zakkai recounted the Zealot's attack and Zeda's subsequent death. The recollection chilled Ishmael but Yochanan seemed to need to tell the story he could never quite grasp.

At first the feeling was a premonition. Ishmael sensed he was being followed. When he reached the end of the market, he was sure. Picking up his pace, he glanced backward and saw a man waving his hand violently. Ishmael started running. When he turned around, the Arab saw three men closing in on him. Ishmael darted to the right into a narrow passageway between two houses. At the end of the passageway, the Arab spun around trying to decide which way to go. Ahead, the alley ended at the back wall of a house. In the opposite direction, he saw one of the men run into the alley. He quickly looked sideways and discovered a ladder leaning against the stucco building next to him. Instantly Ishmael scampered up the rungs to the roof.

Once he reached the top, Ishmael ran across the flat-roofed buildings. At the end of the last roof, he leaped a short distance to the next set of houses. Behind and beneath him he heard men shouting back and forth as if his enemies knew exactly where he was going. At the end of the next row of houses, Ishmael realized what his pursuers must have known all along. The entire block of buildings ended directly in front of him. Ishmael could not go back nor reach another roof. He had no choice but to return to the street. In one single motion the Arab hurled himself to the street.

Ishmael felt momentarily suspended in space, but then a sudden crashing sound filled his ears. His feet broke through boards, slowing his descent, but the cracking and splitting of timber warned him that the pause was only momentary. Strange objects bounced against his body as he collapsed into a pile of brittle shards that punctured his skin. Ishmael was badly scratched and his head was filled with pain. The last thing he remembered clearly was a terrible hollow ringing in his head. The scene faded into darkness.

Ishmael could hear noise and feel hands grabbing at him. He was being dragged but nothing was clear.

"Put your foot on his neck," a man shouted down.

"Keep that swine Arab under control," another voice boomed.

"Got him! Got him!" someone else chattered.

When Ishmael's eyes cleared he was looking across the pavement at a pile of rubble. He blinked and looked again. He had fallen through the shelves of the potter's market. Apparently a large vase had cracked against his head. He offered no resistance when the men pulled him to his feet.

"Look what we have here," a ragged man with a dagger in his hand sneered. "An Arab trying to fly."

"I demand payment!" a vendor shouted into Ishmael's face. "Make this dog of the desert pay!"

"Charge it to Yochanan Ben Zakkai," a deep voice roared and immediately the vendor retreated. "Let me take our catch of the day."

Ishmael turned and peered into the parting crowd. A hulk of a man plowed his way forward. When he gaped at the people around him, his missing teeth left a black hole in his face. Instantly Ishmael recognized Simon Ben Giora.

"You refuse our hospitality?" Simon yanked Ishmael forward by his robe. "Why did you run? Hiding something?"

The Arab looked into the cold, calculating eyes of the Zealot chieftain. "No, no," he muttered. "I thought thieves were attacking me."

"You weren't far from the truth," Ben Giora roared. "Don't you know that I control the Upper City now? Would I allow thieves on the streets . . . unless they served me?" He laughed at his own question.

"I meant no harm," Ishmael answered apologetically.

"Matter of fact," Simon abruptly became serious and lowered his voice. "I've been looking for you. Months ago you and the young Ben Aaron were making inquiries about a family that disappeared during Florus's retreat. Right?"

Ishmael nodded his head mechanically.

"I know where they are," Simon smiled wickedly. "Would you like to know?"

Ishmael hesitated, cautiously assessing the situation. "Any information would be appreciated."

"Bring your little gold merchant to my headquarters at Herod's Palace and I will put your mind to rest."

"Thank you. The family will be relieved. You are a most generous man, Simon Ben Giora."

"Of course," Simon grinned broadly, "I am a benevolent soul. And to demonstrate my generosity I am only going to charge you thirty denarii* for the information."

"Thirty denarii!" the Arab sputtered.

"I have a heart of gold," Ben Giora curtly laughed in Ishmael's face.

Light streaming in through the jewelry shop windows clearly illuminated the wound on Yochanan Ben Zak-

*One month's wages

kai's chest. "Ishmael will return soon?" Luke asked examining the healing tissues.

Ben Zakkai shook his head but said nothing.

Luke poked his fingers forcefully against the old man's ribs and asked, "Does this area hurt?"

"Somewhat, but you push hard," the one-eyed man groused. "You enjoy seeing me squirm."

"I would say you have made remarkable progress." The doctor felt around the scar. "I believe the inner flesh is completely restored. Takes a long time you know."

"I will always be indebted to you."

"No, no." Luke closed his wooden case. "You have more than repaid me. I have finished studying Leah's scroll and met many important people. I am most satisfied."

"You will leave soon?" Ben Zakkai asked too quickly.

"You really don't like these Believers, do you?"

The one-eyed man pulled his robe shut without answering. "I am surprised Zeda and Mariam haven't arrived yet. I would have thought . . ."

Ishmael bounded through the canvas door into the jewelry shop. "The Zealots caught me!" he panted. "Simon Ben Giora himself." The Arab's chest rose and fell in great heaves. "They were watching for me."

"I was afraid of just such a trap!" Yochanan tried to leap up but flinched. "Did they hurt you?" he grunted.

"No, no." Ishmael sank into a chair. "Just terrified me. They caught me before I made it to Leah's house."

Luke immediately pushed Ishmael's dirty robe up his arm. "You didn't come away unscathed. Look at these cuts!"

"Mere scratches." The Arab reached up to feel the large knot on the side of his head. "But I have very important information."

"What?" Ben Zakkai inched toward his friend while Luke dabbed ointment on the abrasions.

"Ben Giora knows where Jewish prisoners are hidden! He knows what's become of the family Ben Ephraim."

"Are you sure?" Yochanan's eyes narrowed.

The Arab told each detail of the chase and conversation. When he finished, Ben Zakkai said nothing. Luke asked a few questions, but the old man maintained a stoic silence.

Finally Yochanan stood up and suggested that it was best to prepare for customers. He quietly settled in behind his work bench, picked up a small mallet, and began tapping on a piece of gold. Solitary as an oyster, Ben Zakkai's mind was obviously captivated by the Arab report. Ishmael arranged gold pieces on the display counter while Luke stared at the silent scene.

"We will try to reach Leah's house tonight after the guards return," Yochanan said abruptly before settling back into his abyss of stillness.

Eventually Luke pulled a scroll from his wooden case and took out the stylus he always carried. As he made copious notes, Luke tried to blot out the scene around him, but he could not escape thinking about what a strange man Ben Zakkai was. Full of contradictions, the old Pharisee was an enigma; integrity and compromise, compassion and cold, calculating intent . . . all bathed in mystery.

"Are you here?" a woman's voice called from outside. A hand parted the canvas flap door and Leah stepped in. "Is anyone home?"

"Leah!" Ben Zakkai jumped up. "What are you doing here? It is far too dangerous for you to be running around this city alone."

"You didn't come." Leah stood indignantly in the center of the shop with her hands on her hips. "Didn't the servant say the matter was important?"

"We had a . . . a . . . a . . . serious problem," Ben Zakkai fumbled to explain. "Ishmael was forcibly detained. All the more reason," his hesitation turned to firm resolve, "that you should never be out without a guard. Never go out alone!"

"I didn't," Leah said smugly with a teasing toss of her head. "I had ample protection."

"What do you mean?" Ben Zakkai turned his good eye sideways to look more directly at her.

"W . . . e . . . ll," Leah smiled. "If you wouldn't come for the surprise, then I had to bring it to you. Look who is here." Leah quickly returned to the door and pulled the canvas back. "Come in," she called outside.

"Shalom," a young man answered as he led a woman in with him.

"Zeda!" Ben Zakkai gasped, rushing toward the pair. "Mariam! Praise be! You have returned!" Yochanan kissed the young man on both cheeks and hugged Mariam. "You are home! Wonderful! Wonderful! Blessed are you, Lord!"

Luke watched in amazement. Ishmael danced around the foursome in utter delight as they laughed, hugged each other, wept, and then overflowed with the same emotions again. *Amazing,* Luke thought, *Ben Zakkai is like a man beside himself.*

"Something to drink?" Yochanan slapped Zeda on the back. "Let us celebrate! Mariam, sit here in the seat of honor."

Instantly Ishmael pulled out a chair from the little table and took a wine skin from a peg on the wall. "Just what we have been saving the best for!" The Arab held the full bag up in the air, whirling around the table. "Let us drink to life! You have returned alive and well!"

"And alone . . ." The words slipped from Mariam's lips as if they had a life of their own. Her hand came to her mouth as if she might call them back, but the joy washed from her eyes.

"They are gone," Zeda said hauntingly. "We come alone."

When the old man once more reached for Mariam,

they broke into sobs. "I loved them," Yochanan choked. "From my earliest memory, Jarius was always there. When I received your letter I did not think I could go on." He buried his face in Mariam's hair.

Once more Luke watched alone in consternation as Leah and Zeda huddled around the old man and woman crying. Ishmael stood at their side weeping as well. For an interminable amount of time, no one spoke until finally Mariam and Yochanan dropped down into the chairs around the little table. As they held each other's hands, Leah and Zeda stood behind them.

"Oh, but they were brave," Mariam said. "What dignity! When the Romans made them walk out on the track to their death, my husband and father were the masters of the day. They stepped into eternity and never looked back."

"Please." Yochanan shook his head. "Later. It is all too much right now. I do not think my heart can bear any more. Later. Tell me much later."

Mariam slowly looked up and began to survey the room. "Oh my, you still have those old strips of cloth on the wall. They are so faded! We must change them tomorrow, uncle."

"Uncle!" Luke spoke for the first time.

Mariam turned, realizing someone else was there. "I . . . I . . . I'm sorry." She tried to stand. "I didn't know anyone else was here. Uncle is *only* a term of endearment. We don't know you."

"This man saved my life." Ben Zakkai beckoned for Luke to come forward. "I was stabbed again after you left, Zeda. This Greek doctor patched me up and has made me like new."

"Doctor?" Mariam puzzled. "Ah, you are the man Leah spoke of."

"I have come a long way to meet you." Luke extended his hand. "I came to read your scroll."

"He's studied it night and day," Leah interjected.

"My name is Luke. I once traveled with Paul."

"Good heavens!" Mariam immediately got up from the table. "I heard Paul speak of you so often. You visited him in Rome. Yes, you kept him well. Paul had the deepest affection for you. And now you have come here."

"I am writing the story of Jesus for the Greeks. I need your help."

"Of course, of course!" Mariam shook the doctor's hand. "But you must also prepare to leave here as soon as possible. The Roman legions are just behind us and terrible days lie ahead. I will gladly help you, but you must depart before the days of war come."

"Come, come," Ben Zakkai beckoned them to gather around the table. "We must not talk about such hard things now. There will be plenty of time for these painful matters. We must savor this good moment and drink its nectar while we can, for we seldom have such goodness poured out upon us these days. Ishmael, run to the market in the Lower City and buy us a lamb, for tonight we feast!"

"I should leave now," Luke said thoughtfully.

"No, no!" Zeda waved him over to sit down.

"You must join our celebration," Mariam insisted.

"Thank you," Luke smiled at the group, "but this is time for you to be together. I will return tomorrow if that is acceptable." He looked at Mariam.

"Of course," she nodded. "I will be glad to help with your questions. But please believe me. You must be ready to leave very soon. We will talk tomorrow."

"Perhaps, first thing in the morning?" Luke asked.

"We will be at the house of Jarius Ben Aaron," Mariam answered. "I will expect you there."

As Luke started through the canvas door, he turned and looked back. Yochanan had one arm around the young man's waist and was holding Mariam's hand with the other. His good eye sparkled with a vitality that amazed Luke. Only then did he fully realize the depth of the depression in the old man's eyes during the previous days. Ben Zakkai was talking and gesturing like a grandfather discovering that his favorite grandchildren had come for a surprise visit.

I don't understand, Luke thought as he walked down the street. *The puzzle has a missing piece.*

VI

The crisp, fresh smell of early morning hung in the air. Luke walked quickly up the lane to the large two-story stucco house of Jarius Ben Aaron. As always, the doctor carried the wooden box at his side. Like all the sandy-brown houses of the city, the exterior was plain and unadorned, but the Ben Aaron house was much larger than most. The Ben Aarons obviously had been a prosperous clan when the Holy City flourished. The deteriorating neighborhood mirrored what political fighting and rebellion had done to the city's market-places.

Luke pondered how long he could stay in the land. Things were certainly coming apart. Standing before the door, he looked up at the well-worn mazusseh and smiled as he touched the metal cylinder, invoking a blessing as was Jewish custom. He knocked on the door.

An old man answered the door and, without a word, gestured for Luke to follow him down the hallway leading to the large gathering room. The wrinkled, worn servant looked like he had been in the family forever. "Please wait here." He pointed to the large room. "She will be here presently."

Luke looked about the room that had become so familiar to him while he had studied Mariam's scroll. Like most Jewish homes, everything was modest and unpretentious by Greek and Roman standards. Next to the

61

central fireplace was a large clay pot filled with flowering branches of an almond tree. The gathering room blended into the dining room, which had another hearth at the opposite end. There were a few plain chairs and a table, but most people simply sat on the pallets around the floor. Near the window was a small table where Luke had studied the scroll.

"Shalom," Mariam's cheery voice broke in from the hall. "I trust you slept well."

"Indeed." Luke bowed in the formal Greek fashion. "God's peace be with you."

"Please sit down." Mariam pointed to the table. A very small woman with intense black eyes, she moved across the room with elegant grace. Flowing, ebony hair streaked with gray was pulled together at the back of her head. Her neck was slender and graceful. Mariam wore the customary black robe of a widow. As she sat down, her pleasant smile didn't conceal a penetrating stare.

"I . . . ah . . . thought," he suddenly found it difficult to express himself. "Er . . . a . . . perhaps, we might deal with a few questions."

"You are a very kind man," Mariam answered. "And the Holy One of Israel has given you a great healing gift. Your hands can extend His touch."

Luke stared at her. He started to speak but didn't know quite what to say.

"Moreover, what you write now will be more important than anything you have ever done with medicine. The risen Messiah will put His hand upon yours. Your words will heal lives for centuries to come. Many will read and find eternal relief for their pain."

"I heard you were like this." Luke spoke hesitantly. "Leah said you can see what is hidden. Truly you are revered throughout this city."

"I hope not!" Mariam laughed. "Let us turn to the facts of my story. You know that Jesus restored me from the land of the dead? I was dying of an incurable disease that no doctor could identify."

"Yes, I have heard the account. They say that when you returned from beyond you had unusual gifts."

Mariam settled back in the chair. "I sometimes forget that I can be quite disconcerting. But I see in your eyes that you can be trusted with all our secrets. Luke, you will help the gentile world know His story. You must translate our Jewish ideas into a form that others can understand."

"That is exactly why I have come." Luke pulled closer to the table. "I have talked to many Believers and studied every scroll I could find. Of course, my journeys with Paul taught me many things."

"Certainly," Mariam acknowledged. "We usually called him Saul. He was a great mind and a wonderful man. Now, what question can I help you with?"

"Why did you write your story in Hebrew? It took me forever to read, and I am still not sure that I understand many of the words correctly."

Mariam smiled. "Jews speak Hebrew in the synagogue. Actually it would have been more natural to write the gospel scroll in Aramaic, but Matthew and I felt that the story ought to be in the holy language. Our people in other countries would understand it better."

"Ah!" Luke nodded his head. "I see, I see. You started with the genealogy of Yeshua so Jews could believe he was of messianic lineage, and then you give us some sketchy details of how Mary was his mother. But I am sure there is much more to the beginning of this story than we know."

Mariam looked out the small window and watched the children playing in the street while she pondered the question. "She's gone now," Mariam finally answered. "Mary and the apostle John left Jerusalem some years ago. Yet, I believe she would want the full story known. During the worst time in my life, Mary told me of how the Holy Spirit overshadowed her and the love of God turned into life within her. Through Mary's story I, too, was able to find a new birth of hope. Both son and mother helped raise me from the dead."

"Please don't stop. I want every detail."

"Mary taught me a song. She sang it often during the days when the scandal of her own pregnancy made life hard and uncertain. I, too, sang her words in the dark of night during the time that I felt so alone and abandoned." Mariam began to hum. "My soul magnifies the Lord; and my spirit rejoices in God, my Savior, who has taken notice of his servant girl in her humble place." She stopped. "Is it not unlike the prayer of Hannah when she prayed for the Lord to give her the child Samuel?"

Luke nodded as he reached for his wooden box with the stylus and scrolls.

"I will tell you about the visit of the angel Gabriel and the overshadowing by the Most High. You should also know the amazing story of Mary's visit to her cousin Elizabeth and Zachariah, the parents of John the Baptizer. All in due time."

Luke put a small scroll on the table. "You have the final details that I need. I want to know more about the beginning of Yeshua's life and what he said about the end of all things."

Mariam nodded her head gravely. "Yes, I know of these matters."

"But I must ask you a personal question first," Luke spoke hesitantly. "Please forgive me if I pass beyond the boundaries of propriety but I am confused about a very important point concerning your family."

"I trust you. Ask what you wish."

"What about Yochanan Ben Zakkai? Who is he?"

Mariam blinked in surprise and a frown crossed her face. "I did not expect that question," she hesitated. "You have touched a painful nerve."

"I meant no harm. Perhaps, it would be best if—"

"No," Mariam studied the doctor's eyes, carefully searching their depths. "Maybe some purpose will be served if you know the whole story, but you must never write these facts down. The truth is forever our secret."

"Whatever you ask."

Mariam again looked out the window into the street where children were still playing. "Once there were three brothers Ben Aaron. My father had an older brother named Zeda. A wonderful man, indeed! He held the family together. When Zeda was killed, it was as if a whole way of life disappeared. Nothing was the same ever again." She turned away from the window. "The three brothers had inherited the family jewelry business which stood forever beneath the great wall. Year after year they worked, happily producing the finest gold jewelry in the city. In time my father, Jarius, even became the president of the synagogue. Even though I was sickly, those were wonderful years with him!"

"You said three brothers?"

"Yes," Mariam said factually. "The younger brother's name was Simeon. His brilliant mind soon propelled him to a place on the Great Sanhedrin. Of the three, Simeon was considered the scholar."

"He died?"

"Simeon was opposed to Jesus the Messiah from the beginning," Mariam continued. "Simeon could not explain my restoration to life at the hand of Jesus, but he considered it to be a work of deception. Many bitter conflicts followed until a great confrontation tore us apart."

"An argument?"

"Far worse. Your friend Paul was involved. You know the story of the death of our first martyr, Stephan?" Mariam's factual tone faded and her voice became very soft.

"Oh, yes. Paul told me."

"Stephan and I . . ." Mariam hesitated, searching for

the right words, "were quite close. My father and I believed Simeon was a part of the plot to kill Stephan."

Luke's eyes widened in astonishment.

"Because of the rift that followed, Simeon disappeared. He was both discredited with us and at the Great Sanhedrin. He just vanished." Mariam shook her head. "In time we learned that he was as much a victim of misunderstanding as we were."

"How sad. Your father was the last surviving brother."

"No." Mariam smiled mysteriously. "Simeon did not die. He returned after several decades. Yochanan Ben Zakkai is my Uncle Simeon."

Luke's mouth dropped. "Uncle," he gasped.

"That's much too long a story to tell you today, Luke. Suffice it to say that Simeon returned to us after many years of working the trade routes to the East. Ishmael, his servant, came with him. It was best for him to remain the mysterious new partner with one eye. When my father and I went to Rome, Uncle Simeon helped my youngest son, Zeda, in handling the family business. During those years, Simeon regained a place of leadership among the Pharisees. He is once again a very important man in this city, and that is why his real identity must be protected."

"Amazing!" Luke exclaimed. "Your secret will certainly be safe with me. I will certainly not let Yochanan know." The doctor laid the stylus aside. "But Ben Zakkai is a very bitter opponent of the faith."

"Oh, yes!" Mariam threw up her hands. "Never underestimate his antagonism. We still struggle to keep from coming to blows. Time has only increased his disdain for our faith. I need not tell you that he has no good words for Paul."

"Mother, mother!" Zeda rushed into the room. "Oh, forgive me, sir. I did not realize anyone was here."

"We conceal nothing from the good doctor, my son. Speak freely."

"Something very important has happened," Zeda spoke rapidly. "Ishmael came very early this morning to tell me that while we were gone he located the Ben Ephraim family!"

"What? Are you sure?" Mariam's eyes narrowed.

"Yes, at least there is excellent reason for hope. Simon Ben Giora has information. We are to go to Simon for the details."

"If I might venture an opinion?" Luke spoke hesitantly. "During my time here I have heard much of this Ben Giora. He is a treacherous beast. Are you sure you can trust him?"

"I doubt it." Zeda shrugged. "But how else can we find out?"

"I don't think your uncle will like it." Luke shook his head vigorously.

"Uncle?" Zeda's stopped. "What did you say?"

"He knows about Simeon," Mariam answered. "We can trust Luke. Perhaps, his help will yet be vital to us."

Zeda frowned, hesitated, and chewed on the side of his lip before speaking again. "You are correct in your suspicions. Yochanan only sent Ishmael today because he thought I should be aware of the facts but my uncle opposes contact with Ben Giora."

"Exactly what did you learn from Ishmael?" Mariam asked.

"Apparently there are many prisoners beneath the fortress at Ptolemais. Ben Giora captured a Roman slave who knows where the jail cells are hidden."

"Ptolemais?" Mariam puzzled. "Zeda, wasn't that where the young soldier was going? The Roman we met on the boat?"

"Exactly!" Zeda pointed his finger toward the north. "Marcus Quintus Cunctator was assigned there. Very fortuitous, is it not?"

"What are you thinking, son? I shudder when I see that look in your eye."

"We have two approaches." Zeda began to pace. "We certainly made a valuable contact with the Roman. Marcus Quintus was very interested in our faith and most cordial. I could easily contact him again." Zeda abruptly turned and started walking in the opposite direction. "On the other hand, Ishmael can talk with this Ben Giora and maybe negotiate something. If one part of the plan fails, then we can go to the other possibility."

"We also have another ally," Mariam said thoughtfully.

"Who?" Zeda pressed.

"Jesse. Remember? The young man who met us at the boat. The one who knows Yosef Ben Mathias."

"We have a three-pronged spear!" Zeda clapped his hands. "I know God is with us. We must carefully lay our plans. I will yet find my betrothed!"

"However, we should talk with your uncle immediately." Mariam stood up. "Even if Simeon is opposed, we must listen to his counsel. I'm sorry, Luke. We will have to continue our conversation later."

"I will be glad to go with you," the doctor replied. "Perhaps I can be of some help. My services are at your disposal."

"Then let us go to the jewelry shop at once," Zeda urged. "We must not waste any time."

Yochanan Ben Zakkai was bent over his work bench twisting gold wire into chain links when Zeda bounded through the door with Mariam and Luke behind him. Ishmael sat in the far corner polishing a gold bracelet with a soft cloth.

"Yochanan!" Zeda extend his arms. "We must talk!"

"I expected you would come quickly," Ben Zakkai grumbled. "Did I not predict so?" He turned his good eye toward the Arab.

"We have new hope!" Zeda shook his uncle's shoulders gently. "We will find the Ben Ephraim family."

Yochanan turned his head to see Mariam and recognized for the first time that Luke was with them. He visibly stiffened. "Perhaps, this is not the time to speak of these matters."

"Luke will help us," Zeda assured him. "We may need a doctor."

"Oh, indeed!" Ben Zakkai responded with unexpected harshness. "You may need the help of the hosts of heaven before this matter is concluded."

"You are angry?" Zeda retreated.

"Deeply concerned." Ben Zakkai pulled at his beard. "We are dealing with a den of snakes. Anyone who does business with Simon Ben Giora plays with the devil. The man is vicious and unpredictable."

"But what else am I to do?" Zeda countered.

Yochanan shook his head and crossed his arms over his chest. "I don't know. I just don't know," he lamented. "There is no question that you should know what Ishmael has discovered, but I wish he had never heard the words. I tell you no one can do business with this tyrant and come away unscathed."

"How can we not inquire further?" Zeda pleaded. "I propose that Luke, Ishmael, and I go to Herod's Palace and see him tomorrow."

"Ben Giora loves to take captives." Ben Zakkai shook his finger at Zeda. "Unless the bargain has a personal advantage for him, you can't trust a word he says. What can you offer him besides a few pieces of gold?" Ben Zakkai turned his back in disgust. "And he is already sucking in all the gold in the Upper City!"

"Perhaps, I have something money can't buy." Luke stepped forward. "Maybe the possibility of medical care would entice a general with wounded soldiers.

"See!" Zeda clapped his hands. "We may have special leverage."

Ben Zakkai glared at the doctor. He pursed his lips to speak but didn't.

"Ishmael, Luke, and I must go see Simon," Zeda talked rapidly. "We can offer money *and* medical care. He will quickly recognize it is to his advantage to deal with us honestly and honorably. It's a perfect plan!"

"In this world," Yochanan snapped, "there is no perfection! Things fall apart. People betray and dreams shrivel. Hear me well. Guard your steps, young Zeda. You are facing an adversary who neither loves Israel nor fears God. Remember this!" He shook his finger in Zeda's face. "Simon Ben Giora is an evil man who only loves power and hates Romans. Unless you serve those two purposes, he will devour you as quickly as he will help you!"

VII

After the family left, the one-eyed sage returned to his work bench. Yochanan held up a gold necklace to the afternoon sunlight. Each fine link reflected exceptional craftsmanship. Satisfied, he once more spread the chain out on his table. Although he worked quickly, he was totally preoccupied with the morning's conversation about Ben Giora. Solitude and fear transported him so deeply within the recesses of his memory that he was oblivious to everything around him. Mechanically Yochanan worked the clasp on the chain while he considered and reconsidered every option his nephew might face.

"You didn't hear me enter."

"Ah!" Yochanan jumped and turned his good eye toward the door.

"I thought we ought to talk again," Luke answered. "I didn't mean to surprise you."

"What do you want?" Ben Zakkai grumbled.

"Since I'm going with Zeda tomorrow, I felt I should know everything possible about Simon Ben Giora."

Yochanan studied the doctor, feeling his own deep ambivalence. Certainly the Greek had proven himself, but he was still a foreigner and a Gentile. "What more can I say?" Yochanan shrugged.

"Please," Luke extended his hands. "What more can I do to prove I am trustworthy? What other purpose

71

could bring me here but to seek the best for the entire family?"

"You will soon leave us," Yochanan said bluntly. "At least if you are smart you will! You mean well but you will not live with the consequences of these actions. We will. You can afford to be charitable. I must be prudent."

"When I walk into that palace with Zeda," Luke countered, "my life is no less on the line. Yes, I will soon depart, but in the meantime I am in no less jeopardy. Can you question my courage?"

Ben Zakkai tilted his head and squinted. After a long pause, he nodded. "Point well made. Sit down."

"For weeks I have watched you." Luke trained his physician's eyes on the old man. "You know more than is humanly possible about what is going on in this city. How is it that you are always so well informed?"

Ben Zakkai scrutinized Luke. "Let me just say that I have contacts everywhere. Whether it be Elezar and his friends in the Temple or members of the Sanhedrin living in the Upper City, I am extremely well informed."

"Ishmael is your link to many of these people?"

"Ishmael is trusted throughout the city," Yochanan said with finality. "Now what do you want to know about Simon Ben Giora?"

"Who really holds power in Jerusalem?"

"No one!" Yochanan barked abruptly. "Elezar and the high priests control the Temple compound and the Antonia Fortress. The Sanhedrin has jurisdiction over the city, but cannot dispatch soldiers." Ben Zakkai shook his finger in Luke's face. "Ben Giora is an evil tyrant! Although he is turning the Upper City into a war machine, he is hated and feared. The priest Elezar Ben Simon and Simon Ben Giora are locked into a battle to gain the upper hand."

"Then Ben Giora could be overthrown?"

"No!" Ben Zakkai pounded on the table. "The fools in the Temple and the simpletons who surround me at the Sanhedrin have failed to realize that Simon has the resolve and temper to be far more vicious than the Romans. He is stockpiling supplies as if he alone were to be our next king. Simon is much stronger than the priests and the lawyers know. He will look for every opportunity to flex his muscles."

"I see." Luke scratched his head. "If I might venture an observation?" he asked apologetically.

Yochanan said nothing but stared at him.

"Your generation has lived under the heel of the Romans. The people understand tyranny, but not freedom. Everywhere I look, your nation seems to be hopelessly divided."

Yochanan contemptuously spat on the floor. He knew the doctor was correct and his accuracy was irritating. "So what's your point?" he groused.

"I fear for you," Luke said earnestly. "My heart is with you, Yochanan Ben Zakkai. You are hopelessly trapped and I know that you are a thoroughly good man. I truly want to be your friend."

Yochanan looked down at the table and his body sagged. Regardless of their difference over religion, there truly was no reason to treat Luke as an outsider. Surely the doctor had proven himself.

"This is very difficult for me," Yochanan said slowly. "Night and day I struggle with the implications of these matters." Suddenly he felt very tired. "Yes, your observations are quite accurate. Unless something unexpected happens, this nation is a house permanently divided against itself. The ceiling will fall down on our heads."

"You cannot stand then," Luke said quietly.

"You are correct," the old man said with steely coldness. "There is a flaw in the national foundation that does not appear to be repairable. Pharisees stand against Sadducees while Essenes flee to the desert. The high priests have no interest in the common people, and the citizens' primary interest is personal survival. The lost mantle of leadership is stolen by criminals like Simon Ben Giora. And now our religion is divided by those who proclaim your Messiah as God. Religious madness makes the repair of the crack all the more impossible."

"There is no hope?" Luke asked.

"Even within this shop," Yochanan sighed, "the divisions are hopelessly unresolvable."

"Jesus predicted this day would come. I don't mean to offend you but even Mariam recorded that He predicted the coming of this moment."

"A prophet or a genius wasn't needed to foresee the outcome of generations bickering with each other," Yochanan answered sourly. "Three decades ago, even I foresaw what divisions his teaching was creating."

"But he predicted the destruction of the Temple—"

"Exactly why we despised the man," Ben Zakkai cut Luke off. "The Galileans never liked coming down here to make sacrifice and Yeshua delighted in attacking temple worship. He's as much a part of our hopeless disunity as is Ben Giora!"

"Come now," Luke implored. "You have many reasons to believe He is your Messiah He healed the blind and raised the dead."

"Listen!" Ben Zakkai slowly began raising his voice. "If that Nazarene had been the true Messiah, he would have thrown the Romans into the sea. We wouldn't want for a leader in this hour. He would be king!"

"Yochanan, my friend," Luke held both hands out and begged. "You sought a man like David, but didn't Daniel and Isaiah predict a spiritual savior who would bring a revolution of the heart and soul? Didn't they foresee spiritual rebirth in all the nations? Could it be you have expected the wrong kind of man?"

"You? A Gentile? Would lecture me, a Jew, about the Torah and the prophets?" Yochanan crossed his arms over his chest. He suddenly felt acceptance turn to contempt. "You come in here and read a few scrolls and start interpreting to me what I long ago memorized? With your pitiable Greek you decipher what I carry in my head in Hebrew? Tell me more, scholar, of our Messiah!"

"Please, please." Luke begged. "I am not trying to affront you. I came to this land to understand the most important truth in the history of the world. Plato, Aristophanes, Socrates . . . none of our thinkers even came close to the extraordinary teaching of Jesus. For centuries, you looked for a military general, but the Lord God Himself came to heal and end the spiritual warfare that has plagued the whole world. Jesus, the Messiah, transcends all barriers of time and eternity."

Ben Zakkai sneered. "Only a Greek could conjure up such nonsense! Madness. You love this 'God in human form' talk that Moses called utter blasphemy! Yes, only a crazy hallucinating fool like Saul of Tarsus would come up with such prattle."

"Look!" Luke began to sound irritated. "The cross of Jesus the Christ was the means by which God reached into our lives and forgave the sin that . . ."

"Forgive your sin?" Ben Zakkai hissed. "Your sin? Your lawbreaking, morally illiterate deeds were wiped out because a Jew was overpowered by Romans and crucified? Now that is ultimate insanity! You had best read the Torah and start living total righteousness before these delusions of Saul eat your brain out. Sin forgiven, indeed!" Ben Zakkai spat on the floor again.

"But everything that Moses and the prophets hoped for, believed in, longed for has now come to pass. Even Jesus looked for the redemption of the whole world. Gentiles can now be included in Abraham's covenant by faith. The blood of Jesus spilled on the cross has—"

"Blood of Jesus?" Ben Zakkai cut him off. "You are attempting to make his unfortunate death a sacrifice for the sin of the world?" The old man snorted.

"God has come in the flesh! Paul says that . . ." Luke tried to call the name back.

"Do . . . not . . . mention . . . again this spineless Saul who was even ashamed to keep his Jewish name. We have tried to work out some sort of accommodation with these Believers who think the Nazarene was uniquely chosen, but to speak of him as divine is absolute blasphemy! It is one thing for Jew to disagree with Jew; it's another for some Greek Gentile to come in here and try to recast every building block our faith rests on. No one can drive a wedge between us as one of you can. People like you and this worthless Saul will do more damage to the nation of Israel than a thousand legions from Rome."

"I only seek to bring God's message to the world that all peoples might . . ."

"All peoples! Don't you understand we are a singular people? Jews are a race, a nation, a clan, a tribe, a family. We stand separate from the world. We have been called to be a nation of priests to the Lord! If you Believers prevail, you will destroy us! People like you will be the death of our nation."

Luke swallowed hard and his face turned deep crimson. "I believe that Yeshua brought fulfillment to everything the Jewish nation has believed."

"You do not bring completion." Ben Zakkai shook his finger in the doctor's face. "You have started a new religion. In the past Jews might differ over interpretations of the holy scriptures but now you have driven a wedge that splits us apart. You rip the sacred scrolls into pieces."

"No! No!" Luke pleaded with upraised hands. "We want to reconcile everyone."

"You are a fool." Yochanan Ben Zakkai's voice was cold and hard. "The path you walk down splits in two separate ways. Either you are right and we are wrong . . . or you are wrong and we are right. There is no middle way. What you, Saul, Mariam, and all the rest believe will divide forever our people against each other. This Jesus brought a sword into the house of Israel. People like you simply push the blade deeper into our hearts!"

"I'm sorry." Luke shook his head. "I did not come here to make you angry. My business is healing, not hurting."

Ben Zakkai opened his mouth as if to shout, but instead he drew in a large gasp of air. Slowly he exhaled clenching his teeth together. "Please leave now," he said firmly. "You came to learn about Ben Giora and I have told you enough. Be as presumptuous as you have been this afternoon and your arrogance will push you over a precipice."

"I'm sorry." Luke backed toward the door. "I only meant—"

"I know," Ben Zakkai waved him on, "you meant well. Shalom."

Luke disappeared through the canvas flap doors without saying anything more. Ben Zakkai slumped back into his chair and rubbed his forehead. "He meant well," he muttered out loud. "Of course they all mean well."

The old man pulled his tallith, which he always wore around his shoulder, over his head. He closed his eye and held his hands toward the ceiling. "Oh, God of Abraham, Isaac, and Jacob save us from those who mean us harm and those who mean us well. Keep us from the stranger's way as well as saving us from the evil designs of despicable men. Sustain us in the disaster that is surely ahead of us. For the sake of Your holy nation, the People of the Covenant, deliver us from this hour of madness." Tears filled his eyes and he choked. Ben Zakkai could pray no more.

Luke, Ishmael, and Zeda left in mid-morning for their meeting with Simon Ben Giora. Because the House of Jarius was not far from the first or north wall, they did not have to walk far to reach Herod's Palace. Just beyond the palace was the garden gate that opened out toward Bethlehem. The second part of the north wall ended at the Antonia Fortress. The tomb of the great resurrection and the Ben Aaron family graves were just beyond this wall. The three men walked toward Herod's high towers, memorials to his treachery, and appropriate headquarters for Simon Ben Giora.

"Let me begin," Ishmael instructed as they walked. "Simon knows me and will expect me to be an envoy. The two of you stand behind me as dignitaries always do when they negotiate for their governments."

"Would Simon know the difference?" Zeda asked cynically.

"Probably not," Ishmael shrugged. "But his arrogance is better satisfied when he is being treated with great respect."

Luke kept looking at the stone façades covering the buildings around them. "I've never been in this section before. These are very expensive homes. There are even marble exteriors on some of these places."

"The most exquisite part of the city," Zeda explained. "The Palace of the Hasmoneans is at one end and Herod's fortress is at the other. Of course, Herod took the best view for himself." Zeda pointed to an immense stone fortress just ahead. "On the other side we will find the lair of Ben Giora."

Armed men milled around the iron gate. They paid little attention when the three friends passed by. Other soldiers slouched against the wall. Moving up and down the broad stone steps leading to the first floor of the palace, the men seemed bored and disinterested. Without uniforms, Ben Giora's troops didn't look any different from other men walking the city streets. They were a motley, undisciplined crew.

"What's your business?" the guard in front of the large, ornate door demanded.

"Simon Ben Giora is expecting us this morning," Ishmael answered. "Please tell him that the family Ben Aaron is here."

The guard tossed his head indifferently and disappeared inside the door. Three soldiers huddled around a fire at the other end of the hallway, roasting a piece of meat over the flames burning on the marble floor.

"The Herods were always hated," Zeda told Luke. "Herod the Great rebuilt the Temple to look important and was all the more despised for doing it. Antipas was nothing but a puppet of Rome. Agrippa isn't any better. I'm sure these beggars love cooking in the hallways and staining the alabaster walls with their greasy smoke."

The inner door opened. "Come in," the guard beckoned.

Lavish tapestries had been torn from the walls of Herod's throne room. Each of the three visitors stared at the large, granite-covered room. Garbage was strewn everywhere. A couple of men were sleeping in the corners. Dogs were wandering around eating the bones left among the remnants of last night's feast.

"Ah, look what we have here!" Ben Giora chided more than invited. He was leaning on a crutch, surrounded by a circle of advisers who were not much better groomed than the dogs. "The gentlemen of the lower city come to visit us. None other than the house of Ben Aaron with their one-eyed partner's Arab spokesman."

"May we speak with you?" Ishmael bowed at the waist.

"Oh, by all means." Simon waved them forward. "Been a while since I've seen you, young Zeda. My eyes and ears in the streets say you went to Rome for a little visit. My, but you Christians are a busy lot."

"I have told my master," the Arab turned and pointed to Zeda, "that you have information about prisoners."

Simon suddenly doubled up and his face twisted in

pain. Two of the aids grabbed his arms to keep him from falling off the couch.

"Stop it," he weakly brushed them aside. "It seems I have a slight problem," his voice was faint. "A Roman put an arrow in my leg, but don't you dare make the mistake of thinking that I am weakened. Just gets me now and then."

"What is it you want for this information?" Ishmael ventured.

"What do you offer?" Simon growled.

"Like the rest of Jerusalem," Ishmael held up empty palms and spoke apologetically, "we are seriously depleted from the lack of business. Pilgrims fear to come because of the a . . . er . . . a . . . unrest in the streets."

"Don't trifle with me!" Simon barked. "You come here to blame me and my troops for your business failures. I want five talents of gold before I even begin to talk."

"Such is impossible!" the Arab held his hands together as if praying. "No one has that kind of money now."

Simon grimaced again and drops of sweat began to form on his forehead. "Then what could you possibly offer me?" he sneered.

"The opportunity to become known as a great general," Zeda suddenly spoke. "I met the new commander of the fortress at Ptolemais as we returned from Rome. In addition, I have contacts with the forces of Josephus in the north. A successful raid would make Simon Ben Giora even better known as the future leader of the entire country."

"So you think you know something about Ptolemais, do you?" Simon bit his lip. "You flatter yourselves. I might let you talk with my new boy, Shamir, who knows *all* the secrets of the fort."

"You have men sitting around wasting," Zeda continued. "I could help them find the exercise that makes soldiers strong. Is that not a worthy objective for a great leader of the people?"

Simon wiped his forehead. "You are suggesting that I need you worse than you need me?" he snorted.

"We have mutual interests that exceed mere money." Zeda smiled accommodatingly.

"Don't toy with me," Simon snapped. "You had best have the money or our discussions are ended."

"Perhaps, I might offer a better proposition," Luke stepped forward. "You are in pain that no amount of money can cure. Wouldn't relief be worth more than talents of gold?"

Simon held his side. "What are you suggesting?"

"I am a Greek doctor," Luke answered. "Surgery is my specialty. If I can heal your wound, would you accept my success as adequate payment?"

The advisors turned and stared at Simon. He inhaled a deep breath, exposing the side of his face where his teeth were missing. "So, young Zeda, you want information and my soldiers to free your friends. You come without a denarius in hand to suggest that I do battle for the sake of my reputation." He tried to laugh but couldn't. Simon's eyes squinted so tightly they became slits. "The idea is not quite as crazy as it sounds. Yes, my men need a little exercise."

The advisors nodded to one another.

"But none of this interests me like the proposal the doctor offers." Simon suddenly whipped his robe aside. The gaping hole in his thigh was red and swollen. Streaks of red ran down his leg. "Yes, physician, I can read the signs, too. There's a metal arrowhead buried in there somewhere. I know if it doesn't come out quickly I need never plan a battle again. Your offer is the best I've heard today."

Luke nodded gravely.

"Now, I will make *my* offer." Simon gently closed the robe over his leg. "If the doctor can heal my leg, we will ride with you to explore the caverns beneath the Ptolemais fortress. Along the way we will even kill a few Romans for sport." He suddenly waved his hand in the air toward Zeda. "Yes, yes, I know you are one of the Christians who won't kill anything. I know all about your mother's powers. If I can fight again, the battle will cost the Ben Aarons nothing."

"Excellent!" Zeda exploded.

Ishmael reached for Zeda's hand instinctively to stop any premature response.

"And my final terms," Simon clinched his teeth as he spoke menacingly, "are that young Ben Aaron does not leave this room until the surgery is successfully completed. If I am well, you may all go and prepare for our attack on Ptolemais. If I should not survive, then each of you will sleep in my grave with me. Those are my terms. The matter is settled." His voice trailed away. Simon feebly waved toward the back and two guards immediately locked the doors.

VIII

Luke carefully placed a narrow wooden tray from his carrying case on a small table next to Ben Giora's couch. He opened his varied collection of surgical instruments. Some scalpels had sharp narrow points, others curved blades or hooked cutting edges. Luke quickly found a long metal sheath holding an ornate lancet. He pulled the lancet out of the case and gingerly touched the slender blade with the finely honed edge. "I think we are about ready." He put the special knife back in its case.

"What do you want me to do?" Zeda asked.

"You are to strap his legs together." Luke pointed at several of Ben Giora's soldiers. "These men are to hold him down at all costs. He must not be allowed to move. Zeda, be ready to hand me whatever I ask."

Two soldiers stepped solemnly to the end of the couch, but their eyes were locked on the doctor. They stared suspiciously.

"Don't fail," one soldier grumbled and shifted the knife in his belt. Ishmael pushed his way through the crowd of men standing around the couch. "Here is the vinegar and water." He placed two small bowls on the table next to the surgical instruments. "Can we begin now?"

"I want two strong men to pin Simon's arms against the couch." Luke beckoned two burly guards forward.

The unkempt soldiers stepped into place.

"We only have a short amount of time to conclude the operation," Luke spoke directly to Zeda. The doctor pointed to the veins in his hand. "If such a vessel had been severed in the battle, Ben Giora would have died on the spot. Should I accidently sever a major vein, he will die quickly." Luke handed the young man a small ligature. "Bleeding is not a problem, but hemorrhaging is! My only hope would be to use this clasp. Hand it to me immediately if I call."

Zeda nodded his head solemnly as he took the ligature in his hand.

Luke looked around the room and then down at Simon. "Your skin has grown over the top of the wound. I will have to reopen the hole to find the path of the arrow into your leg. I have an anodyne made from herbs that will help the pain some, but relief will be slight."

"Get on with it," the chieftain grunted. "A little pain is no problem for old Ben Giora. Forget the medicine." Simon sneered and waved for Luke to begin. "If you fail today, you won't need any medicine for your condition either, Greek."

The doctor slowly pulled the lancet from the sheath as he pulled back the cover over Simon's legs. His right leg was swollen to nearly twice the size of the left; the entire upper area of his thigh was an angry red. The old wound was ugly and festering around the edges. "Tie him down tightly," Luke commanded. He inhaled deeply and closed his eyes for a few moments before beginning.

Luke felt the feverish skin around the place where the arrow had entered and then dropped to one knee. With one quick flick of his wrist, the doctor cut an opening through the crusty scab. With his other hand, Luke carefully pushed a long metal probe into the incision. Suddenly a yellow-green liquid oozed out of the cut. The doctor laid the lance down and pressed on the other side of the man's leg. The pus erupted in every direction. The stench caused Luke to stagger backward and gag. Zeda and Ishmael took several steps back from the couch.

"Ah!" Ben Giora exclaimed. "I already feel relief."

"Hang on," Luke sputtered and pushed the long probe back into the wound. Simon abruptly clenched his teeth and squinted his eyes. The chieftain gasped. With quick short thrusts, Luke sank the surgical instrument deeper into the arrow's path. Suddenly he felt metal touch metal. "I've found it! Quickly!" He spoke to Zeda. "Take the flat piece of metal on the box and pull the side of the wound open. Quickly."

The young man timidly slipped the spade-like instrument into the skin and cautiously pulled sideways against the skin.

"Give me those tongs!" Luke barked at Ishmael. "I hope to get the arrow tip on the first try."

Instantly, the Arab handed the doctor the long, thin tweezers. Luke carefully worked the tongs down the side of the probe until he felt contact again. Letting go of the probe, he clamped the sides together and yanked upward. Luke looked at the corroded tip a moment and then held the bloody instrument with the metal arrowhead up in the air. "Got it!"

Applause broke out across the room.

Luke looked carefully at the wound again. A small piece of leather stuck out the top. Once more he worked the tongs into the opening and slowly pulled a leather lace out. "Held the arrowhead on the shaft," he concluded. Once again a foul odor filled the room as Luke held the rotting leather up. "Pour the vinegar into the wound," he instructed Ishmael. "Wash it out thoroughly."

At once the Arab poured the bowl of vinegar over the thigh and washed the corruption away. Ben Giora flinched and moaned deeply. "Don't let the wound close," he nodded to Zeda. "We must keep the cut open so the leg will drain. We are not out of the woods yet. The infection is terrible."

"You've done it!" Zeda clapped his hands.

"Assist me," Luke answered his young friend. "Put your hands on his leg and pray."

Luke closed his eyes, laid his palms on the swollen thigh, and began praying under his breath. Intense silence fell over the room as the soldiers watched the unexpected sight of a doctor acting like a priest or one of the holy men who often attended the sick. Ben Giora moaned several times keeping his eyes closed. Ishmael kept staring at the soldiers and the figure on the couch as if he feared a violent reaction, but did not move during the lengthy time the two Christians prayed.

Luke finally lifted his head and took his hands away. "Our prayers are as important as the operation. I think he will be all right now. Keep the wound open and let it drain. We have finished our work. We will return tomorrow." He closed his instrument case.

"No!" one of Ben Giora's general commanded. "You are not to leave this room until we know our leader lives. You will sleep here tonight. Only Simon can release you."

Late the next morning, the soldiers assembled once more around the couch of their leader. Luke and his two friends examined the drainage. Luke nodded his approval.

"I'm astonished at how the swelling has gone down." Zeda handed a cloth bandage to the doctor.

Simon flinched when Luke squeezed the sides of his leg. "The operation made the whole leg more tender," Luke mused. "Typical. I think we can safely cover the wound now."

No one spoke as Luke gently placed the final cloth bandage over Ben Giora's massive thigh. The rebel clenched his teeth and stared straight ahead while his aides huddled around carefully watching the doctor's motions. The physician's agile fingers quickly tied the compress down.

"A day and a night have made quite a difference." Luke straightened up. "We can say confidently the tides have turned. Time is all that is needed now."

Simon bounced an arrowhead up and down in his palm. "A little thing can cause so much damage." He smiled slightly. "We shall be such a thorn in the side of the Roman Empire. Yes, my leg is much better."

Zeda stood next to the window watching the morning sunlight fall over the city and trying to breathe fresh clean air. "Now you will release us? Or at least start making plans to march on Ptolemais?"

"You doubt my word young Ben Aaron?" Ben Giora's grin widened exposing the toothless black hole in his mouth. "Maybe you have just grown weary of our hospitality?"

"Two days is a long time to stay in one room," Zeda said soberly.

"You should have been lying in my bed," Ben Giora growled. "At least I'll give you credit, doctor. My body is covered with scars. I've lost count of how many times my hide has been stuck. Three arrows were pulled out of me, but never have I started to heal as quickly. You have good hands."

"You didn't make a sound." Luke picked up the iron arrowhead from Simon's hand. "It was lodged against the bone. I didn't think I could get it out quickly." Luke turned the sharp point over.

Ben Giora snatched the arrowhead out of Luke's hand and threw it past Zeda out the window. "Give me a week and then we will ride north. Go on! Send a runner to make contact with this Jesse, the lackey of Josephus. Do what you wish. I'm going to live and that's all that counts." Simon waved his aides away. "Let them go and get out. I need more sleep. When I'm ready to move out, I'll let you know." He turned over and pulled a cover over his face.

"You heard him!" One of the aides barked at Zeda. "Be thankful that the Holy One of Israel was with you. Now get out of here. When we are ready to attack we'll send men for you. In the meantime, speak to no one of what you have seen in this room. Don't trifle with us. We can attack in the lower city as easily as we do up here."

Ishmael pulled Luke and Zeda behind him and hurried down the stairs. "Don't linger," he said under his breath. "Move!"

"You saved his life," Zeda said as they scurried out to the street. "He was in very bad shape."

"I'm not sure we've done the nation a favor," Luke said sourly. "Maybe we've only perpetuated a disease!"

Nothing more was said as the three men rushed toward the jewelry shop.

A week later Mariam gathered the Ben Aaron family in the large room where for three decades every significant decision had been made. Even at high noon the largest room in the house of Jarius Ben Aaron was filled with shadows. Mariam felt the presence of Philip, Stephan, Jarius, Saul, and Peter hovering in the corners.

Luke and Ishmael did not seem out of place. Ben Zakkai sat next to Zeda. Leah and her husband sat at the dining table in the back trying to keep their children occupied and quiet.

"I oppose it!" Yochanan Ben Zakkai's voice was shrill. "I told you in the beginning that everything Ben Giora touches drips with treachery. Have we not already lost enough loved ones to the Romans? Will we foolishly expend more lives on a whim?"

"Please," Zeda begged. "We have extremely good reason to believe the whole Ben Ephraim family is imprisoned at Ptolemais. Would we want them to do less for us?"

"Did I not foretell exactly what would happen if you went to Rome?" Ben Zakkai pointed his finger at Mariam. "Why will you not listen to me?" He turned his face toward the wall.

Leah stepped over her son, Amon, who was playing on the floor, and came forward out of the dining room. "Zeda is quite right. I would hope if one of us was chained up in a dungeon we wouldn't decide the matter in some unemotional, businesslike way." She whirled around and went back to the children.

Ben Zakkai clenched his teeth and closed his good eye.

"By now our messenger has surely made contact with Jesse." Zeda continued. "We might even be able to enlist support from Yoseph Ben Mathias. Would this not be an even greater reason for optimism?"

Yochanan did not open his eye but jutted his chin forward even more defiantly.

"We owe a debt to the doctor," Leah interjected from the back of the dining room. "Without his intervention our position would be hopeless."

"Hmph!" Yochanan opened his eye. "It would have been much better for the whole city if the vile beast had died. The doctor did us no favor."

"There is no point in arguing," Mariam said firmly. "The decision has been made and the journey is set. Ben Giora told us that we leave in three days. We must decide who stays and who will go. Let us not waste time bickering," she looked hard at her daughter.

"Of course, I'm going." Zeda glanced at Ishmael who immediately looked away, avoiding any eye contact. "No one should feel any pressure to travel with us."

"I must go," Mariam said quietly.

"No!" Ben Zakkai leaped from his chair. "A thousand times no!"

"Please, Uncle," Mariam spoke kindly but gestured resolutely for him to sit down. "I seem to have developed a taste for danger in the last few years. I have lived with worse than this journey offers."

"No! No!" Yochanan repeated. "The Roman galleys have landed. No telling how many legions are wandering around in the north. Besides, what possible value could you be in a battle at a seaport?"

"I spent many hours talking with Marcus Quintus Cunctator while we sailed across the Mediterranean and even prayed with him. I think I know his heart." Mariam smiled slyly. "I may have a better plan than that which Simon Ben Giora proposes."

"What could you possibly offer?" Yochanan walked over to Mariam, holding out his hands begging her.

"I think I might accomplish more by talking with this man than he will ever achieve by attacking his fortress. At least, I believe I can persuade him to tell us if the Ben Ephraim family is truly being held there before more lives are lost."

"That's brilliant, Mother." Zeda beamed.

"We must do everything possible to be peacemakers," Mariam continued. "That is our way. The Roman was sincere in his inquiries about our faith. He knew the story of our friend Honorius and his death at the hands of Nero. Marcus Quintus was eager to learn everything we could tell him."

"In spite of what your nation has faced," Luke spoke up, "I've found many Romans to be quite honorable and reasonable. I think Mariam might succeed."

"And I think we might never see her again!" Yochanan retorted bitterly. "*Nothing* is predictable anymore."

Silence descended over the room as everyone but Ben Zakkai looked toward Mariam.

Leah spoke sarcastically. "Is nothing predictable, mother?"

Mariam did not speak but gave her daughter a hard look.

"Yes, yes." Ben Zakkai waved his hand aimlessly in the air. "I read your scroll and know of the predictions as well as any of you do. Any fool could make such conjectures about the possible destruction of this city. Heaven knows you've given the soothsayers ample material for their babblings."

Mariam winced. The room again became silent.

"Some of us call *that* blasphemy against the Holy Spirit," Leah retorted coldly.

"Stop it!" Yochanan pointed his finger at his niece. "We can't have these divisions. We must stay together. It's our only hope for the future. No, I don't accept the prophecies of Yeshua, but we must present a unified front against the Romans or they will cut us to shreds. It doesn't take a prophet to recognize that simple fact."

"Uncle," Mariam pleaded, "you don't understand us. Most surely I do not wish to offend you further, but you must see our position. We truly believe that we know what lies ahead."

Luke stepped forward. "What is it? I've waited a long time to hear the answer from your lips."

Mariam closed her eyes and rubbed her temples. "I believe the hour is at hand," she lamented. "Yes, I must believe what Daniel predicted and Antiochus Epiphanes fulfilled in his desecration of the Temple is about to be repeated. Yeshua said not one stone will be left standing. He was not against temple worship, Uncle. He was pointing to the day that is at hand."

Ben Zakkai crossed his arms over his chest and stared at her.

Mariam continued, "In addition to this trip to Ptolemais, we must soon flee the city. All who stay will perish. A way of life began to die when your brother Zeda was killed thirty years ago. Whether you blame the changes on Yeshua or the Romans, it has been so. The final funeral dirge will shortly sound across this city and the walls will become as one great coffin. We must leave before that moment."

"We?" Ben Zakkai's voice was hardly audible.

"Our people. The Believers. Yes, Uncle Simeon, and you, too. We don't kill and we won't go to war. We must seek other cities of refuge."

"There are so many of you," Yochanan whispered. "You will be branded as cowards, traitors. We must have your people to unify the city. You are known as reconcilers. Possibly you can help mediate the disputes."

Mariam shook her head sadly. "To not heed the words of our Messiah would be disobedience. We have no choice. Zeda must go north and in the very near future we must leave Jerusalem."

"N . . . o . . . o . . . o," the old man wailed. "Not again! No, no. Not again." He buried his face in his chest and covered his head with his arms.

"You must go with us," Mariam reached out for him. "There is no hope for you if you stay here."

Ben Zakkai pulled away. "Never! Never. I would gladly die here before I will abandon this Holy City."

Mariam tried to speak compassionately. "You misunderstood our Messiah. He did not mean to destroy our traditions. He came to fulfill them. You must not allow living things to die with the perishing."

"No more!" Ben Zakkai grabbed Ishmael by the robe and pulled him toward the door. "I can talk no further. I do not want to hear any more of your plans. My ears are already filled with pain." He bolted for the hallway, towing Ishmael behind him. The door stayed open as the two men disappeared down the street.

Mariam wrung her hands in despair. "I was afraid it would come to this."

"I've never seen him like this," Zeda answered. "He

is always so detached, reasonable . . . even when he disagrees."

"His world is about to end," Mariam spoke almost to herself. "He is more despairing than fearful. He knows that I am right. Yes, in his heart of hearts he knows that what I said is true. Like the winds from the wilderness blowing in the scorching heat of the desert, the days ahead will dry up all life. Simeon is a good man but each event strips him of another layer of hope. He is being pushed beyond his limits."

"Obviously, Ishmael will stay with him to the end," Zeda observed. "But I know the Arab will go with us to Ptolemais."

"We will not need Ishmael," Luke added.

"We?" Mariam turned to the doctor. "We?"

Luke looked surprised. "I'm not sure I understand."

"You must not go." Mariam's voice was resolute.

"What? Not go with you?"

"No. I know well what can happen when we underestimate change. I've seen sacred scrolls disappear in the night when attackers suddenly appear out of nowhere. If you wish to preserve the story you have been writing, you must leave now."

"But . . ." Luke stammered. "You may need a doctor . . . and . . ."

"Your work is too important," Mariam stopped him. "You were quite right to believe that the story of Yeshua must be circulated in Greek rather than Hebrew."

"I don't agree." Luke shook his head. "I . . . a . . . mean . . . I don't agree that my writing is in danger."

Mariam shook her head. "My uncle was also quite right about the danger. The chances are high that none of us might return from this venture. When we go to Ptolemais you must turn aside and sail from Caesarea."

"Really!" Luke sounded exasperated. "I have been through many dangerous situations with Paul and—"

"My son." Mariam put her hand on his shoulder and

looked up in the doctor's face. "You do not yet understand, but your writing is the most important work of your life. We will all pass from this scene, and if the Messiah delays His return, what is left behind can guide generations yet unborn."

"But the Messiah will return," Leah interrupted. "As soon as the city falls, He will come again."

"This has been revealed to you?" Mariam asked curtly.

"Well," Leah puzzled, "everyone says so."

"Everyone?" Mariam smiled cynically. "Everyone makes up your mind for you? I would suggest we do well to not put words in the mouth of the Messiah."

Leah started to speak but stopped. She blinked uncomprehendingly.

"We cannot measure the length of the future," Mariam spoke forcefully. "You must write as if your book were going to travel to the ends of the world. To be prudent is not a lack of courage. I have seen the Evil One's personal interest in stifling the publication of the story of Yeshua."

"Mother is seldom wrong about such matters." Zeda smiled at Luke. "When the Believers hear of her conclusions, they will begin to leave the city. Now is the right time for you to go."

Luke raised his hands as if to punctuate his protest, but no words came out of his mouth. Slowly he dropped his arms and shook his head despondently. "Perhaps I should prepare to go to Alexandria."

"Let us set our house in order." Mariam began to pace. "We must have two plans. First, we must think through what is to be said to the Believers after the attack on Ptolemais. We do not want people to panic, but they must understand the implications of the Messiah's teaching." Mariam held up two fingers as she thought out loud. "Second, we must have everything in place if . . . if none of us returns."

PART TWO

"For then there will be great tribulation,
such as has not been since the beginning of the world
until this time, no, nor ever shall be."

Matthew 24:21

IX

The seven generals standing before Yosef Ben Mathias could not conceal the weight of their concern.
The splendor of Herod's northern palace no longer offered reassurance. Even the gentle breeze blowing in
from Galilee did not offer the usual solace of spring in
Tiberius. Each man looked worn and worried.

"So what did you learn, Jonah?" Ben Mathias smiled
cynically but spoke calmly. "Reflect on our military defeat at Sepphorius. What are your conclusions?"

The Galilean stuck his hands up the long sleeves of his
large brown robe, crossing his arms tightly across his
chest. Jonah glanced uncomfortably around the room.
"We should never have trusted the people of Sepphorius
to rebuild their own walls," he said sourly. "They were
traitors from the beginning. The wealthy aristocrats betrayed us! They're the ones who sued Vespasian for a
separate peace. They literally opened the gates of the
city to him and his army! The citizens sold out the future
of the nation to save their worthless hides."

"Sepphorius is the largest city in Galilee!" Old Tabor
wailed. "The richest! We lost the gem of the north."

Yosef acknowledged their accuracy, nodding his head
unemotionally. "And why could we not take the city
back? Why did our campaign to take Sepphorius fail?"

No one answered.

"Yoel, you have spied on the Roman camp. What can you tell us?"

"Placidus, the tribune, got his revenge for the humiliation we heaped on him earlier. The thousand horsemen and the six thousand foot soldiers Vespasian sent into the city tipped the scales."

"But what did you see?" Yosef Ben Mathias bore down.

"Romans travel and fight as if they have a single mind. I am amazed, terrified. I watched them move with the precision of the legs of a centipede. Each part is in complete coordination with the rest of the body. Nothing happens by accident. Even their camp is completely encased and divided like a portable city. No one could surprise them or penetrate their outer walls. They even have carpenters who immediately go to work erecting barricades and entrances as if they were preparing to stay forever."

"And the soldiers?" Yosef waved his hand for the young man to continue.

"Absolute discipline. They live together quietly and decently. No one even eats alone. Everything is according to well-ordered practice. Nothing is done without a signal. The soldiers awake to trumpet blasts and immediately salute their superior officers. The day is spent in military drills and mock combat. When the general appears, his crier asks the assembled legions if they are prepared for war. They answer enthusiastically, 'We are ready!' Never have I seen anything like their rectitude."

Yosef again nodded his concurrence. "And what did you observe when they marched forth from the camp? Ehud, what did you see?"

The big man lumbered forward. His voice rumbled, "They march without noise. No one breaks rank, and they walk as if at any moment they expect attack. Nothing is left to chance."

"Your reports are quite accurate." Yosef showed no

emotion. "Now you have met the enemy and you know our adversary. While our countrymen at Sepphorius were betraying us, the Romans moved with a common mind and soul. Yes, my friends, such is the nature of the foe. Never, never underestimate their resolve. Now, why did we fail at Sepphorius?"

"We are divided," Bildad of Ginnesar answered. "Our people have one God but nothing else binds us together except personal survival. Obviously the people of Sepphorius did not even look to Jerusalem for help. We lost because there was no heart to win."

"Exactly!" Yosef slammed his fist on a table. "We must want our land more than the Romans desire to take it from us. Unless we close ranks, Vespasian will cut us down person by person, piece by piece, city by city. Our people must believe in and trust each other or there is no hope."

"Years of rule by the Hasmoneans did nothing to create common cause." Tabor wrung his hands. "The decades of Roman domination have only deepened our divisions. I have difficulty in rallying the people in my district."

"Unless you do, we are lost!" Ben Mathias exploded. "We have fierce warriors, but they must stand on the shoulders of the people if our soldiers are to prevail." Yosef spun the map on the table around so the seven men could see it. "The hour is late." He plunged his finger at a point on the map west of the Galilee and north of Sepphorius. "Jotapata. See it? Yes, I have long known that this city would be the great test. The time has come for us to march to the defense of Jotapata."

Yoel pointed to Ptolemais. "Titus has followed his father out of the fortress. They march down the Plain of Esdraelon and will soon turn north. Placidus is already slowly moving up from Sepphorius. Their legions will soon converge on Jotapata."

"Exactly." Yosef thumped on the map. "Jotapata is

our opportunity to overcome the division among the Galilean people. A defeat of the legions at this city could reverse the tides of the war."

Jonah pointed to the door. "My son, Jesse, awaits with an important communique." He clapped his hands and beckoned for the guard to open the door. "We sent Jesse to spy at Caesarea. He has spent a great deal of time at Ptolemais as well."

The young man walked quickly into the room, bowing and nodding respectfully to the assembly.

"Son, you have a report?" Jonah put his arm around Jesse's shoulders.

"A contingent of Judeans is coming north from Jerusalem to search for political prisoners possibly held beneath the Fortress at Ptolemais." Jesse stood at rigid attention. "They ride with the troops of Simon Ben Giora. They are requesting that we send troops to help them."

"Ben Giora! Hmph!" Yosef tossed his head. "Who rides with him?"

"Zeda Ben Aaron, a young man I met at Caesarea. He and his mother, Mariam, were returning from Rome when I stood at the pier . . ."

"Indeed!" Yosef leaned forward. "Why would the house of Ben Aaron do business with a criminal like Ben Giora?"

"I only know they are searching for friends who were captured when Florus caused the revolt in Jerusalem two years ago. They ride with a considerable army."

"We need *them* at Jotapata." Yosef spoke rapidly. "Of course we won't send soldiers. There are no Romans left to attack at Ptolemais. Heavens, prisoners would have died or been sold as slaves long ago! Send them a letter. Better yet, Jesse, return at once. Intercept their march. Tell them I command the soldiers of Ben Giora to join us in the great battle. We must have every able-bodied man we can find."

"Will they come because of your demand?" Tabor asked carefully.

"If they don't," Yosef shot back, "they will be clearly and publicly branded as marauders and traitors. I don't understand why the Ben Aarons would deal with such men. Certainly Yochanan Ben Zakkai would not condone such a thing."

"Yes," Ehud's deep voice resonated across the great stone room, "we must create unity in the land."

Yosef shook his head. "Go, Jesse, and fetch the Ben Aarons and this reprobate they travel with. We will give Ben Giora a chance to redeem himself at Jotapata. For surely we will live or die there!"

The sun was low in the sky when Jesse found the camp of Simon Ben Giora's men. For three weeks he had wandered the countryside trying to locate the Ben Aarons. Only after he had received advice from a sailor near Caesarea had he turned back toward Scythopolis. The old seaman had seen a great band of Jewish soldiers gather near the port. Strangely enough, they had sent only one man, a Greek, to the harbor. The crew had bragged that they were on their way to free prisoners held by the Romans. After Jesse left Scythopolis and passed Mount Tabor, the trail was easy enough to follow. Ben Giora did not leave friends in his wake.

Just beyond the little town of Gabec, the caravan settled in for what appeared to be a long stay. The country was rugged and mountainous and the soldiers had chosen a well-concealed gorge for their camp. Fires were beginning to send curls of smoke up into the darkening sky, and Jesse quickly recognized there was no order or scheme to how the camp was laid out. Soldiers milled around aimlessly talking and arguing as Jesse rode unchallenged through them. Finally he guessed the largest tent in the center must belong to someone in charge.

"What's your business?" the guard demanded. "And get off your horse. No one rides into the center of our camp as if he owned the place."

"I am on a mission from Yosef Ben Mathias, the general of all Galilee." Jesse dismounted. "I come at the request of Zeda Ben Aaron."

"Oh, really!" the guard answered indifferently. "Stay put until I see what they say." He disappeared inside the tent and quickly returned. "Follow me," the ugly little man beckoned.

"Jesse!" Zeda rushed forward out of a circle of men. "Welcome to our camp." He hugged the traveler and kissed him on both cheeks. "Simon, meet our ambassador from the northern country."

The large hulk of a man in the center of the group did not move. His piercing black eyes were fierce and cold. The men standing behind him were no more inviting. The tent was large and dim, making it difficult to tell just how many people surrounded the man with the missing teeth. A few oil lamps hung beneath the skin-covered ceiling but none were lit. The air was humid, ominous, and foreboding.

"Meet Simon Ben Giora." Zeda bowed and made a sweeping gesture toward the leader. "Undoubtedly, you have heard of our renowned general," he said ingratiatingly.

"Indeed," Jesse answered stiffly. "I bring you greetings from the commander of Galilee, General Yosef Ben Mathias. He has received your communique and sends his response." Jesse stepped forward and handed a small scroll to Ben Giora.

In one sweep Ben Giora passed the scroll on to Zeda with the uneasy flourish of a man who would not want to reveal his reading abilities. "What's he say?" Simon spoke for the first time.

"He bids us to join him at Jotapata where a great battle is about to begin," Zeda read aloud.

"By now the siege is underway," Jesse added. "The war is on."

Zeda continued, "The general writes that there is no point in attacking Ptolemais since all legions have marched toward the north."

Ben Giora smiled for the first time, further revealing the black hole in his teeth. "So! There will be little resistance," he mused.

"The general indicates the battle at Jotapata is crucial for the future of our nation," Zeda concluded. "We are to listen carefully to Jesse's instructions."

"Ah, the good general would command my army." Simon rose to his feet. "My, but these Sadducees love to wield power. Of course, we are his dutiful servants." Simon made a mocking curtsy.

Zeda stared at Simon. "You . . . you are ready to comply?"

"Simply confirms your mother's plan," Ben Giora was uncharacteristically gracious. "She can talk to her friend Marcus Quintus Cunctator. The two of you ride in and talk to this Roman tribune and find out the lay of the land. We will be preparing for the march further north. The whole matter will save our energy."

Zeda looked puzzled.

"Should some problem arise, we will be standing by," Ben Giora rambled. "If the prison cells are empty, you can accompany us to the north. Should this Roman friend of yours release the Ben Ephraim family, you can return to Jerusalem with them. The matter is settled."

"Certainly," Zeda sounded surprised.

"Take the general's messenger with you." Simon waved Jesse away. "I'm sure he knows the city of Ptolemais well. Undoubtedly he can lead you in as well as my boy, Shamir, could."

"Definitely," Jesse acknowledged.

"I keep my bargains," Ben Giora leered at Zeda. "You saved my leg and I told you I'd get you to the city. One way or the other, we will make sure no prisoners remain in a Roman dungeon."

"Thank you," Zeda backed away. "I will bring Jesse to talk with my mother now. We take our leave." Zeda offered the scroll, but Simon waved it away and the two young men quickly left the tent.

Simon watched the flap swing shut behind them. "Well, well." He suddenly laughed aloud. "Today we've learned two very important bits of information." He beckoned his aides to gather around him. "All the Romans and the Jews will be gathered at that nasty mountain fortress. My guess is they will spend half the summer killing each other over an impregnable city. If this Ben Mathias thinks he's the general of the north, then we'll teach him another lesson by summer's end."

X

The rising sun slowly emerged above the mountain peaks. Yosef Ben Mathias bolted upright on his bed. His dream woke him even before the first rays of the morning bathed his face. Yosef quickly covered his eyes, supporting himself with his other hand on the flat pallet. He pulled the single covering over his closed eyes, but he could not block out the images that had shaken him to the core.

Once more the dream of swarming locusts surged through his half-awake mind. A great eagle flew above and before the ever advancing pestilence. He and his friends rushed forward with brooms and sticks to smash the hideous insects. They killed thousands and thousands of the pests, but the eagle kept diving into them with open talons, slashing and tearing into them with its murderous beak. The overpowering bird picked up Yosef's helpers and carried them away one by one. Suddenly Yosef had a flaming torch in his hand. Even though he burned thousands of the locusts, the eagle kept carrying away his comrades until Yosef alone was left to face the oncoming devastation. Finally Yosef retreated, looking once more at the terrifying scene. The great eagle sat perched on a charred cedar stump above an insurmountable mountain of burned and crushed carcasses of the detestable insects. As he looked, Yosef recognized the mangled bodies of his comrades lying in

105

the midst of the locusts. Retreating in horror, Yosef looked back only to discover that the heaps of insects and bodies had taken the shape of a giant number forty-seven.

Yosef pulled his knees up under his chin and pondered the terrifying dream that returned nightly since he had established his command in Jotapata. Dreams were never dismissed. His priestly training included the study of God's strange night speech. Moreover, he had returned to reading the ancient prophets and considering their indications of future destruction. Little reflection was needed to understand the meaning of these dreams.

Yosef eventually stood up and walked to the window. The city was built on an unusually high precipice surrounded by deep gorges that disappeared into long valleys. The cliffs were so steep that the fainthearted avoided looking over the edge of the huge fortress. Behind Yosef's palace was the great wall that divided the north end of the city from the plain that quickly rose up into the mountain. The encircling mountains offered further protection to the city. Only eagles soaring to such heights would not be impeded by the barriers of walls and gorges.

The fall of Gadara immediately came to mind and Yosef pondered the merciless way the Romans not only burned the ancient city to the ground, taking all the men and women as slaves, but murdered all the youths of the city. Oh yes, Placidus and his one thousand Roman horsemen had been humiliated and General Ebutius was defeated afterward, but now Vespasian and his legions were camped round about in the valleys below and just beyond the north walls of Jotapata. The locusts had arrived and were already devouring the crops. The Roman eagle raised high on the wooden pole in front of the marching soldiers would begin ascending the sides of the supposedly unassaultable cliffs of Jotapata today.

Of all the symbols of the dream, the number was the

most ominous. Far more precise than his own estimates, Yosef had come to a frighteningly close approximation of fifty days in calculating how long his troops might hold out without reinforcements. No, the cipher was a word from the Lord. The only consolation was the implication Yosef would survive the epidemic of death awaiting Jotapata.

Yosef let the cool breeze of morning wash his face. The horror of the dream could not quench his awareness of the overpowering beauty of this amazing city. At this early morning hour nothing concealed the river's roar cascading in the valley below. He inhaled deeply and wondered if the hoped-for arrival of Ben Giora's contingent of troops might yet change the outcome of his nightmare.

A sharp rap on the door ended Yosef's reverie. Jonah walked in unannounced and uninvited. Wearing his predictable coarse brown Galilean robe, the aide snapped to attention. "I have the latest briefings for you, General."

"And what does today, the fifth of Iyar,* bring that requires uninvited entry?" The breeze gently stirred Yosef's light homespun nightshirt, which hung loosely from his shoulders. "You seem rather rushed."

"The beginning of the great battle." Jonah lowered his head respectfully. "Vespasian's troops marched till late in the night. Their tents are now pitched along the northern side of the city on a small hill about seven furlongs from us. They have a double row of soldiers before the city walls. Vespasian's cavalry is set in place behind them to keep everyone from escaping. The Romans are firmly in place."

"And our people?" Yosef walked to the table and sat down. "What is the disposition of the citizens?"

"The people of Jotapata are not yet fully aware of the situation, but they will shortly fill the ramparts of the

*April to May

wall trying to catch sight of the Romans. Consternation will soon grip them."

"Marching until late?" Yosef smiled. "Perhaps this is the day to turn local consternation into courage." For a few moments he rapped gently and reflectively with his knuckles on the thick planks of the table. "Any word from your son, Jesse? Is Ben Giora coming to help?"

"No report." Jonah puckered his lips. "But I have total confidence that Jesse made contact well before now. Surely the new contingent of soldiers will arrive shortly."

The commander of all Galilee looked solemnly at his subordinate. Yosef's raised eyebrows silently conveyed his melancholy reflections on his dream. "Nothing is certain, my good friend. Nothing."

"What do you suggest, General?"

"Assume nothing, but prepare to fight for life itself. I suggest we command our men to attack as soon as these weary Romans crave sleep. We shall teach them the meaning of boldness! If Vespasian hopes to intimidate us with his blockade, let us instruct him on the cost of such presumption. I will personally lead the attack. Before the sun sets, we will shame our adversary!"

The morning sun had moved halfway toward the center of the sky by the time Zeda, Mariam, Ishmael, and Jesse gained entrance to the fortress in the center of Ptolemais. They could feel that the cold damp winds blowing in from the ocean had warmed. The Roman garrison was built on the cliffs overlooking the Mediterranean. Standing before the gate, Zeda could hear the waves beating against the rocks far below. Because the Ben Aarons spent the night on the edge of the village that surrounded the walls of the Roman garrison, they were in a position to seek entrance early in the day. If the Romans had turned them away, Ishmael would have had ample time by the afternoon to get a message to Ben Giora that attack was necessary. On the other hand, Simon's firm agreement was that if no report was received by nightfall, his troops would begin their march immediately to aid the citizens of Jotapata. But the four travelers did not have to wait long before the massive entry into the garrison opened before them.

A stern-faced guard quickly led the foursome across the open commons, silently marching the trio past small groups of foot soldiers who eyed the Jewish intruders suspiciously. Only a small contingent of Romans was left inside the walls.

Once they reached the inner wall, Zeda led the way as they were ushered up stone stairs into the tower where a commander could survey his men working below. Marcus Quintus Cunctator received them as if they were long-separated friends, immediately launching into a discussion of their health and how Zeda and Mariam had found their family upon their return to Jerusalem. Ishmael and Jesse stood in a corner near the door, observing.

"And this faith of yours," Marcus talked while beckoning for a servant to bring wine and fruit, "I want us to talk more of your belief in your Messiah, the Christus. Your arrival today is a rare opportunity for me to continue learning the truths we discussed on the boat. There is almost no activity since the fortress is nearly abandoned right now."

Mariam smiled but looked apprehensively around the cold, stone chamber. In the center of the distant north wall was only one large window covered with thick iron bars. The floors were made from the same granite blocks that were piled one on top of the other until the rock almost disappeared in the darkness, far above where huge beams supported the ceiling. The severe starkness of the chiseled rock matched well the faces of the soldiers and servants.

"You have learned more about our way of peace?" Mariam asked while looking warily at the rack of steel-tipped spears lining the south wall.

"No. I'm afraid not." Marcus Quintus poured a goblet of wine and handed it to Mariam. "We have been far too busy since I arrived to do much more than stay within the walls of this forsaken place. Once Titus arrived from Alexandria and joined his father, reorganization developed at a feverish pace. Titus brought with him the preeminent fifth and tenth legions to join with the fifteenth legion under his father. The fortress was packed with soldiers and confusion."

"But the commons were nearly deserted when we came in," Zeda puzzled. "We only saw a few men guarding the ramparts and walkways."

"It is no secret," the primus pilus said factually. "The march is on. Even as we speak, Titus and Vespasian prepare to attack Jotapata. I must tell you as your friend that there is no hope for your people in that city. Kings Antiochus, Agrippa, and Sohemus have each contributed a thousand archers. Malchus, the King of Arabia, has sent a thousand horsemen and five thousand foot soldiers. There will be at least sixty thousand soldiers ready to storm your city and take the surrounding countryside. These are simply the facts."

Pain swept across Zeda's face. "We are not military people," he said respectfully. "But we love our people and believe our land was promised and given to us by God."

"I have offended you," Marcus apologized. "I meant no personal offense but simply to clarify the present situation. I remain in Ptolemais only to finish preparing this fort for prisoners after the battle is finished."

"We understand," Mariam's gentle voice was reassuring. "As Christians, we pray daily for peace and the well-being of both Romans and Jews."

"Amazing!" The centurion shook his head. "How can you possibly do such a thing?"

"Our ultimate allegiance is to the Kingdom of God that will one day encompass all people with the love of our heavenly Father," Mariam explained. "We do not seek power or authority, but the opportunity to do good."

"A Roman should be repulsed by such a notion." Marcus settled back in his chair. "Our empire is built on raw, naked strength. We do not seek or court the affection of those we control, only respect born of fear. And yet . . ." His voice trailed away. "And yet I have seen enough killing for ten lifetimes. I long to believe that your way will finally prevail."

"Our Savior is the prince of peace," Zeda added. "The seat of His power is the heart, the place of love and righteousness."

"If such a promise is possible, I want to claim it." Marcus Quintus looked squarely into Mariam's eyes. "I hunger for decency and justice. Betrayal, obscenity, and debauchery have consumed my life for far too many years. My soul is sick and I long to know a remedy."

"What we have received was freely given and so we give freely," Mariam smiled. "I, too, am glad we came today, Marcus Quintus."

"We do have one urgent concern," Zeda added nervously. "Perhaps, it is not the moment to ask, but we beg a favor."

"Anything!" The commander turned to the young man. "If it is within my power, it shall be done at once."

Zeda scooted to the edge of his chair, nervously clasping his hands together. "We have reason to believe that the woman to whom I am betrothed might be kept in a cell in the caves beneath this fortress. Possibly her family is with her," he added cautiously.

Marcus Quintus looked pained. "Why would they be here?

"In the revolt started by Florus's raid on the Temple, they were mistakenly taken captive during his retreat." Zeda began speaking more rapidly. "Honestly. She is but a girl. The Ben Ephraim family are not rebellious Zealots, seditious people. Just hard-working, decent merchants. I know if you met . . ."

The commander held up his hand to stop the plea. "I have no doubt that anyone related to you is innocent of any crime. It is simply that . . . no young woman would be left . . ." He stopped and breathed deeply. "Prisoners have been shipped out to the slave markets or turned into personal servants of officers." Marcus looked sadly at Zeda. "You know how it is. I am so sorry. This is the injustice and evil I hate, I deplore."

Silence settled over the room. Mariam looked at the granite floor and Zeda toward the window covered with iron bars.

"There is no hope?" Mariam finally asked.

"I have not yet seen the dungeons in the caves down below the fort," Marcus Quintus answered thoughtfully. "But I will go with you to search. I am afraid the area was built for the results of such a campaign that is now in progress at Jotapata." Suddenly the primus pilus stood up. "Let us go at once and take a look." Raising to a commanding height, he clapped his hands. Two soldiers marched in from a side hallway and stood at attention.

"At your service," the larger of the two men answered.

"We are going down to the prison," the commander instructed. "Go and prepare torches. Find the jailer. I want to inspect every cell."

The two soldiers bowed their heads, turned, and were gone.

"Perhaps you would choose to stay here," Marcus said to Mariam. "Dungeons are terrible places. I understand the caves are near the opening where the ocean comes in under the fortress. Damp, covered with slime, most unpleasant. I think you might be better . . ."

"I'm sure I have seen worse sights," Mariam answered resolutely. "Perhaps it would be best if I accompanied my son."

Marcus looked at her carefully. "Your humility is not a substitute for courage. Yes, you are remarkable people. Even coming inside this fortress was an act of courage." He picked up his sword from the corner and strapped the sheath around his waist. "Let us go and see what lies in the darkness below."

At the same moment Zeda reached the stairs to the dungeon, Yosef Ben Mathias hurried down the stone steps around Jotapata's central gate in the center of the city's outer wall. On the other side were the Roman soldiers. The sun had barely crossed the center of the sky when Yosef leaped out of the huge gateway in the city's strategic northern wall, calling for his army to follow him. The bright red cloak draped over one shoulder and tied at the opposite waist guaranteed no one would fail to recognize the leader of the protectors of Galilee. Immediately, a multitude of Jewish soldiers surged out behind the general. Yosef quickly saw that the Romans were surprised by his preemptive strike. However, their discipline would automatically reorder their front ranks. Yosef swung his flashing sword in the air and ran forward. "Strike!" His command soared toward the sky.

The roar of Jewish battle cries echoed across the surrounding mountains, assuring the general that his bravery had inspired his troops. He did not stand alone before the pestilence.

Yosef's soldiers surrounded their general and rushed on toward the forming line of Roman shields. The sheer weight of the Jews and the press of their charge sent the first row of the Roman soldiers tumbling backward.

Swords swung in every direction as the invaders were quickly forced to retreat.

Yosef slung aside his bright cloak so the enemy could not distinguish him from any other soldier. At once he moved with complete abandonment into the fray. Romans fell on the left and right. Spears, swords, and knives flashed on every side, but none touched the Jewish general. When the initial line broke, there was nothing to keep his soldiers from surging onward.

About fifty feet ahead on the gentle slope, the next row of soldiers began digging in and setting up their shields. Yosef leaped on a tree stump and waved to the archers waiting near the gate. Immediately their bows went up and a shower of arrows filled the sky. Roman soldiers fell backward, leaving gaps in their previously solid front. Jewish javelin throwers stepped to the fore and heaved spears as the soldiers charged forward. By the time the Jews hit the Roman line, there were many holes in the impaired defense. Again the wrath of the Galileans was not to be denied. The second line of Roman defense crumbled.

Yosef turned his head slightly, catching sight of a large Roman charging toward him. The man's heavy leather helmet with the side protectors was tightly tied under his bearded chin and his head was bent like a rampaging bull. Across his shoulders and around his chest, heavy leather straps formed protective armor; the rest of his body was protected by a shield. His sword was slightly cocked above his shoulder as he ran forward. Yosef squinted straight ahead as if he did not see the attack coming. The Roman ran even harder.

Slowly Yosef lowered his guard, offering an unprotected shot at his chest. Immediately the Roman lowered the shield and lifted his sword high above his head. At the last possible second Yosef swung his sword sideways, slashing the Roman across his exposed throat. The soldier's helmet tumbled backward. There was no sound when his chin collapsed into his chest.

When an arrow whistled passed Yosef's head, he grabbed the Roman's shield from the ground and pulled it in front of him. Without hesitation, Yosef rammed into the remaining segment of the Roman defense before him. Breaking through, Yosef ran his sword through the man in front of him. He jerked his sword out and slashed the soldier to his left across the back of his neck.

"They are retreating!" Yosef yelled. "The Romans are in flight!"

Five feet away, a Roman foot soldier stumbled backward, terrified at the general bearing down on him. The warrior started to run but tripped over a log and fell to the ground. Before he could regain his feet, Yosef was on top of him.

The young soldier looked as if he might be in his teens. Instinctively he hid his face, peering out behind gnarled dirty fingers. Yosef looked into his pleading eyes and hesitated for a moment before ramming his sword through the leather straps into the soldier's heart. His final gasp of pain was short and quick.

"We have prevailed!" Yosef shouted above the roar of the battle. "Finish the work! The hand of God is with us!" Yosef began retreating behind his soldiers, looking to the left and right for his battle commanders. "Press on!" he encouraged the troops. "Vespasian will long remember how the sun set on this day!"

XI

Mariam huddled close to Zeda to keep from slipping on the stone stairs that wound downward to the cells. The jailer held a torch, leading the way toward the caves lost in the darkness far below. Marcus Quintus brought up the rear, carrying his own torch.

Small shafts of light came in from the cracks in the rock slabs overhead. The distant opening out to the sea made the end of the cavern somewhat visible, but the pathway was murky, the rocks were slick, and the moss-covered walls were treacherous. No railing protected them from a sudden plunge to the rocks far below. Jesse stayed on a landing near the top where a torch was fixed to the wall.

The dungeon had been cleverly and diabolically constructed to take advantage of the natural cavity created by centuries of sea erosion opening under the great rock slabs that formed the sea cliffs of Ptolemais. Time and natural drainage from above had cut many pockets and caves in the porous caverns. Slave laborers carved the winding steps that followed the natural curvature of the cliffs. At the bottom, other prisoners of Rome had chiseled out numerous footpaths that led to the natural cells in the hollows of the rocks. Massive iron bars were set in front of the damp holding tanks.

Dying prisoners were simply pushed into the boiling sea, ebbing and churning through the center of the cav-

116

ern. The tides quickly carried their bodies out to sea, with anonymity being added to the ignominy of their deaths.

The air was cold and stale. The closer Mariam came to the cells, the more repugnant was the stench. Huge rats scampered for cover as the flaming lights came closer. Bats darted back and forth, far overhead.

"I'm sure these cells are far worse than usual," the jailer said defensively. "No one has been down here in some time." He stuck his torch through the bars of each cell as they passed and in each instance the shadows were empty.

"Records are not kept," Marcus Quintus explained apologetically. "One of the tragedies of war," he mumbled. "All we know is the last slave boats left a week ago."

When they reached the bottom landing where the sea came in, Mariam stopped. Slimy moss made the flat rocks extremely unreliable. Even though the heat of summer was bearing down outside, she pulled her cloak around her arms. All Mariam could see overhead was opaque darkness.

The jailer walked up the sloping path toward the back of the cavern. "There's one final holding tank back there." He held the torch high above his head. "I have the keys."

The barred door swung open, and Zeda and Marcus followed the guard into the last segment of the prison. The space was vast, appearing to reach the fort above.

"Look!" Zeda pointed. "There's something over there."

The jailer held his torch in front of him and walked to the farthest corner. The tide gulped part of the tidal pool out of the cavern, sucking the stale air out with the foaming sea water. Immediately a ghastly nauseous odor hit the three men and swept toward Mariam.

"It's a body!" The jailer covered his mouth. "Must

have been missed." He hurried for the cell door, gagging. "Could have been dead a week . . . ten days."

Zeda doubled over and fought to keep from vomiting. Once he was on the other side of the door, Zeda held to one of the bars to regain stability. Far down below Mariam watched her son fighting to gain his composure.

"No one is here." Marcus Quintus could barely speak. "I'm sorry. Terribly sorry." He spoke softly. "We need to get you out of this place. It's hopeless . . . pointless to continue."

The jailer put his hand to his mouth and shouted one last time. "Anyone in here?" His words echoed across the expansive rock cavern and then, like everything else that lingered there, died on the rocks down below.

"We can go now." Zeda sounded far off. "There is no hope here."

Marcus Quintus joined Zeda and Mariam on the landing. "My friends, I am deeply sorry, but I pledge that I will do everything in my power to seek information. Yet, I must be honest. I know of no way to locate anyone who traveled through this place. There are far too many left in watery graves." He shook his head ruefully. "I am so very, very sorry."

Zeda did not answer. Mariam put her arm around her son's shoulders. "Thank you for trying, Marcus. We appreciate your willingness to help us."

"We had best leave here as quickly as possible." Marcus moved ahead of them, holding his torch high so Mariam and Zeda could see the steps. "Stay close to the wall," he warned as they slowly ascended the rock staircase.

Halfway up to the first landing a strange pounding began to vibrate overhead. Muffled distant shouting filtered down. Jesse hurried down toward them.

"An attack is going on outside," Jesse warned them. "Men are fighting. I heard swords clashing."

"Can't be!" Marcus Quintus turned to the jailer bringing up the rear. "Hurry! Get ahead of us and find out what's going on."

The guard carefully slipped past mother and son and bounded up the steps. He turned into the passage that led into the fortress courtyard and his torch light disappeared.

"Quickly, quickly!" Marcus snapped. His military discipline became automatic. "Time must not be lost."

The strident sounds of war were overwhelming. Men were running, shouting, horses charging, blows being struck. Only the thick planks of the door stood between them and the battle.

Marcus Quintus drew his sword. "Put Mariam in the rear. You two stand between me and her. Protect her at all costs!" The commander lunged forward, pushing the heavy gate open.

Marcus Quintus stopped and stared at the front of the door. The jailer was pinned to the wood by a broken spear rammed through the center of his chest. The rest of the broken shaft on the ground was burning in the flames from the guard's torch.

The commander immediately crouched, ready to defend himself. Invaders were swarming overhead, on the ramparts of the fortress. Roman soldiers were falling right and left. The main gate was wide open and fresh attackers on horseback raced into the commons.

"We are completely outnumbered!" the commander muttered in disbelief.

Marcus Quintus did not hear Zeda push past Jesse or realize he was looking over the commander's shoulder. Watching the army press forward, Zeda saw faces he recognized. "Ben Giora!" he exclaimed. "Simon Ben Giora is behind this! He lied to all of us!"

"Get back in there!" Marcus whirled around and pushed Zeda backward. "Don't come out again!"

Marcus Quintus turned his back to shut the door and did not see two horsemen riding straight toward him.

Only at the last minute did he discover the charging horses. Edging his way between them, Marcus leaped up and thrusted his sword in the chest of the man to his right. The rider on the left tried to slash the commander, but instead speared the side of the other horse. Riders and horses tumbled over each other and sprawled over the great stones of the commons.

Both riders lay on the ground, immobilized. Marcus Quintus's sword was sticking through one man's body; the other attacker began rocking back and forth in pain. The terrified horses fought to regain their footing. One finally hobbled away, but the other sunk back to the pavement.

Marcus Quintus crumpled in a ball on the ground, his knees drawn up toward his chest and his leather helmet several feet from his face. Marcus's leg was turned at a strange angle, the large bloody imprint of a horse hoof stamped on the side of his right thigh. The skin on his left cheek up to his scalp was scraped and torn.

"Get Marcus Quintus back in here," Zeda shrieked and motioned violently for Jesse to help him. "Get Ishmael to help us." The three men hovered over the fallen Roman, trying to move him. "Gently lift him without bending his right leg in any direction." Zeda pointed to the door. "Get him back in the cavern. We must hide him." The attackers riding past seemed indifferent to the kneeling men dressed just like any other Judean.

Carefully the cortege scooted Marcus Quintus across the granite pavement and through the door. Once inside, Zeda led the way down the passageway until he found a small side cave. The commander was carefully pushed to the back. "Quickly," Zeda commanded. "Cover the man with your cloak."

Zeda returned to the door and watched through the crack. Ben Giora's soldiers were slaughtering the outnumbered Romans. As the fighting in the commons area slackened, the rampaging horde surged into the buildings inside the fortress. Only then did Zeda push the door open slightly.

Cautiously, he peered around the edge. Everywhere he looked, men were dead or dying. Arrows protruded from many bodies. A few horses huddled near the side of the wall, riderless and bewildered.

Suddenly the heavy door in front of Zeda was yanked open. The jailer's body fell from the front of the door with a thud. The burst of sunlight momentarily blinded Zeda, and he tried to shield his eyes.

"Kill the swine," a man screamed. "No Roman will survive this day."

"Wait!" another voice cautioned. "He's not a Roman."

Before Zeda could escape, he was jerked forward, landing with his face on the pavement and the wind knocked out of his chest. His cheek and nose stung and burned. He felt a foot on the back of his neck painfully bearing down.

"Who are you?" someone growled from above.

"Zeda," he barely stammered. "Zeda Ben Aaron, and if you hurt me Simon Ben Giora will cut you into pieces."

"What?" insolence turned to bewilderment. "Simon?"

"I warn you that *I* brought your troops to this fortress. Dare you violate allies of Simon?"

Immediately Zeda was pulled to his feet. Rough hands began brushing him off. "You're sure you are one of us?" one of the men asked skeptically.

"If you're lying, it will be even worse for you," the other growled.

"Want to chance it?" Zeda snarled.

"Simon is coming down from upstairs," the smaller of the three men advised his comrades. "We'll know quickly enough."

Zeda felt his nose and burning face. His fingers quickly became bloody. His knees and ribs hurt, but his discomfort was quickly replaced by burning anger. Zeda realized how completely Ben Giora had deceived him and even used his mother as a decoy to lure Marcus Quintus into a false sense of security. Ben Giora had lied, deceived, and manipulated the Ben Aarons into his murderous scheme.

Zeda's mind raced as he tried unobtrusively to close the door behind him. *Simon had used his mother as an instrument of his evil intent and put her life in immediate danger. Her death would have been of no matter or concern to him.* Zeda's hot anger turned to icy fear. *Uncle Simeon warned of the cost of doing business with this devil. Once again Simeon's judgment was vindicated.* Zeda shuddered.

"Ah, look what we have here!" the loud, oily, arrogant voice of Simon Ben Giora roared across the courtyard. "My comrade at arms, Zeda Ben Aaron, the Believer!"

The two soldiers began slinking away, leaving Zeda standing alone before Simon, surrounded by his lieutenants. Ben Giora swung a bloody sword at his side. Zeda spread his feet and braced himself.

"Find your Roman friends?" Simon asked casually. "Were Jews in the dungeon?"

"No," Zeda answered coldly, "the prison was empty. They're gone."

"Sorry. Sorry to hear it," Simon answered with uncharacteristic respect. "Well, whatever happened to them, we avenged their memory today. There's not a Roman left alive . . . or there won't be by the time I leave."

"I thought you were going to wait for our message before attacking." Stopping short of a challenge, Zeda's tone was more caustic than respectful.

"No point wasting time," Simon's mood shifted to cynicism. "More fun this way!" He suddenly laughed. At once his lackeys around him broke into coarse snorts of laughter.

"What's next?" Zeda's voice was flat.

"We'll burn the place and leave." Simon's eyes became

glazed and strangely empty. "Burn the whole town as well. Take everything. Kill everyone who's Roman or collaborated with them. Ravage what remains. Sack the place."

"We will need our horses," Zeda retorted coldly, "for my mother and associates."

"Take what you want," Simon gestured aimlessly across the commons to the steeds by the wall. "Take as many horses as you need. My gift. If you hadn't brought us here, we'd have missed a great victory." Simon turned away.

"When you are finished today, will you go east to join Yosef Ben Mathias at Jotapata?" Zeda called after him.

"Ah!" Simon turned to his cohorts. "Our young Christian wants to join us for the big battle. You desire to be one of my soldiers?" he taunted.

"We don't kill," Zeda called in measured tones.

"What a pity! You miss such adventure. You Believers are hopelessly moral in a totally immoral world. Such a pity." Simon waved to Zeda. "I suppose we'll have to go alone without you."

"To Jotapata?"

"To fight under this Jew who calls himself Josephus?" Simon shook his fist at Zeda. "Never! I take orders from no one, much less a Jew who Romanizes his name. By the time the summer is done, the world will know that I am the Jewish general to be reckoned with. Go back to Jerusalem and tell everyone that Ben Giora didn't need any assistance in taking and destroying Ptolemais. Let them know I made a leisurely afternoon's work of this place. Tell them to see how long it takes this Josephus to accomplish his task . . . if he can succeed at all. I set my own course."

Zeda bit his lip.

"Good luck to you." Simon called over his shoulder. "We should do business again another day. Your Greek doctor was good, very good. Thank him for me again.

When you return to Jerusalem tell everyone I am the master of the North." Simon and his men did not look back again as they walked confidently toward the center of the commons.

Zeda picked up the broken shaft of a spear before backing into the cave. When no one appeared to be watching, he secured the door behind him, cramming the pole through the latch, and made sure it would be very difficult to open from the outside.

In the small cave, the torch illuminated his mother, Jesse, and Ishmael, huddling over the cloak-covered form of Marcus Quintus. Low groaning noises arose from beneath the covering.

"Simon Ben Giora's killing everything in sight," Zeda spoke in low, hushed tones. "He used us to achieve an easy, meaningless victory. The swine never had any intent of joining forces with Yosef Ben Mathias. He'll portray himself as the protector of the north."

"What'll we do?" Jesse nervously wrung his hands. "I must get word to Jotapata."

"Go secure horses for us," Zeda pointed to the commons. "If anyone asks, tell them that Simon gave the animals to the Ben Aarons. Tie them to the doorway."

Jesse quickly hurried out.

"What do you think?" Zeda huddled near his mother. "What does the Lord say to you?"

Mariam closed her eyes and rested her head on her knees. After a few moments she said, "I think that the Lord has a special use for our friend Marcus Quintus. If Simon's men catch him, they will either kill Marcus or torture him for information. We must do everything we can to protect him."

"But where can we go? If we stay here, the Romans could return at any time. Then we would be in jeopardy."

"Not so far from here is a special place," Mariam answered. "Gennesaret is a secluded village by the blue waters of the Kinneret. Long ago when I was a sickly, dying child, my father took me there. In that place the Master said to me, *'Talitha cumi,'* and life began again. I believe this would be a very good place for us to nurse Marcus back to health."

"We will have to wait until Simon's men are completely gone or at least until it's dark," Zeda thought aloud. "We could make a stretcher and carry him between two horses. In the meantime, you must pray that the commander lives. I know his leg is broken and the sword wound is bad."

"God has just begun to work with Marcus Quintus. Our journey will be under divine protection." Mariam put her hand on the moaning form beneath the covering and closed her eyes.

After a few minutes, quiet filled their small shelter. "You are deeply disappointed," she said to her son.

"I thought they would be here," his voice trailed away.

"I have lived in the house of mourning many times," Mariam sighed. "I know all too well the emptiness of that place. But defeat must not become despair. God's grace is tested, but not thwarted by these times."

Zeda leaned back against the wall of the cave. Even though the torch flickered overhead, his face disappeared in the shadows. "Nothing is the same anymore. Everywhere I look, the world crumbles like sandstone. Every day another piece of a cherished dream flakes away and disappears like powder in the wind."

Mariam reached for her son's hand, but Zeda had drawn himself tightly into a ball.

"There is no assurance of justice or equity in this world." Mariam patted his shoulder. "But we aren't alone in our struggle."

"I simply want to laugh again . . . like we did before you, Stephan, Father, and Grandfather went to Rome . . . when we lived in Jarius's house like one happy family. I want things to be like they were."

"Permanence? Oh yes, I know what it is to crave continuity. Like links breaking in a chain, the destruction of order cuts us loose from our foundations. At such times the ache is unbearable."

"I do not ask much," Zeda spoke under his breath. "I want Ephraim Ben Ephraim to walk into our house on some quiet evening with the final details of the dowry. In an hour, the agreement will be struck and plans will be made for the great feast and the wedding. In a month the wedding will follow, then I can take my rightful place in the jewelry shop as all my ancestors have done before me. I want life to go on like it always has." He ground his teeth. "I must find Sara."

"Nothing can ever be the same again," Mariam lamented. "We have no abiding place here . . . even in this holy land. He who was crucified must be our peace, or we find none in this age."

The draft sucked the flames overhead toward the cavern and the torch burned low. Marcus Quintus's moaning had turned to troubled sleep. Silence settled between mother and son. The noise of battle was gone, but the echo of the incoming tide far down below filled the passage with a final empty, lonely sound.

"I must keep looking," Zeda concluded.

XII

Each morning during the past month, Yosef Ben Mathias had begun his reverie by looking out of the tower window of his bedroom. The beauty of the deep valleys rushed up at him, but Yosef could not shake the strange dreams that continually shook his personal confidence. He had to fight to fix his mind on promises that might renew his hope. The rugged beauty of the towering mountains and plunging gorges inspired him to recite the Psalms and prayers of the day.

Unexpected noise abruptly interrupted Yosef's meditation. He looked down at soldiers starting to march in early morning drills through the streets below him. Above the young warriors, workmen hastily slammed bricks together on the new towers that Yosef had ordered built on Jotapata's north wall. He was pleased at the speed with which the entire length of the wall was rising. Beyond the ramparts Yosef could hear the Romans moving heavy catapults into place beside large piles of boulders and rocks. He could see several companies of the tenth legion marching down from their encampment beyond the city. And yet the signs and sounds of the approaching battle could not obliterate the beauty of the peaks and gorges surrounding Jotapata. Yosef inhaled deeply and drew new strength from the enduring silhouette of the everlasting hills. He ended his prayers with a determined, "Amen." Having restored his soul, Yosef

127

returned to his planning table and unrolled the small scrolls he had started writing the day before. Yosef set out the little pot of sepia ink, then sat down and slowly reviewed his composition.

> Dear Yochanan Ben Zakkai,
> My trusted friend, we have needed your wisdom many times in these past weeks. Our defense of the city is now in the twenty-first day and we press on. I send you this report for the Great Sanhedrin and the Temple so there will be no question or debate about my true position. If the Holy One of Israel ordains, Jesse Ben Jonah will deliver this account into your hand. He will be wrapped in animal skins and sent over the wall during the night. The Romans will take him for an animal and Jesse will make a swift escape.
> Let no one in Jerusalem misunderstand the truth! Simon Ben Giora attacked a defenseless city conquering nothing but a handful of unprepared Roman foot soldiers. If he had joined our forces, this dog of the desert might be counted a true hero of Israel. In contrast, Simon roamed the hillside attacking both small contingents of Romans and our own people who refused to supply food and treasure for his marauding horde. The man is to be feared only for the unpredictability of his animal instincts . . . certainly not for intelligence's sake. Simon is both coward and traitor. Publish this report throughout the city with my name attached!

Yosef smiled approvingly. Jesse had informed him well about the debacle at Ptolemais, and he intended the whole world to know the facts. Unrolling the scrolls farther, the pumice and chalk used to polish the lamb-skin into parchment rubbed off on his fingers and his long nightshirt. Only then did Yosef start to write once more.

> Let me apprise you of the results of our defense of the city. Our troops have made constant forays into the

Roman lines leaving behind many casualties. Our successes have caused no small embarrassment among the highest levels of their commanders. In response, Vespasian made his first attempt at conquest by building a high embankment parallel to our walls, hoping to invade over the top. I simply commanded the fortress to be built higher.

Vespasian next came at us with a monstrous ram. The beam was larger than the mast of a ship. After the Romans erected a huge balance apparatus, the beam was pulled backward by soldiers and then released, causing the head to smash into the city gate. The impact shook the entire wall! In time the gate and the towers would have fallen. However, I instructed our men to fill large sacks with wheat chaff. These bags were lowered in front of the ram, absorbing the shock quite effectively. While the Romans studied the matter in great consternation, we showered them with arrows and spears.

Before Vespasian could withdraw his machine of war, Elezar Ben Samaias rolled a large stone from the wall knocking off the head from the shaft. Elezar leaped from the ramparts onto the beam and began slaying soldiers. Even though he was wounded with five darts, he did not cease to kill the invaders. Soon his brothers, Netir and Philip, joined him, putting the remaining soldiers to flight. Whereupon I marched out the gate and our men burned the apparatus. In exasperation, Vespasian ceased this approach and began hurling boulders with his machines of war. We have not yet been significantly affected by this strategy. Spread the word throughout Jerusalem of the bravery of my men who fearlessly fight the real foes of our people! Incite warriors to join us!

An archer even shot an arrow that struck Vespasian in the foot. Great disorder followed. Titus himself came forth in panic to assess the injury to his father. Make no mistake! We have given a good account of ourselves!

What I tell you now must be used with great

discretion but these facts will fully clarify our position. I was unable to retake the city of Sepphorius. Our own people capitulated to Rome, trading their freedom for bondage. Vespasian easily recaptured Gadara and burned it to the ground. In addition, he burned all the villas and small cities in the area. The inhabitants were taken away into slavery. No less a fate awaits the people of this city if we fall.

We desperately need reinforcements to attack Vespasian's legions from the rear. Support at this time would lead us to the crucial victory that would save the country. Delay will be to the detriment of all Israel. Our only hope for the future is unification. Division is deadly. Unfortunately, I must report the people of Galilee do not stand together. I need soldiers from the south.

Now a personal word to you, my friend. I have great concern for the next twenty-six days. If we fall, then every prediction I made of the fall of our Holy City will soon follow. You must be prepared to relocate should such eventualities follow. I think I know the right place for you. Near the coast, not far from Jerusalem, is the little town of Jamnia. Think about this matter. Time may be shorter than we think.

At night, images of dissolution and destruction arise in my dream. Life ebbs away and despair pushes forward. Such signs are to be taken seriously.

I remain eternally your friend and servant.

Josephus

Yosef rolled the scrolls tightly together and bound them with a small leather thong. He changed under-shirts and prepared to put on the leather vest he wore to protect his chest. At that moment, a dull thud shook the entire building. The dreaded whirling sounds of speed-ing missiles filled the air. Rushing to the window, Yosef watched in horror as rocks of all sizes flew over the walls striking everything in their path. Beneath his window, the huge boulder which had slammed into his own tower lay in pieces on the pavement. Out in the streets people ran in all directions seeking cover.

Beyond the north wall, Yosef watched catapults being cranked back into loading position to fire again as others were released. The next wave of rocks landed with a sickening thud like bodies being smacked against a wall. Each time a sling was shot, the terrible, gyrating noise added to the bewilderment of the frightened citizens of Jotapata.

Far below, a young man ran toward an overhang on the north wall. As the general stared, a small boulder dropped from the sky on the man's head. More rocks fell like hail, and three more soldiers dropped on the plaza. Stones showered from every direction pounding the pavement and buildings mercilessly.

Yosef did not hear the door behind him fly open. "We've counted at least one hundred and sixty catapults," Jesse yelled. "The city is in chaos! What should we do?"

Yosef grabbed the young man by his robe. "Listen carefully," the general talked intensely. "Get prepared to go over the wall tonight at the darkest moment of midnight. Find animal skins to wrap yourselves in. You will scale the wall at the steepest point. You must get this message to Yochanan Ben Zakkai." Yosef pushed the scrolls into his hands. "Do you understand?"

The young man nodded mechanically, his eyes fixed wide open in consternation.

"No one must see my communiqué. If you think the Romans are about to catch you, bury the scroll in the ground and get away from the place. The letter is more important than your life. No one must see this message but Yochanan Ben Zakkai! Now prepare yourself. This writing is more urgent than what is happening down below. I will take care of the city. You get the letter through!"

Yosef slipped a kolbur, a linen undergarment with

short sleeves, over the leather protector on his chest, crammed his helmet on his head, grabbed his sword, and was gone, leaving Jesse staring at the small bundle in his hand.

The rock storm continued relentlessly throughout the entire morning. Yosef hurried from shelter to shelter, encouraging the people and giving directives to his leaders. Near mid-afternoon, the barrage stopped and Yosef's soldiers hurried out to complete his earlier instructions.

During the attack, soldiers dragged injured animals inside, then killed and skinned them. At the lull, they set up reclining stretchers on which the skins were loosely tied. Piles of older hides were stacked behind the wooden poles. Other hide-covered looms were placed in front of doorways and across open areas beneath the walls.

"Leave enough slack to cushion the impact," Yosef called up to the men. "We want the hides to absorb the blow of the rocks and let them slide to the ground."

"Brilliant!" Ehud, the Galilean commander, exclaimed. "Arrows will slide off the fresh hides and flames won't even kindle on them."

"The Romans will be quite frustrated when they discover that their rock assault has been no more successful than was the battering ram." Yosef smiled slyly. "Vespasian must still be astonished that I could build the north wall quicker than he could raise his embankment against us from the outside." He pointed to the masons already back at work laying bricks behind the stretchers. "He'll get the report quickly that his rock attack hasn't even slowed our building."

"I have a question," Ehud's deep voice rumbled. "Vespasian has us bottled up in the city. I'm sure he knows we have ample food to wait him out, but he must also be aware there are no springs in the city. They can see our men measuring out small quantities to drink." The big man pointed to the barrels along the top of the wall's walkway. "He has to know we are already rationing water."

"Yes," Yosef spoke slowly stroking his beard, "I have foreseen the problem. As soon as all their rock throwing has stopped, I have planned a little exercise that will frustrate the good Roman general even further. You are to take sheets, soak them in water, and hang them over the edge of the wall, letting the water drain down the sides until the fortress looks like it's swimming in water. Make the wall look as if we washed everything in sight. Everyone knows there will be no rain during this hot season of the year. Vespasian will be forced to conclude that we have a secret supply of water. Our extravagance will drive him to despondency."

Ehud shook his big fist in the air. "Yosef, you miss nothing. Regardless of the level of our water reserves, I believe we can endure."

"Of course!" Yosef smiled and slapped him on the back. "Keep the faith!"

"I will carry out your directions at once." Ehud dashed toward the ladder leading up the wall.

Yosef's confident smile faded as he watched this good man bound up the wooden ladder to the walkway on the wall. Yosef's face sagged and his mouth drooped at the corners. *Not many days are left,* he thought. *The water may yet last longer than we do.*

In contrast to Jotapata, the last twenty-one days in remote Galilee had been completely free of strife and war. The journey from Ptolemais took the Ben Aarons two arduous days, but the trip was without delay. Although wracked with pain, Marcus Quintus Cunctator survived. The little town nestled by the Sea of Galilee was slightly less than a day's journey from Jotapata and about two miles north of Tiberius. The Ben Aarons' family house near the shore was part of an estate that had been in the clan for generations. Distant cousins maintained the family land and always made the house available when kin from far off Jerusalem came north.

As was true of all Galilee, the brown, stucco-covered stone house was small, plain, and one-story, but a spacious veranda opened toward the placid blue waters. Swallows diving through the trees and squawking sea gulls circling the lake were the only sounds disturbing the tranquil day. After the noon meal, Marcus Quintus stretched out on a simple couch.

"I am amazed at the progress my leg has made," the Roman commander told Mariam as she worked. "I would never have believed such a bad break could heal so quickly. Your prayers are truly amazing."

"The wound on your side does well," she observed, setting a wine jug in the corner. "God has saved you for His holy purposes."

"It seems so," Marcus Quintus acknowledged soberly, "though the reason for His generosity completely escapes me. Nothing in my past commends me."

"You have told us very little about yourself during these past days," Mariam sat across from the young man who might well pass for her son. "We learned little about you on the boat trip from Rome. Of course, we are glad to tell you about our lives and our faith, but we want to know more about you."

Marcus looked beyond the open doorway and shrugged. "I am a professional soldier. What more offensive thing could I tell a Jew? I stand for everything that violates your dreams, your freedom, and your way of life. I have killed without mercy and survived by being more vicious than my opponents."

"And we didn't know these facts the first time we met you?" Mariam gently mocked. "Come now, you didn't come into the world by yourself. You must have a mother, father, maybe even a brother or sister? Marcus

Quintus, you are among far more than friends. We are quite ready to accept any fact of your life."

The Roman smiled sheepishly. "Forgive me. I suppose there are many reasons I don't like to talk about myself. I have kept certain facts from you. For one thing, I knew I had to sort out the truth for myself, and it has been hard for me to believe you would not deceive me."

"Still think so?"

"You've saved me," Marcus answered earnestly. "I would have been butchered if you had not risked your lives for me." His smile changed, fitting the poignancy in his voice. "I came seeking knowledge and you gave me life. I must be completely honest with you."

"Good!" Mariam settled back in her chair. "Tell me about Marcus Quintus."

"My father's name is Flaccus Postumus Cunctator. Our family name means 'he who holds back.' Rather appropriate for my natural reserve. *Postumus* tells you he was born after his father died. No sisters and fortunately, I didn't inherit the big ears the name Flaccus denotes, but my younger brother did.

"As a matter of fact, Grandfather was in a campaign in North Africa and killed just before Father's birth."

"You don't sound like you are particularly fond of your father."

"Am I so obvious?" Marcus stirred uneasily on the litter. "Yes, if it were not for him I would not be here. But my father was of noble birth and ran with officers of the Praetorian Guard. Even though he was short of funds most of the time, Flaccus Postumus always kept acquaintances with nobility of unlimited means. In fact, for a period of time one of his best friends was general over the Praetorians. Flaccus Postumus's military hero had also spent more than a little time in this part of the world."

Mariam turned her head sideways to catch his every

word. She blinked several times. "You're not speaking of General Gaius Honorius Piso?"

"None other."

"Why, why he was our dearest . . ."

"Friend," Marcus finished her sentence. "Yes, I knew this was the case soon after we met on the ship. A fact I carefully avoided mentioning earlier, as well as telling you that I already knew of your work in Rome."

Mariam's mouth dropped.

"My father was deeply offended and disillusioned by the brutal execution of this thoroughly good man. He admired the great change he saw in Honorius's life through the years as did many others. Nero made a serious mistake when he executed the general."

"But how did you know about us?"

"Rome really is quite a small place when one reaches the top rungs of the social ladder. Gossip is the daily bill of fare for the patricians and the nobilis. Seductions, adulteries, betrayals, and new allegiances are routine conversation. However, when a public hero deviates from degradation in the direction of virtue, that is genuine diversion for the talebearers. The arrival of Peter, Paul, and your family became a well-known topic of interest among my friends."

"Why didn't you tell us any of this on the boat coming over?"

"Several reasons." Marcus Quintus shifted his weight carefully as he tried to move on the narrow couch. "I had my eye on Priscilla Rutina Laenas long before your son Stephan appeared. I suppose my old infatuation with Priscilla clouded my judgment somewhat. Unfortunately, the romantic attraction was one-sided on my part and really a matter of families negotiating a match. But I wanted to carefully survey this Jewish family who not only converted my jewel of Roman society to their faith but managed to snatch her away as a daughter-in-law. No small feat."

"Priscilla has proven to be an extraordinary woman as well as an excellent wife for my son," Mariam acknowledged. "I dearly miss both of them."

"I suppose I feared you might have met or known of my father. I didn't want his name mixed up in what I was seeking to learn for myself. He always hovered over me, trying to manage both my life and my career as if I were one of his better conceived commercial interests. Since most of his investments went bad, I suspect he saw me as the last hope for a secure old age. Here again, his connections proved misguided."

"Misguided? I don't understand."

"The very man he hoped would be his ultimate security became our downfall," Marcus sounded bitter. "General Piso was to be the Cunctator family ticket for a permanent place with Rome's upper crust. When Honorius fell, Nero also brought Flaccus Postumus Cunctator down with him."

"Your father was arrested with the Christians?"

"No, no. Father cared nothing for religions per se. We were all simply discredited because of our relationship with Honorius. I was forced to take this assignment as a veiled threat to all nobility of what could happen to one's children if loyalty to the emperor became in any way suspect. There's no honor in being yanked up out of Rome and ordered to come to this land of sedition and strife. I must prove my worth and dependability in this war if I am ever to return to a place of acceptance near the aristocracy. You can see there is much at stake in what I decide to believe. My life and career are on the line."

"And have you come to any conclusions?"

Marcus looked down at the bandage across his side. "Not only did you risk your lives to save me, you literally prayed me back to life. You arc in touch with a greater force than I have ever known and I know your work is not accomplished by magic. Never have I experienced the caring, and the love that I find among you people. Cures, potions, and doctors come and go but you have the capacity to heal hate and to restore hope. You impart peace to the soul as well as health to the body. Yes, I think I am in a position now to have clear perception of the truth."

The warm, gentle lake breeze of summer blew across Mariam's face. "In this very room the Master gave my life back to me when I was a child. Sometimes I find it difficult to comprehend all that has happened in the nearly forty years that have passed since that hour, but it becomes clearer every day that His way is much greater than any of us can comprehend." She turned around and spoke forcefully. "I tell you, Marcus Quintus, that you have barely touched the edges of this truth that will someday reshape the whole world. When the Master healed your body, He gave you back much more than your physical existence. He offered you a renewed future with eternal promise."

The Roman ran his hands through his tangled hair and sighed deeply. "No, I can't comprehend such thoughts." He swung his leg to the floor and tried to stand briefly before sinking back on the couch. "Look at me! I am supposed to be the flower of Rome's most noble youth. Look at me!" he bellowed in disgust. "I have squandered my youth in wild orgies, banquets of such proportion that even the surplus is obscene. I have gorged myself only to purge my stomach in order to make a glutton of myself again. I have seen enough debauchery to shame the barbaric hordes of Germania."

"Need, not perfection, is the only criterion for entering our way of life," Mariam said compassionately.

"Ah, but avarice is not the worst mark against my name," Marcus anguished. "I've listened and plotted with the mighty to ensnare the weak. I've seen and been a part of friend betraying friend without a second thought. You know the truth. We, the people of privilege, have polluted the world." He stopped and shook his head soberly. "My body is on the mend but my soul is sick. I am young and yet my spirit feels decrepit."

"But your life is about to begin again," Mariam answered. "When I first prayed for your survival, I sensed that beneath the armor of the soldier lay the heart of a gentle, good man. Brutal experiences have worn calluses on your soul, but by no means have they obscured the best that is you. Our Messiah can restore your life and bring the bud you have not yet discovered to fullest bloom."

"I do not think there is a place for me in the world in which you walk," Marcus struggled with his words, "and I don't see how a Roman can embrace your way and still survive as a citizen of the empire. The division within me is deep. As I come closer to your teachings, I sense I lose the place I hold in my world."

"Death brings a strange clarity to all things," Mariam answered gently but firmly. "Important matters convert to trivial distractions. Urgency loses its drive. Necessities become optional. What we thought was so ultimate is only relative. Nothing heals the division within us like discovering the perspective of eternity. Sometimes we must die to truly live."

"And is that the secret you have found?"

Mariam looked back toward the blue Galilee. "One of them," she answered confidently. "And there are others. Each secret is like a key that will open a treasure room within your heart. Whatever you give up is nothing compared to what you will receive. I know. I have spent my life facing great losses and learning the lessons that only the transformation of suffering can teach. Fear not, Marcus, you are not far from the Kingdom of God."

XIII

The steady cracking sound of steel splitting wood interrupted the usual tranquility of Galilee. From the house, Zeda and Mariam watched Marcus Quintus exercise on the shoreline. Running and walking briskly had corrected most of the soldier's limp. His adversary, an old gnarled tree stump, was slashed with new criss-crossed marks from Marcus's constant sword practice.

"One more week has made a great difference in his strength. Marcus could leave now. By tomorrow he will be ready to return to the army," Zeda said pensively. "And we can go south. I am more than ready to go home."

"We have been here nearly thirty days. I'm sure your uncle frets daily over our safety," Mariam added. "I'm glad we sent Ishmael back! Hope he got through. Reassurances about our well-being will help but they won't satisfy Simeon."

"I'm not so sure. Things have changed." Zeda turned away from the window. "I sense Uncle Simeon is different, distant, as if preparing himself for a great change. Since we returned from Rome I sense a greater gulf between us than was there before."

"Too many deaths," Mariam shook her head. "I think the martyrdom of your father and grandfather pushed Simeon over a line. He blames our faith for their deaths."

"Yes," Zeda agreed. "He says little but his tolerance is

diminishing. I notice his irritation especially when Leah is around."

Mariam nodded and silently returned to watching the sweating soldier make quick thrusts at the tree stump. Even the constant breeze made little difference. Finally Marcus wiped his forehead, stuck his sword in the tree, and plunged into the lake. Once cooled, he began a slow halting walk back toward the house.

"We must avoid battles with Simeon." Mariam stood up. "And that may not be an easy task. I must fix a cool drink for our warrior."

Zeda walked out on the veranda. "You completely defeated the stump," he called out good-naturedly, "splintered his dreams. A mighty victory."

"Certainly." Marcus grinned. "But last week that tree beat me. I'm making progress!"

"How do you feel? Your side?"

"Excellent." Marcus sat down on the ground in the shade of the house. "In a week or so I won't even have much of a limp left. I'm ready to go back."

"To war," Zeda's voice betrayed a hint of disgust.

Marcus Quintus looked down at the sword in his hand. "Afraid so."

Zeda smiled weakly. "I'm going down to the village square to see if there is any news." He backed away. "I'll bring you the report." Zeda hurried away.

"A cold, honey drink." Mariam handed Marcus a clay cup. "A summer drink that we often find refreshing."

Marcus reached up for the cup. "I deeply regret our time is coming to an end. I trust the return to our own worlds will not end our relationship." He paused. "I have come to have a deep affection for Zeda. I hope that continues."

"Of course." Mariam sat on a little bench under a fig tree. "But I know that what happens at Jotapata can change everything."

"Yes," Marcus spoke hesitantly, looking again out

across the placid lake. Only agitated sea gulls broke the still. "I wish I could stay here forever." He emptied the cup. "You are right. Nothing is predictable in combat. The tides of war will take all of us to other shores."

"What will happen?" Mariam asked earnestly, "Can we prevail? Will Yosef Ben Mathias stand against your legions?"

"No." Marcus Quintus said resolutely. "I regretfully tell you that Jewish victory is not possible."

"Why?" Mariam threw up her hands. "You know you can be honest with us."

"I suppose I must tell you my final secret." Marcus pursed his lips and groaned. "Even though I was ordered here because of the displeasure of the emperor, I am a man of unusual military background. In Rome I was considered somewhat of a scholar because I studied manuscripts, scrolls, and records of the past. For several months I read about the previous military campaigns in this land. Nearly every piece of correspondence was scrutinized. I was sent here to advise General Vespasian about your history. I know a great deal about the nature of the Jewish people."

"And what did you read?" Mariam asked earnestly.

"The dispatches of Procurators Gessius Florus, Albinas, Antonius Gelix, Ventidius Cumonus . . . everything that Honorius ever wrote, the annals of Pontius Pilate, the communiqués of the Herods, the writing of Ben Sirach and the records of the civil wars between the Hasmonean dynasties when Rome first took control of this land. I even read Philo's philosophic reflection."

"Your conclusions?"

Marcus pushed himself upright against the wall, his countenance changed; his expression was stern. "Romans have always been the masters of divide-and-conquer strategies. We know how to wait and let our enemies defeat themselves. This was the secret of our first conquest in this land. General Pompey stood back and let the civil war between Hyrcanus and Aristobulus destroy the throne of Israel. We purposely allowed the Herods to rule as Rome's regents because the Senate knew the sons of Antipater would add to the natural divisions among your people. With the exception of Agrippa, were not Herods a despised lot?''

Mariam nodded. ''Of course. Your logic has a cold, deadly edge.''

''Yes, I know a great deal about Ben Mathias whom we call Josephus. The general is respected by Rome but he is surrounded by legions of fools.'' Marcus shook his head disdainfully. ''Oh yes, your army could stand against us and even drive Rome from your soil if there was one will to do so, but your long-standing animosities will defeat your people . . . not Vespasian's legion. Remember? I now have a personal experience with Simon Ben Giora. Our soldiers will only seize the opportunities such fools as Ben Giora present to us. I do not mean to be blunt but this is the truth.''

''And what do you expect to happen at Jotapata?''

Marcus drew a circle in the dirt with the tip of his sword. ''The city's natural protection is quite formidable. Deep gorges and long valleys make the back side virtually impenetrable.'' Carefully he traced lines out away from the back edge of the circle. ''Undoubtedly Josephus will use these geographic barriers well and force us to pay a significant price for our victory.'' Marcus drew another circle around the first one. ''But in the end, Vespasian will keep Josephus and the entire army from escaping. The Jews must fall unless reinforcements come from the south. In the end the city's greatest asset will cause its demise.'' Suddenly the Roman cut the circles apart. ''After the city falls, Josephus will no longer have an army to defend the north. The Galilean rebellion will be over.''

Mariam took the heavy sword from his hand. Her arm sagged under the weight. The black steel blade was pitted and the sharp edge nicked. Dark brown stains blotched the leather strap wrapped around the handle. Marcus Quintus's battle sword was stark and grim. Using both hands, Mariam traced a line to the south, away from the broken half circles. "And the rest of the country?"

"Vespasian and Titus will quickly clean out all pockets of resistance in the north. Then the legions will sweep to the south and take Jerusalem. Rome must make an example of this nation for all other countries that might consider rebellion. I suspect that little will be left standing when the campaign is through in that ancient city."

Mariam's head dropped and she let the sword fall to the ground. "I presume there will be no mercy for the people who stand in your way?"

Marcus Quintus picked up the sword and wiped the dust from the blade. "You touch the division within me. I have been trained to think with a military mind, but now you teach me what you Christianios call righteousness, justice . . . love. Compassion was not one of the lessons offered in training. As never before, this military campaign tries me as much as it does my adversaries."

"Like the family of my son's betrothed, will we become slaves for the auction block?"

"Listen to me, Mariam." Marcus dropped the sword and took both of her hands in his. "You must stay out of the way of our army. No one will harm you if you keep away from the conflict." Marcus picked up the sword and quickly drew an outline of the country with Galilee in the center. He pointed north. "Once we have ended all resistance around Galilee, the legions will go south to the capitol city. Only maintenance force will be left here. You must go to the east." He drew a line straight across from Jotapata. "Somewhere on the eastern borders of your country will be a safe place."

"There are the ancient cities of refuge," Mariam mused. "Towns like Pella . . ."

"Yes," Marcus said enthusiastically, "the expeditionary forces will never travel in that direction. You could begin again. You must move your families before we descend on the south. For surely Vespasian will put an end to even the most remote possibility of any future revolts. Not only will Jerusalem be destroyed, but the rebels will be pursued and obliterated."

"Jesus predicted this day," Mariam said resolutely. "I have watched the final hour coming as surely as the sun setting over the Galilee. Nearly four decades ago, the Messiah gave us instruction to prepare for this time. Now I must lead our people to the new place the Redeemer has prepared for us, for surely the center of the Jewish world is about to collapse."

Marcus balanced his sword on the point. "The center? I thought Rome was the heart of all existence before I came here. Now I am not so sure. How does one know where is the real center?"

"When we are young, the answer is simple. Parents, family, the way things have always been. Our dreams. The core seems so constant and predictable. We assume we will simply step into the parade moving past our door each day, but time exposes the truth. More subtle and pervasive spheres of influence lay claim to our true devotion. Power, wealth, security, position, and a host of contenders already vie for our devotion. An unseen passion, a not yet identified authority, becomes the hidden turning point in our universe. The clouds conceal our true north star; our lives are spent driven by task masters in disguise."

"And what if the force loses its drive? What if we no longer have an axis for our existence?"

Mariam smiled at the earnest young man. "I was fortunate. I was even younger than you when that moment came for me. A fine young man of virtue and intelligence was the hub of my world. His tragic death destroyed my confidence in all of which I was certain. Out of that dark time, I discovered what the ancient Jews learned in their wanderings. Sooner or later the supports of life always fall away. We discover what we believed to be permanent is made of clay, dust, and ashes. Only an eternal center can endure. All else must perish with time."

Marcus scooted away from the wall and laid the sword across his legs. "Tell me this secret of the everlasting for surely you know the most important mystery of all."

"Jews call this great truth the shema. We say in worship, 'Hear O Israel, the Lord our God, the Lord is One and you shall love Him with all your heart, mind and soul.' When all else is swept away by the winds of time, the Holy One and the Holy One alone stands."

"But how can I be devoted to something or someone I cannot see?" Marcus Quintus protested.

"The Messiah is the answer. He is the one who shows us how to find the divine center. In His face, we have seen the face of God—not like Greek stories of human beings who turn into gods—but in the love of the Most High taking flesh in Jesus. Through our Messiah, we have found both the heart of God and the meaning of life. Not even death can destroy this balancing point. In simplest terms, the name of this place, this axis, is love."

Marcus slowly raised the sword up in front of his face. "Strength and power I understand. Conquest, preeminence, victory I comprehend." Slowly he lowered the blade. "Love is not a way I recognize."

"My young friend, love is the only road that travels into the abode of death and comes out the other side. Unless you learn this path, no other route can take you home."

"And where do I find my way?" His sword slipped to the ground.

"The way both begins and ends at the Messiah's cross." Mariam removed a little gold cross from around her neck and handed the chain to Marcus. "My family made these symbols to explain our faith to the people of Rome. Keep this gift as a remembrance of your time with us. I know a Roman finds difficulty in seeing anything of value in this torturous means of death. Yet His crucifixion revealed that love is the strongest force in the world."

"A man dying like a common criminal?" The Roman's forehead wrinkled and his eyebrows raised. "You touch the hardest part of your story. Obviously this Messiah's death was not a demonstration of authority. When it was all said and done, was not malice the victor?"

"My father was there on that dark afternoon. He heard Yeshua's final words from the cross. After that afternoon my father was never quite the same again."

Marcus looked at the cross in his hand. "Not the same? What did he hear?" Marcus closed his fist around the cross.

"You know what a crucifixion is like," a harsh edge slipped into Mariam's voice. "Pain and anger devour what's left of humanity as life slowly drains out. Men curse their captors and die in complete despair. No death is quite like this Roman form of execution."

Marcus looked at his closed fist and avoided direct contact with both her eyes and words.

"But what my father saw and heard was of another order. Yeshua surveyed the barbaric scene beneath Him and prayed . . . not just a prayer for survival or even for death. Father heard Him as He looked to heaven and said, 'Father, forgive them for they know not what they do.' Those final words cracked my father's inner world open. Quiet hate and desire for revenge had worked morning and night in this otherwise thoroughly good, religious man, but that afternoon Jarius Ben Aaron saw a new vision of a greater truth than justice. He knew the love and mercy of God were greater than mere equity. Love could change what justice could never correct."

Marcus opened his rough hand once more and looked at the gift. The gold gleamed in the bright sunlight.

Slowly he closed his hand over the cross again. "I must leave tomorrow and go to Jotapata to join Vespasian in the battle. I may never see you again, but I am sure on my dying day I will remember this conversation."

"In the morning we, too, will leave . . . for Jerusalem." Mariam covered his closed fist with her hand. "Find your own true center, Marcus Quintus, and He will be there. The Messiah will teach you the meaning of love and love will reveal the Messiah."

Marcus picked up his sword and opened his palm with the cross. In one hand was black steel and the other gold. He slowly looked back and forth.

XIV

The undulating sides of General T. Flavius Vespa-sianus's massive tent swayed gently in the wind sweeping down from the mountain tops. Although Marcus Quintus Cunctator's eyes were fixed straight ahead and his body rigidly at attention, he felt irritated by the distracting motion. Before him on each side of the entry, a guard in full battle attire stood with spears and shields in hand. Constant breeze made their red, horsehair plumes quiver along the ridge at the top of brass helmets. Each man looked straight ahead as if Marcus weren't even there. He thought the soldiers' indifference seemed particularly arrogant. Their polished metal breastplates forced an obviously poor comparison with his own scratched dull leather protection, covering beneath the torn sagum, Marcus's regulation military cape, which hung limply from his shoulders.

The tent flap parted and a tall, muscular soldier quickly stepped out. Although not wearing a helmet, or battle sword, the commander had a longer red cape attached at the shoulders and the usual military dagger always close to the side. "Marcus Quintus Cunctator, you are fortunate that I am the legate of your legion. No matter that you are the primus pilus! Your situation would have been very hard to sell if I were not your friend. Fortunately you are considered a political subversive by Nero and that sits favorably with the general. I

149

had to talk a lot, but he finally accepted your account of the past forty days."

Marcus's body sagged in relief. "Thank you, Clodius Augur." He rolled his eyes. "You are a true friend."

"You look terrible." The legate shook his head. "Couldn't you have at least escaped with something that looked a little like nobility? A commander?"

"Thank the lares!" Marcus stopped, uncomfortable in invoking the gods of Rome. "I should say thanks to my Jewish friends who saved me."

"Don't say much about them." Clodius frowned. "Jewish virtue isn't a popular topic with any of the commanders. These rebels have given us a bad time. Just stick to the military facts of how you escaped. You look so shabby that no one will doubt you've crawled out from under a hay stack. And don't hesitate to limp. Drag your leg. Wouldn't hurt to remind everyone why you took so long in getting here."

"Who's in there?" Marcus pointed to the tent.

"Most of the legion commanders as well as Titus." Clodius leaned close to Marcus's ear. "We picked up a deserter who may prove to be the final breakthrough we've needed to wrap up this attack. We're not sure he's trustworthy. Could be another trick by Josephus but he's being interrogated carefully. Come in and listen. When the questioning is done, Vespasian will have a word with you. Then I should think you can return to business as usual."

Marcus Quintus rolled his eyes the opposite direction. "I hope so. I don't need any more trouble with the powers that be."

"Did you know there wasn't one survivor from the attack on Ptolemais . . . except you? How in the world were the raiders able to completely surprise your men?"

"Is that an issue?" Marcus answered defensively.

"It's sure a question."

"I'll have an answer when they ask."

"Make sure you do." Clodius Augur opened the flap and gestured for Marcus Quintus to follow him.

The general's field quarters were impressive. The luxury gripped Marcus's attention. Large furs completely covered the ground. The spacious tent was lavishly furnished with oil lamps hanging from massive poles across the top. Carved chairs with leather seats were sitting around the wide open spaces. Tables of various sizes were covered with everything from maps to dishes and personal effects. In the center of the command room, a rough-cut man sat on a plain wooden stool answering questions the Roman legionnaires fired at him from every direction.

"Jews don't desert their own people," a burly soldier snarled in the little man's face. "Why would you turn traitor?"

"I want my family spared," the captive shot back. His eyes darted nervously back and forth around the menacing circle. "I know you are going to win. I'm here because I don't want my children killed."

"Why should we trust you?" a commander at the edge of the circle barked. "Perhaps Josephus sent you as another one of his clever tricks."

Marcus Quintus stayed near the edge of the tent, carefully sizing up the situation. As he listened, he looked studiously at the general's personal effects for some hint of the status of the assault. Near the general's bed, his parade armor was draped over a frame. An ornate scabbard with a massive sword hung over the side of the armor. The highly ornate commander's helmet sat next to the rack on its own stand. To the left was Vespasian's rack of medals. His leather cuirass that protected his chest and back was covered with the awards of battle, gold and silver awards of successful campaigns. Eight small silver spears were reminders of eight successful, single, hand-to-hand victories with long-since dead adversaries. A vexillum, his cloth embroidered in gold, was covered with memorials to other victories in single combat. Silver-covered shields were attached as awards for military victories gained against impossible odds. Never had Marcus seen such an array of decorations.

But the laurels of victory were covered with dust. Obviously the armor had sat untouched for a long time. Vespasian had not marched in a parade of triumph since setting foot on the shores of this perverse land. There were no signs of any decisive victories. Perhaps, the general's staff respected the tenacity of their adversaries and would have some sympathy with the debacle at Ptolemais.

"I tell you the city is ripe for the taking," the Jewish informant insisted. "The soldiers are spent and rations are near depletion. Yosef Ben Mathias has cleverly misled you. He's very low on water. His troops are close to the end of their tether. Now is the time for a night strike."

"Very interesting," a deep bass voice rumbled authoritatively. "Perhaps we should test your assertions."

Marcus Quintus edged forward. When T. Flavius Vespasian spoke, every word was taken with infinite seriousness. Not that Marcus had not seen and listened to the great man many other times, but his fascination with the personal power and authority of Vespasian never ceased. Although Marcus despised his own father's propensity for attachment to men of stature, he shared the same fascination for rubbing elbows with the elite of Rome. No one knew the extent of the general's personal fortune, but rumor was that during previous campaigns he had obtained both silver and copper mines that poured unending wealth into his personal coffers. Everyone knew that money ruled Rome. Anything and everything was possible to those who had the leverage only wealth could provide. Vespasian held the world in the palm of his hand.

"I think our newfound friend might wish to lead our attack on the city. A place of high honor," Vespasian's low voice mocked his prisoner. "Surely, you can take us to exactly the right place to attack. Correct?"

The Jew blinked nervously.

"Yes, we will give you the prestige of leading the charge." Vespasian grinned, exposing large teeth. The general's jaw was square and massive, his features, angular and blunt. His unusually opaque black eyes were penetrating enough, but were set beneath massive bushy black eyebrows that met in the middle of his head which made his stare more than disconcerting. No one would trifle with him. "You will take us to the place you described as the vulnerable point of attack. The legion will follow *you* over the wall. If you are telling the truth, you have nothing to fear."

Once more the deserter looked about the sea of hostile faces. "Acceptable," he grunted.

"You had better not be toying with us." Vespasian leaned closer to the man's face. In contrast to the Jew's long hair, the general's hair was cropped close and combed down on his forehead in typical Roman style. Huge muscles bulged on the side of his neck. Everything about the general conveyed strength. Vespasian naturally embodied what the people of Rome called auctoritas, a unique combination of authority, power, and position.

The Jew peered into Vespasian's face and then looked away.

"Should deception of some order be another ploy by Josephus, I will personally see that you are kept alive until we locate this precious family of yours. Each one of them will be marched before your eyes to have their throats cut. Then you will be hung before the city gates to die after we have removed the skin from your back and legs. Am I clear?"

The man's mouth dropped in horror but he nodded mechanically.

"Good!" Vespasian patronizingly patted him on the back. "We will attack tonight. I want to get this place far behind me as fast as I can." The general turned to his son. "Make the preparations with as little commotion as possible. We don't want to send out any signals. If it is a trap, they will not anticipate attack until after they see a flourish of activity. Tell the men to appear to be taking a day of leisure. We want no fires when we move tonight. The charge must be silent, swift, and unsuspected."

Titus was unusually tall for a Roman, but as muscular as his father. "Your command will go out at once." Titus struck his breastplate with his closed fist. "The men will assemble for the march at the midnight hour."

"Excellent!" The general smiled proudly at his son and winked. "Perhaps, we will have an enjoyable evening. Put our newfound Jewish friend by your side when you descend on the city gates."

Although there was an obvious facial resemblance to his father, Titus lacked his father's compelling aura of sovereignty. Yet Titus had extraordinary presence for a twenty-nine-year-old man.

"He will stand behind me when I personally kick the gates down," the son arrogantly reassured his father.

"Thank you for past perseverance, gentlemen," Vespasian spoke to each of the commanders. "Our meeting is ended. We shall conclude our business tonight. Let us be on our way."

The legionnaires quickly and confidently broke for the canvas door. Two commanders took the Jewish prisoner in tow between them. No one appeared to notice Marcus Quintus. He felt relieved that he aroused no particular interest or concern. Titus passed him with his usual aloofness as if the primus pilus hadn't been standing two feet from him. Clodius Augur stood to one side, waiting for the right moment to speak.

Vespasian spoke quietly to three aides for a few moments and then looked around. "Ah, Augur. You have the centurion with you, I see."

Augur snapped his heels together and bowed at the waist. "Your servants await your pleasure."

"Bring young Cunctator here." The general pointed to the small stool the Jewish deserter had vacated. "We want a full accounting."

Marcus Quintus instantly stepped forward, struck his chest with his fist, and sat down. Only after he was seated did it occur to him that he should have limped more. He felt undone, nervous, and his heart beat like a runaway horse.

"You look awful," Vespasian sounded disgusted. He began walking slowly around Marcus. "How could you have possibly lost the fortress and every man defending the place?" Vespasian's voice rumbled like an approaching thunderstorm.

"I had gone to the caves to inspect the cells in anticipation of an early victory at Jotapata." The line came out just as Marcus had rehearsed in his mind a hundred times. "I expected slaves and prisoners to be coming in a few days." He watched the general's face hoping that memories of swift success would cause Vespasian to recollect his own difficulties in handling the Jews. "While I was in the bottom of the caves, the marauders attacked. They were not soldiers, but common criminals. Our patrol on the ramparts couldn't have detected any difference from the other people of the village. I believe that the guards on the walls simply did not suspect an approaching enemy."

Vespasian shook his head. "Never saw anything like these Jews. They love pain . . . obstinate to the core!"

Marcus felt immediate relief. His ploy worked. The general was accepting the explanation.

"But you escaped!" Vespasian's mood swung violently in the opposite direction. "Why didn't you die with your men?"

"During the battle I was severely wounded." Marcus immediately began unstrapping the leather breastplate covering his scar. "When my leg was broken by the two horses that fell on me, I was knocked unconscious."

"Two horses?" Vespasian raised his eyebrows. "Two? Not bad."

"I was saved by Christian Jews caught in the cross-fire. They don't believe in killing and felt a mission to nurse me back to health."

"Christianios? Hmph!" Vespasian snorted. "I understand this latest scourge of Rome began as a pest in this country." He turned to the aides. "Can you believe the sect doesn't believe in killing their enemies? Very strange group."

Marcus exposed the bright red scar. Edges of the torn skin were still dotted with ugly brown scabs. He turned his leg sideways and pointed to the imprint of the horse's hoof that was also edged in red.

Vespasian puckered his lips and looked at Marcus out of the side of his eyes. "I know your father, Flaccus, and have always liked him. I hope that during this campaign you can bring honor . . . ," Vespasian paused to consider his words carefully, "and any vindication your family name might require. We need your insights into these maddening Galileans who seem to prefer death to life. I am accepting Clodius Augur's full report and your explanation. A report will be sent throughout the camp that you performed acceptably and were wounded in the due course of battle. Your record will reflect honor in this matter."

"Thank you, thank you," Marcus Quintus stammered. "I live to serve Caesar."

A look of disgust dropped over Vespasian's face. "Just do your job," he said flatly. The general suddenly pointed a finger in Marcus's face. "And next time make sure you die with your troops! Don't get yourself saved again. That's not the Roman way!"

Marcus Quintus bowed at the waist, reached for his drooping breastplate, and began backing away.

"Will you be ready for the battle tonight?" Vespasian asked warily.

"Of course! If it is your wish."

"Good." The general smiled. "Bring your limp and we will let you join the fun."

Marcus and Clodius Augur both bowed and left the tent quickly.

Once outside and beyond the hearing range of the guards, Clodius turned and beamed. "The gods do smile on you, Marcus Quintus Cunctator. You've walked out of this disaster nearly a hero. Whatever you offered the lares was the right gift."

"Yes," Marcus said thoughtfully. "One detects a divine touch."

PART THREE

"Therefore when you see the 'abomination of
desolation,'
spoken of by Daniel the prophet, standing in the holy
place . . .
then let those who are in Judea flee to the
mountains. . . .
For wherever the carcass is,
there the eagles will be gathered together."

Matthew 24:15–16, 28

XV

Shortly after midnight a heavy mist settled over Jotapata. The Roman legionnaires believed the descending fog was an omen of favor from the fates. Later Josephus concluded quite the contrary, thinking along the same lines as the ancient prophets Jeremiah and Isaiah. Surely the Lord alone had sent such disaster at a strategic moment. The loss of visibility was Vespasian's final stroke of fortune, precipitating an overwhelming victory on the forty-seventh day of the siege.

Marcus Quintus Cunctator watched the clouds drop from the sky and conjectured that the night would be unusually dark. The opaque sky made a perfect cover for any soldier to scale the wall. Domititus Sabinus, one of the general's tribunes, climbed at Titus's side while Marcus Quintus observed from a distant hill the shadowy shapes of the fifteenth legion following behind their leaders. Like silent cobras, the invaders cut the throats of the night watchmen and quickly fanned out across the top of the wall. Shortly thereafter, Titus waved a white flag from an opening in one of the citadel towers signaling that the city's first line of defense had fallen.

Cerealis and Placidus led the next wave of attackers up the wall. By the time the steady stream of unopposed soldiers mounted the ladders, fog engulfed the city. Marcus Quintus knew success was inevitable. The Roman strategy unfolded with the precision of a skilled gladiator

161

luring his exhausted opponent into the final maneuvers, leaving the victim's throat open to the fatal thrust. Why would the Jews have allowed so few men to stand guard unless their numbers were seriously depleted? Marcus Quintus reasoned correctly that the citizens would quickly panic and forfeit any final vestiges of defense.

Once the massive city gate swung open, Marcus Quintus Cunctator raced down the hill with his own unit. His troops waited patiently beside the crowded bridge while attacking soldiers surged through Jotapata's main gate. The mist was very thick by the time they crossed over and were inside, but there was no need to see far. Every soldier could hear the cries of panic. The entire city was in flight.

Marcus quickly found Jotapata to be a city of narrow winding streets. His men easily climbed to the roofs and struck from above, while other soldiers blocked the exits. He watched the legionnaires slaughter every man, woman, and child they found. By the first light of day the bloodstained streets were covered with bodies of every size and shape. Marcus found the overwhelming victory hard to stomach.

At dawn the legionnaires swept the northern end of the city, forcing the people and soldiers toward the citadel's steep walls. The people of Jotapata were either butchered where they stood or were plunging over the edge of the wall.

The campaign at Jotapata had been costly and difficult. Josephus's clever ploys evoked respect that quickly turned to contempt. In the end, Roman anger reverted to a grudging admiration for the man. Yet any remaining esteem for Josephus did not deter the underlying rage of the foot soldiers. Now the tables were turned, and mercy was inconceivable.

The pincers of the final Roman attack closed. The remainder of Josephus's aides retreated to the towers on the north side of the city, and fighting continued fiercely until the end of the first hour.* The sun slowly burned away the fog to reveal the plight of the defenders. Retreat was not possible and further resistance was hopeless. One by one the valiant Jews resolutely stretched their necks over chopping blocks. Comrades severed their friends' heads in one quick blow. Just before the first Romans broke into the towers, the last survivors fell on their own swords.

From the scrolls, Marcus Quintus knew most Galilean fortresses had vast systems of caves, like the ones beneath Ptolemais. Because of his knowledge, he was assigned to lead the task of ferreting out escapees who sought refuge in the caverns. The only Roman casualty suffered on the final day was a centurion named Antonius, who was killed while probing one of the shelters. A defender lurking around a corner rammed a spear into the centurion's stomach.

As the day wore on, the dead were collected, searched, and piled in heaps for disposal. Vespasian immediately sent out search parties to locate the body of Josephus. The general reasoned that the exhibition of his corpse would crush all Jewish hopes. But as the sun set, Vespasian was confronted with a final frustration from his crafty adversary. Josephus was not among the dead nor found with the living. Thus it was in the thirteenth year of the reign of Nero on the first day of the Roman month of Panemus, Vespasian effectively ended the rebellion in Galilee.

The next day Marcus Quintus and his men once again searched the caves. To their surprise, many women and children were still huddled together in the winding passageways. By dusk the recesses of the earth had coughed up more than twelve hundred new slaves.

*Sunrise to 9:00 A.M.

At nightfall, Vespasian summoned Marcus Quintus to his headquarters. Inside the tent, Marcus found Titus and five aides standing around the supreme commander seated at his planning table, studying a scroll. "These calculations indicate that we have slain at least forty thousand people since the attack began." Vespasian pushed the scroll aside. "This victory must be a supreme lesson for the Jews. The city is to be burned to the ground. The entire fortification is to be torn completely to pieces. I want Jews to be terrified of what will happen if there is further resistance." He slammed his fist on the table so hard the scroll tumbled to the ground.

"Ah, Cunctator!" The general beckoned him forward. "I understand you've found the chattel to fill up those prison cells you were preparing at Ptolemais," he chided.

"More than twelve hundred were apprehended today." Marcus kept his eyes fixed straight ahead.

"Not bad for a cripple with a broken leg," Vespasian smiled wryly. "How many more caves are there to search?"

"We have at least half a day's work left. Many of the caverns are vast and deep. We are proceeding carefully to avoid any further casualties."

"Yes, yes." The general pursed his lips and frowned. "I want you to take the lead in the rest of the search."

"As you wish." Marcus looked puzzled. "Is there a specific task I am to perform?"

Vespasian nodded his head. "We have not found the body of Josephus. Unless we find him in one of those caves, we must conclude the sly fox has eluded us. A defeat in the midst of such a great victory!"

"I will personally lead the search." Marcus sounded authoritative and sure.

"Should you find the man," Vespasian spoke in measured tone, "the recovery would certainly cover a multitude of your past sins." The general broke into a broad smile and laughed crudely. "I like you, Cunctator. Go find my nemesis and things will go well for you."

"At once!" Marcus Quintus struck his breastplate with his closed fist and hurried out of the tent.

That evening the primus pilus summoned his personal group of aides and instructed them the search would begin before dawn. Marcus had an opportunity that must not be lost. He rested that night with eager expectation of the dawn.

Deep sleep wrapped around Marcus like a warm blanket. The worries of the day disappeared in the haze. Only with great difficulty could he later understand the sound of someone telling him to get up. Slowly the face of Clodius Augur came into focus.

"Wake up!" Clodius kept shouting.

He felt like he had barely gone to sleep. *Perhaps it's a bad dream.*

Clodius Augur persisted. "I have important news for you."

Marcus sat up on his bed. "We're being attacked?" he muttered.

"Come outside. You need to hear the night watch's report. It's nearly morning."

Pulling the blanket around his shoulders, Marcus slowly stood up. Small rocks in the dirt made him hobble behind Augur. He searched the pitch black tent for his sandals.

Outside a soldier in battle dress stood at attention. Augur beckoned for the man to step forward. "Tell the primus pilus what you saw."

"I was on the walkway when a man came up out of the shadows. He was big, strong, and obviously one of their soldiers. He began creeping around the edge of the wall looking for a way out. Of course, all the exits are guarded. When he stepped into the moonlight I noticed that he wore an unusual white tunic . . . nothing like what you would see on the common people or their soldiers. Just as I was ready to leap from the wall, he popped into one of those doorways that conceals an entrance to the caves you searched yesterday."

"What did you do?" Marcus let the blanket slide away.

"I immediately went to the doorway and cautiously pushed it open, but the man had disappeared into the cave."

"Know the area?" Clodius asked Marcus.

"Certainly," Marcus spoke rapidly. "Below the entry shaft are several small caves that empty into a very large chamber. That area was raided yesterday. Either the man was missed, which I doubt, or he is moving from place to place under the cover of night."

"I'm sure you are aware that this Jew may prefer death to captivity and could well try to take you with him."

Marcus Quintus shrugged. "Give me a company of ten men and I'll be at the entrance as soon as I arm myself."

When the primus pilus arrived at the entrance, the first light of day silhouetted the soldiers against the plain wooden doorway that concealed the shaft to the cave. The detachment stood in formation awaiting his instruction.

"We have no choice but to use torches," Marcus lectured as he pushed the door open. "Without light we could walk past an elephant and never know it was down there. Hold the flames high and away from your body or you'll make an easy target. Understand?"

The company nodded and began lighting the torches.

"There may be a connection to another tunnel that was missed earlier. Walk carefully. Do your best to avoid killing anyone. I want the prisoner alive at all costs."

Marcus Quintus darted fearlessly into the dark tunnel. The torch cast some light over his shoulder but he crouched and walked fast enough so that he would not be an easy target for anyone lurking in one of the recesses. The soldiers tediously searched the first two small caves until Marcus was satisfied nothing had been missed.

"I am concerned about the big cavern that should be ahead," he addressed his men in hushed tones. "We must enter quickly and use surprise to our advantage. If any men are hiding, we may cause them to run. I will stand in front. When you see my sword drop, charge and listen carefully."

Racing forward into the darkness, Marcus immediately sensed how enormous the cave must be. Torchbearers spread out on either side of their commander, but the light barely revealed the depth and breadth of the stone chamber. Far to his right, Marcus heard the telltale noise of men scurrying for shelter. He charged toward the sound of scattering rocks.

At least a dozen men were trying to conceal themselves behind boulders and under rock ledges. As the Romans surrounded them, the rebels' swords reflected the light. Marcus suddenly realized his prey probably outnumbered his men. A battle would only be to the detriment of his purposes.

"Josephus!" the centurion called out. "Flavius Josephus! I have not come for your life." He waited, hoping for a response. "We offer amnesty to you and your friends."

The ring of opposing rebels tightened, but no one answered.

"We have killed enough." Marcus stepped forward. "There is no honor in turning my soldiers loose on your small miserable number. Honor is not served by slaughtering you like animals caught in a trap. Let us meet face to face like men. You have earned your dignity."

After a long period of silence, a man in the shadows answered. "What do you propose?"

"I will step forward away from my legion. Come forth from these few. Let us talk face to face."

"We prefer death!" the rebel shouted back. "Prepare to die with us."

"No, Jonah," another voice spoke. The figure in the shadows said resolutely, "Do not be foolish."

"Don't go out!" a voice warned in more subdued tones. "They will only humiliate us before turning us into slaves."

"Not so!" Marcus took another step toward the enemy. "Romans honor bravery and always treat men of valor with respect."

"Don't leave us!" the rebel turned his sword toward the unseen figure. "We have come too far to fold now."

"God wills otherwise." A powerfully built man wearing a soiled white cloak edged in gold stepped into the torchlight, and boldly pushed his comrade's sword aside with his hand. "Living may take more courage than dying."

"You are Josephus," Marcus's query was half assertion and half question.

"And if I am?" the Jew stepped between the groups of soldiers.

"Then I seek you." Marcus cautiously edged forward, trying to see the man's eyes.

"I would speak to you alone," the man sounded unintimidated.

Marcus motioned with his sword toward the side of the cave. "Walk slowly and keep your hands in front of you."

The captive's stride was assured and surprisingly casual. When they were about thirteen feet from the others, he turned and faced the primus pilus. "I know how many men you have with you," he said bluntly. "I heard their footsteps in the tunnels and saw the shadows when you entered. I am not deceived. I outnumber you and we are far more desperate."

"Your point?" Marcus tried to sound unimpressed.

"We may fall but we can take your squad down as well," the rebel continued unemotionally.

"Your price?"

"If Josephus is handed to you, let the rest of these

men go. Escort them to the city gate and release them. They are no longer a threat without their leader."

Marcus knew he did not have the authority to approve such a thing, but his predicament was clear. Anything could happen in a black cave and Josephus could well escape down some side tunnel. "I would expect to walk out of here with Josephus's hands bound."

"Agreed. Tell your soldiers to take the men to the city gate. The one who remains is Josephus. No treachery! I expect the command to be given from where you stand."

Marcus turned slowly toward his men. "Take these Jews out to the city gate and release them to the countryside. They will lay their weapons down at their feet now and no one is to harm them. If any ask by what authority you set them free, give my name." No one moved.

"Do as the Roman said!" the Jewish commander barked in Hebrew.

Slowly the rebels laid their arms down and the Romans cautiously circled them with their torches. "We will not let you lay down your life for us," a defender cried out.

"Jonah," the commander called back across the dark empty space, "you are too valiant and good to die in this black hole. The future needs you."

"No!"

"Go on," Josephus answered. "Take Jesse and go back to your village. These matters are now in the hands of God."

Marcus Quintus watched the torchlight procession move away, and then turned back to the man who stood in front of him. He was keenly aware of the precariousness of being alone with such a proven warrior. "Why do you surrender?" Marcus asked cautiously.

Josephus casually reached for a dagger in his belt. He smiled when Marcus raised the point of his sword, but the general dropped the small blade to the ground. "I have never been in charge," he spoke gently, "and neither has Rome. You have prevailed because the Holy One of Israel decreed that it should be so. You did not win; we lost." He gestured with his hand toward the door as a friend politely defers to another. "Let us go."

"Put your hands together," Marcus Quintus demanded.

The Jewish commander immediately complied.

"I would have expected more resistance," Marcus answered cautiously, setting the torch between two rocks. With his free hand he quickly wound a piece of rope around the man's wrists.

"The last forty-seven days were not enough for you?" Josephus chided.

The knot was tied tightly. Marcus looked probingly at the legend who stood before him with the grace of a captor, not a captive. "You have motive in what you do. Speak honestly. I respect your intention."

"I have a message for your commander. Take me to Vespasian and I will tell you clearly what is on my mind."

"As you wish." Marcus Quintus gently pulled on the end of the rope. "Let us go."

When the two men emerged from the cave, a mass of soldiers crowded around the doorway. The legionnaires broke into cheers and some even mockingly jabbed at Josephus with their swords. Marcus Quintus pushed past the troops and marched his prisoner through the main thoroughfare toward the city gate. A contingent of soldiers fell in step surrounding the two men as they trudged up the hill toward Vespasian's encampment. By the time they reached the command tent, soldiers had formed two lines leading to the entrance. Men applauded and beat on their shields with swords.

Vespasian arose immediately when Marcus Quintus led his prisoner into the general's tent. The aides surrounding Vespasian and Titus stepped back, forming a semicircle around their commander. Vespasian barely acknowledged the primus pilus as he extended his hand to Josephus.

"We are honored to meet so noble an opponent." Vespasian began untying the Jewish leader's bonds. "You certainly humbled us on a number of occasions. Please meet my son, Titus."

Josephus and the young general bowed to one another.

Vespasian clapped his hands. "Wine for the general. I am sure you must be hungry after the last several nights. Perhaps a little bread for breakfast?" He pointed to a platter sitting on his table.

"Your hospitality is appreciated." Josephus stood stiffly.

"Rome honors courage." Vespasian pointed to a chair. "Sit if you wish."

"No, thank you. May I ask how you intend to make disposition of me?"

Vespasian turned to the aides. "Josephus is to be cared for with the utmost caution. His person and needs are to be attended to as if he were in his own chambers. Of course bonds will be necessary."

"And then I will be taken to Rome?"

"I should think you would want to meet our emperor. I intend to present you to Nero myself."

Josephus smiled knowingly. "And then I will be marched in your triumphal parade. In my finest attire you will exhibit me down the length of the Palatine for the crowds to jeer. I will walk past the great Forum Romanum and around the Temple of Vesta. Perhaps, even up to the stairs of the temple of Jupiter Optimus Maximus as you pause to make your sacrifices. Then you will take me on to the Tullianum on Arx hill where I will be pushed headfirst into the pit to die."

Vespasian's hospitable casualness ceased. "You know Roman custom as well as I was told you did."

"I have not surrendered without considerable forethought." Josephus looked around the room carefully.

"Nor have I come forth with any misgivings about my fate. I do not stand here because I have chosen to do so, but because I am sent on a divine mission. I would speak to you alone."

The general frowned and looked uncertainly at his captive. He grimaced before nodding his head. "Titus . . . Marcus Quintus stay . . . the rest can wait outside."

The dismayed staff filed out of the tent and Vespasian sat down, staring at the commanding Jew.

"I have come to address Caesar and his son." Josephus looked straight into the general's eyes and then at Titus. "I did not capitulate, but I have been sent as a minister of the most high God to Caesar."

"Caesar?" Vespasian interrupted him. "What do you mean?"

"Bind me to your side, emperor, for I am of far more worth to you than Nero, who will soon fall in Rome."

"What are you saying?" Vespasian sat upright in his chair.

"I am a priest of the most high God of Israel and am granted dreams and visions. I knew we would face defeat on the forty-seventh day. I saw no point in wasting extra men's lives guarding the walls. It was no accident that you found so little resistance. While I waited for the day to come, I was granted another dream of the future. You, Vespasian, are to be the next emperor and your sons will rule after you."

"Caesar?" Titus sputtered.

"Do not plan to waste me on a ruler who will be dead within the year. My God has a mission for me among your people."

"No one must hear what you have uttered." Vespasian abruptly stood up. "This conversation must not leave this tent." The general looked hard at Marcus Quintus before turning back to his captive. *"Caesar?"* He stared at Josephus.

"You will succeed and ascend," Josephus continued,

"because it is the will of God that you do so. The fog did not come by accident of nature or design of the fates. Adonai decrees you should rule the world."

"You jest with us?" Titus put his hands on his hips.

"Jews never speak lightly of the Divine or His intentions," Josephus answered. "How could I have continued to oppose your army once I came to see the matter so clearly? If Rome has become the instrument of the purposes of the Holy One, opposition is not only foolish but wicked. I have come to minister to your needs in His name, mighty Caesar."

"You are either the most clever or the most brash man I have met in my life." Vespasian's eyes narrowed. "Unless, of course, you are truly a prophet. Well, we shall see. Indeed, we will see. At the appropriate time, we will find out if you are a seer. Yes, my friend, if you speak the truth, you will live to bless the day you came to me with this message. If not, I will push you into the Tullianum myself."

Josephus picked up a goblet in toast. "In less than two years!"

Vespasian's composure returned. "Tonight you dine with us. In the meantime, the centurion will care for your every need. I do not think there will be further need for the rope but chains must be fixed to your wrists until we prove this capacity to know the future."

Josephus bowed to the general and turned toward Marcus Quintus. "I await your orders."

Mechanically Marcus pointed to the entrance of the tent and then followed the Jew through the throng of soldiers. Marcus was so distracted that he hardly noticed the tumult of soldiers surging around him and his prisoner. The dazed primus pilus walked on completely distracted by the implications of what he had just heard. *Vespasian, the Emperor? Caesar?* He turned and looked at the man who walked at his side with the regal bearing of one who had conquered. *Who is really in control here?* he thought to himself.

XVI

Simeon Ben Aaron, or Yochanan Ben Zakkai as he was known to most, dated the year after the fall of Jotapata as 3622. Romans calculated the victory occurring in the fourteenth year in the reign of Nero. Jews who believed that Jesus was the Messiah remembered it was the thirty-sixth year after his resurrection. Then again, no one measured the seasons as did the Jews. Generally the ancient world counted years in terms of a personage, an empire, or a conquest. Jewish memory commenced with the creation of time itself and was the continuous story of the intervention of the Creator in the mundane comings and goings of kings and commoners. Humans had a pivotal place in the grand cosmic scheme. Caesar and citizen, general and soldier, laborer and leader, slave and free, stood on a certain ultimate par with each other.

During the year that followed the fall of Jotapata, the Roman army moved to permanently end all rebellion in Judea. In early summer, Vespasian returned to Ptolemais and filled the caves with prisoners before marching on to Caesarea-by-the-Sea. Rome had learned well from Antiochus Epiphanes' failure to quell the Maccabean revolt two centuries earlier. The Greeks' mistake in not taking seriously the Hasmoneans' potential resulted in their defeat and the beginning of the disintegration of the Seleucid empire. Vespasian would not make the same error.

174

Two legions camped in Caesarea for the winter to take advantage of the warm coastal climate. The tenth and fifth legions were sent to Scythopolis, where the winter was equally mild. Once these units were in place, Vespasian and Titus began a systematic campaign to end all resistance.

Nothing went well for the rebels. The remnant of Josephus's army regrouped at Joppa. When the Romans pressed the conspirators, the rebels attempted to escape by the sea. A violent wind caught the fleet and dashed the ships against the rocky coastline. The Romans watched the sea turn bloody and waited to fish out any survivors, who were then butchered on the beaches. When the piles of bodies were counted more than four thousand two hundred Jews had perished. Joppa was taken without opposition and utterly demolished.

Sephoris had always been a pro-Roman town and the citizens saved themselves from the wrath that fell on their neighbors. John of Gischala tried to unite the people of Gabara, but he could not hold the loyalty of the peasants, who promptly deserted as fast as they were conscripted. In turn, the Romans fully exploited the lack of unity.

The people of Gamala put up a formidable defense, but the Romans were able to undermine one of the high towers in the city wall and pull it to the ground, weakening the city's defenses. Titus and two hundred handpicked horsemen marched into the city as efficiently and effectively as they had entered Jotapata in the night. The slaughter was on. By the end of the twenty-third day of Tishri,* Gamala was razed.

While Titus conquered the rebellious countryside, Vespasian made a foray north to visit the kingdom of Herod Agrippa. The Herodian dynasty understood power and wouldn't tolerate foolish speculation about the vulnera-

*September to October

bility of Rome, much less challenge its authority. Rome had put the first Herod into power. Later, Emperor Caligula made his boyhood friend, Herod Agrippa, ruler over all the territories across the Jordan. Agrippa's prudence had expanded these boundaries without shooting one arrow.

Herod Agrippa greeted Vespasian as supreme royalty. In turn, Vespasian made sure the local administration was in good order, efficient, and loyal to Rome. Agrippa wisely provided sufficient assurances that sent Vespasian and his army on their way after a month of consummate pleasure.

During this time, the story of the fall of Jotapata slowly filtered through to Jerusalem. Because of the total destruction of the city and the lack of eye-witness accounts, Josephus's death was assumed and public mourning followed. For thirty days the Holy City's streets were filled with lamentations of the personal and professional mourners.

However, once Josephus's survival and capitulation were known, the condemnation was even more passionate than the adulation. His exalted status as a prisoner only added to the indignation. The hero had become a traitor. Yochanan Ben Zakkai was no less perplexed, although he still assumed the honor of his friend. Yet the defection of the priest-general only added to Ben Zakkai's overwhelming dread of the future.

Yochanan's fears were well-founded. Having failed in the north, John of Gishcala made a bid for power in Jerusalem. His murderous forays and the mindless assaults of the Zealots turned the city into an open camp of terror and sedition. High priest Elezar Ben Ananias and the Sadducees could only hold the Temple compound and the Antonia fortress under their control. Without the insight of men like Josephus, the remaining priests' leadership was more reactionary than insightful. As a result, the citizens made the blunder of asking Simon Ben Giora to restore order to the city. The wolf had become the guard of the lambs. Nothing pleased the instincts of the ruthless rogue more than his recognition as a legitimate arbitrator of power. Simon's idea of stabilization was to kill everyone who disagreed with him. At the last desperate moment when the Holy City most needed every man to defend the walls, the street gutters ran red. During these weeks of mayhem most of the Believers began moving out of the Holy City to Pella, one of the ancient cities of refuge.

However, the civil war that now gripped Vespasian's attention was not in Judea but in Rome! During the fall of Jotapata, Nero met his own demise. Persistent rumors about his burning Rome were compounded by stories of excesses, delusions, and incompetence. Three provincial governors rose in open revolt and soldiers rebelled in Spain. Finally, the Praetorians deserted Nero. Pressed on every side, the despot committed suicide.

Marcus Quintus first heard the astonishing news when he was summoned to the general's tent. Aides and centurions were so crowded inside the tent that it was not easy to see the supreme commander sitting behind his makeshift desk.

Vespasian waved a worn scroll in the air as he spoke. "The latest from Rome, gentlemen. The ink was barely dry on the scroll telling us that Galba is our new emperor when he was slain in a Roman market." He tossed the communiqué on the table. "We must halt our entire campaign until this business is settled."

Silence settled over the crowd.

"Otho was made emperor in Galba's place, but currently he is locked in battle with Vitellius. The legions in Germania put him up as their choice. Of course, civil war followed immediately. Before long we should receive another letter telling us who won. We can't attack Jerusalem until we know who leads us."

Aides broke into grumbling and angry mumbling.

"Yes, yes." Vespasian waved his hand for silence. "Fools and opportunists are having a sporting time at everyone's expense, including ours. I dare say we have seen the last of the Claudians as emperors, but only the gods know who comes next. We must wait and see."

Marcus Quintus listened to the uproar as the news spread through the camp like an epidemic. Legionnaires were openly agitated and angry. Instability at the top meant treachery at the bottom of the social ladder and everywhere else along the way. Civil war posed jeopardy for everyone.

Two months later, Marcus was summoned back to the command tent for another briefing. This time he found himself only a few feet in front of the general as he spoke.

"The latest report has come." Vespasian crossed his arms over his chest. His voice was flat and glum. "Seems that Otho chose battle with two of Vitellius's best generals, Valens and Cecinna. Good men," he sneered. "Otho lasted two days and saved Vitellius any inconvenience by killing himself. We now salute Vitellius as Emperor."

"No!" the group roared.

"Never!" Men's voices rumbled across the tent.

"Who is Vitellius that the lazy elite of Rome should foist him upon us? Let our legions choose their own Caesar!"

"We elect Vespasian."

Applause filled the tent.

Vespasian's eyes met Marcus's quizzical gaze. The general blinked and smiled.

"No more," he said sharply. "We will see what comes next from Rome. Obviously the matter is far from settled."

By the time the latest report spread through the camp, the legionnaires' response was virtually unanimous. The soldiers were more than ready to declare their commander the new emperor.

Marcus Quintus listened to the heated exchange among the soldiers, and thought often of Josephus's predictions. What seemed an absurdity a few months earlier was quickly becoming an accepted fact.

"No one could seriously compare this lascivious Vitellius to a general such as ours." One foot soldier shook his finger in Marcus's face. "The new emperor has proven to be a barbarous tyrant in his previous commands. He'll be no better than Caligula or Nero!"

"And Vitellius has no children," another man added. "Once he's gone, civil war starts all over again. Not only do we have Titus, but the general's son, Domitian, is in Rome even as we speak. Two fine sons! That's stability!"

"Not to mention Vespasian's brother, Flavius Sabinus, who commands his own soldiers. I say we push our commander to the top!"

Marcus listened daily to the growing swell of support, not knowing that Vespasian had already written to Tiberius Alexander, governor of Egypt and Judea, asking for his endorsement and allegiance. A letter was returned quickly with Alexander's oath of fidelity. Emissaries began appearing from every realm with similar pledges of support.

Apparently Vitellius did not fully realize how tenuous his hold on the throne was. His defeat of Otho had given him false confidence. Even though Vitellius's soldiers put Domitian to flight and were able to capture and kill Flavius Sabinus, Vitellius's days were numbered. Vespasian's ally Antonius descended with his army and seized control of Rome. One sunny afternoon, unsuspecting Vitellius finished a lavish lunch, strolled out on the veranda of his palace, and was abruptly swarmed by his enemies. His opponents carried him out to the mob that beat, stripped, and humiliated Vitellius before cutting his head off.

Domitian came out of hiding and was proclaimed interim ruler, pending his father's arrival. Immediately,

Rome broke into festivities and the fate was sealed. Late in the month of Chislev,* 822 years after the founding of the city of Rome, Vespasian took up the laurel wreath of emperor. While waiting to take a city, he had captured the world.

On the eve of his departure for Rome, Vespasian called Marcus Quintus to his tent to witness a unique ceremony. Titus was already present with two other commanders. Aides stood around the back of the tent. Josephus stood in the middle of the group. Vespasian was already speaking when Marcus arrived.

"As I commented earlier, your defense of Jotapata was brilliant, but I have not called you here to restate the obvious. Rather, I wish our legions to know that you accurately predicted that I was to become Emperor even before the death of Nero. Marcus Quintus Cunctator was witness to these words the very day he brought the prisoner into this tent."

The primus pilus nodded his head in acknowledgment.

"Obviously the lares have been gracious to me," Vespasian continued. "I would do nothing to offend the gods who have blessed me so greatly. Josephus is a priest and attributes his amazing insights to the Jewish god. We must do him and his deity honor."

Titus stepped forward. "Father, according to Roman tradition, if we cut his chains to pieces, Josephus will become as a man never imprisoned. Let us make him a free man."

Vespasian ceremonially nodded to the aide on his left. The man drew his sword, took the chain holding Josephus's hands together, and put the links over a large block. In one fell swoop he severed the bonds.

"You are free to leave," Vespasian pointed to the entrance to the tent. "You are also free to stay. You have a

*November to December

future with us, for the destiny of the world lies with Rome."

"I came by choice," Josephus answered, "because I believe my God sent me as His minister. I stay by choice. Perhaps I will yet serve my people best by remaining with you."

"Settled!" Vespasian beamed. "I will yet bring you to Rome . . . but not as you might have feared." He picked up a wine goblet from the table. "We drink to your decision, Josephus."

With the click of a gold cup Yosef Ben Mathias, the Jewish priest-general, crossed the final line into the Gentiles' world where he would be forever after known as Flavius Josephus, collaborator with Rome, never again able to be considered fully one of his own people. No choice was left but to set his face toward the west across the Mare Internum.

XVII

Yochanan Ben Zakkai slowly trudged up the cobblestone path from the marketplace toward the large house that had for so many years been the home of his brother Jarius. He thought on the many strange twists and turns of event. Could it be that Vespasian was truly emperor and Josephus his confidant?

Everything about the journey left him feeling unsettled. Because the old house was in the Upper City, he had entered the territory controlled by Simon Ben Giora. Walking any back streets was dangerous enough, but getting close to Herod's palace was sheer foolishness. His bodyguards had long since been pressed into other military service. Nevertheless, he walked boldly onward.

When he turned up the final hill, he was reminded of how much the dull brown stucco house always looked like a fortress compared with the smaller homes of the neighborhood. Certainly Jarius's house had been a bastion of stability during the past turbulent decades of such catastrophic changes in Jerusalem.

The pain of old age rumbled through his muscles. Yochanan stopped and rubbed his back. *Could it have been nearly four decades since my brother Zeda and I hurried up this same street to discover if the miraculous recovery of our niece was true? All the trouble started when the rabbi was given credit for her recovery.* Yochanan shook his head and walked on.

182

As always Yochanan gently rubbed the slender mazus-seh attached to the doorjamb, inviting the blessing of the Holy One of Israel. He paused, wondering if he would ever again invoke the prayer from Psalm 133, which he and Jarius had so carefully chosen to seal within the oblong box. The fragment had been the adage of their family! "How good and pleasant it is when brothers dwell in unity." The plea remained hauntingly true, though their many intercessions seemed tragically doomed.

Yochanan walked in without knocking. Once he crossed the threshold of this house, he could no longer be the strange mysterious Ben Zakkai. Simeon, the surviving brother of the Ben Aaron clan, had returned. No servants were left. Mariam's domestics were members of the despised Christian sect and had fled the city months earlier when Leah, her new baby, and her family departed with the other Believers to the north.

The hallway was dark and his footsteps sounded hollow and empty; the large living room seemed hopelessly devoid of promise, of life. Decorations and ornaments had been stripped from the walls. He slowly looked around the room at the stark walls. The fireplace was filled with cold, gray ashes. Simeon sank down in one of the two remaining chairs.

Tears came to his good eye when he remembered his reunion with the family in this very room. Everyone had assumed him forever exiled, or more probably dead, the night he walked in.

How I loved Stephanos! But now my nephew is the one forever banished, living in Rome like a common Gentile. The thought was almost more than Simeon could entertain, but the memories would not stop. *Jarius wept on my shoulder like a child. Mariam and her family hugged me so often throughout the evening I thought my back would break . . . perhaps, the most important night of my life.*

"Uncle!" Mariam suddenly appeared in the doorway. "I didn't hear you come in."

The woman standing before him looked much older than she ever had before. "The door was open. Dangerous habit these days. Not smart at all!" He tried to push lingering sentiment away.

"I suppose that won't make much difference after the next few hours." Mariam smiled pleasantly.

"Hummph!" Simeon folded his arms across his chest. "Young Zeda is here?" he asked sourly.

"He has gone to secure a donkey to carry some of our things."

"Do you really think they'll let you out the gate, looking like you're leaving the city?" He stuck his chin out defiantly.

"Our things will be covered with flowers and we will put sacks of spices on top." She continued smiling. "We will go out the Ephraim Gate because it is close to our family tombs. The guards will accept the fact that we are visiting graves. Of course, many people often visit the place of the great resurrection and return to the city. It will not be hard to get beyond the third wall."

Simeon rolled his eye at the word *resurrection* and shook his head. "Only Providence will get you out of the city now. Simon Ben Giora has sealed everything off."

"Perhaps we should have left months ago when most of our people did," Mariam said thoughtfully. "At least Leah's family and the new baby are in Pella by now. But you convinced us to remain . . ."

"Without apology!" Simeon snapped. "If your sect had stayed to defend the city with the rest of our people, there might have been some hope of reconciliation in the future between our factions. What Jew will not remember that the Christians ran before the last showdown with Rome?"

"Have you come to fight with us in this final hour, Uncle? We have discussed this matter a hundred times.

We cannot forget, Yeshua told us this time was coming."

"It didn't take a prophet to make wild assertions about confrontation with Rome. Any politician could have said the same thing."

Mariam's smile was thinner and tighter. "We discussed this last night when we said good-bye." She started back through the door. "Perhaps I could get you something to drink?"

"Your desertion will be the final blow to all relations between our two groups. If *you* stay, at least there would be a symbol of an attempt at solidarity among our people."

"Please, Uncle. This is not the time for us to quarrel. Please."

Simeon abruptly remembered his last conversation with Luke. He had called the doctor a fool that day and predicted the encroachment of Gentiles would cause an irrevocable split between Jews. The man who saved his life left with the impression they were enemies. Yochanan's pain always seemed to come out as anger.

"You know the defense of the city is hopeless," Mariam answered. "Now that the Romans have settled their political differences, nothing will stop them from assaulting the gates of the city. The fall of Jotapata over a year ago signaled the inevitability of our defeat."

"The Lord most high will defend us!" Simeon waved his arms in the air. "The power of Adonai will strike any Gentile dead who sets foot on the holy soil of the Temple."

"You not only sound like one of the street corner Zealots, you don't believe a word you're saying." Mariam shook her head. "I've heard you argue with your friends that if the Temple fell once, it could fall again. You told the Great Sanhedrin that Scripture gives no reason to believe that a second great exile is not possible."

Simeon angrily jerked his head sideways and began nervously stroking his beard.

"We hope to be able to get a letter through to Stephan in Rome once we are settled in the north." Mariam's voice suddenly took on a lighthearted air. She walked to the window and pointlessly adjusted the curtains. "Once we are in Pella, it should be easier to reestablish communication. I am so concerned to know what is happening with his family. Heavens! Who knows how many children they have by now?"

Simeon understood her intent but he resisted. "And Zeda will go on forever thinking he can find his betrothed out there somewhere when everyone else in the world knows the Ben Ephraim family is gone, banished, dead." His voice was hard and argumentative. "Simply chasing lost dreams!" he snorted.

Mariam ran her hand down the coarse fabric of the curtains a long time before answering. "Lost dreams? Yes, we all have our lost dreams which will not fade even in the most brutal light of day. What shall we do with our disillusionment, Uncle? For surely despair can destroy the time we have left."

Simeon bit his lip and tried to hold the tidal wave of emotion back, but tears seeped out. When the trickle ran down his cheek and dropped on his hand, he was undone. Abruptly he reached out for his niece. "I may never see you again!" he blurted out. "This may be the last conversation we ever have."

"Oh, Uncle Simeon, we have struggled so hard over these years, loving and disagreeing with each other so passionately. I know my convictions have been like a knife in your heart. None of us ever wanted it to be so!"

Simeon hugged her fiercely. She felt so frail and small, and yet he had learned long ago that Mariam's size was no measure of her capacity. He tried to speak but the knot in his throat made it nearly impossible. "Today may be our last day," barely slipped out.

"No! No!" Mariam buried her head in his chest. "We will not allow it to be so."

Simeon finally turned away. "Once you cross the threshold of this city and start north, the future is decided. The Romans will seal up what Ben Giora and the Zealots won't let out. When the final attack begins, the Romans will settle for nothing less than total conquest. Yes, probably not one brick will be left standing before they are finished."

"You can still go with us," Mariam pleaded.

Simeon shook his head. "What I believe and what I am are too interwoven. I could never assimilate among your people." He hesitated, feeling the implication of his own unexpected words. "Yes, those Believers have become your people now. The wedge has been driven. A new way has been unleashed on the world that cannot be called back. No longer is the problem a difference of opinions. We are two different religions, two diverse ways, separated peoples. If my world is to die, then I must die with it."

Mariam pressed her closed fist against her mouth, gently shaking her head. "We must keep trying to touch. We can't stop."

Simeon's body sagged. "Whatever happens, I continue down the path the Holy One of Israel has given me to walk. I·can't leave this city."

"And I can't stay. If we linger, we may be trapped."

Simeon reached inside a leather pouch at his waist. Carefully he lifted out a piece of velvet and unfolded it in his palm. "Zeda gave this to me last night." He held out a flawless large black pearl. "Stephan sent the gift to me in return for the ruby I gave him years ago. He said my little present saved your lives."

"Indeed!" Mariam's eyes moistened. "Your Spidel Ruby bought us out of the clutches of death. Stephan hoped to return your priceless gesture with this pearl of great value. He wanted you to know there are some things worth giving up everything for."

"So, Stephen has sent me a little parable as well!"

"Hide it carefully, Uncle. You know better than I that men would kill quickly for such a treasure."

Simeon slowly returned the pearl to the pouch. "Whatever happened to our world, Mariam? Was it so long ago that three brothers worked happily in the shadows of the great wall? Life was stable and our dreams so simple. I asked nothing more than to study the Torah, balancing the opinions of Hillel against Shammai. Everything had its place and its way. We seemed to stand on bedrock. And now all that is left are shadows and the faded outline of those hopes."

"And my dreams are no more secure." Mariam ran her hand through her graying hair. "Many of our people believe we are at the end of the world." Mariam slowly sat down. "They believe the Messiah will return soon for the final judgment. We often speak of the last days. Shadows do that to one."

"Oh, yes." Simeon looked down at her. "The end of an age is at hand. No doubt about that! Everything is falling apart. Some days I can't even remember where I am. Like the waves of an incoming tide, the relentless forces of time push me onward. I see only a curtain of destruction hanging before us."

"Uncle, you will always have a place with us. We can't let our differences separate us forever. Our people would welcome you."

And I would have to arise and go to them, Simeon thought. *No matter what Mariam says, I would be the constant object of their arguments, trying to persuade me to accept their beliefs. Such would be worse than death.*

"We could start a new business in Pella. Ishmael could come with you."

Simeon shook his head heavily. "I had best go now. I did not think I could stand to say good-bye to Zeda again, but I had to come one more time." He got up slowly and shuffled toward the door.

"But we will not be that far away," Mariam called out. "Only several days travel . . ."

Simeon couldn't say anything else, neither could he look back. He dragged himself down the hall and out the front door. Even when Simeon heard Mariam call after him, he looked straight ahead. At the corner where he normally looked back to make sure everything was all right, he pulled his tallith over his head and set his face toward the marketplace where so many years ago his older brother Zeda had been killed in a Zealots' attack. The possibility of personal attack no longer made any difference.

XVIII

haos was so common in Jerusalem that Yochanan Ben Zakkai listened to the noise of battle as
one does the constant chirping of birds. Silence was far
more apt to capture his imagination. The sound of ma-
rauding bands of thugs, assaulting each other at every
opportunity filled every side street, as the constant struggle for control of the city continued relentlessly day and
night. Consequently, Yochanan and Ishmael stayed in
the jewelry shop behind boarded windows most of the
time.

"Not much to eat this noon." Ishmael poured hot,
thick porridge into Yochanan's bowl. "But there's no
selection left in the market these days."

"*Baruch atah Adonai Elohaynu,*" Yochanan prayed as he
took the bowl, "*melech ha-olam.*"

"Who gives us bread," Ishmael responded. "Amen."
He took a small gulp and grimaced. After a pause he
asked, "You going to their meeting at the Temple
today?"

"The gathering the priests called? Yes. Not often do
the Sadducees want the company of a Pharisee much
less his advice." Yochanan looked in his bowl with an
air of glum solitude.

Both men ate silently for awhile before exchanging
puzzled looks.

"Strange," Yochanan mused. "It's quiet. Unusually quiet."

Each began to listen intensely.

Ishmael set his bowl down and looked out between a crack in the boards on the window. "No one's in the street. Best take a look."

The two men inched their way out behind the barricade blocking the entrance to the shop. Surprisingly no one was even walking down the winding corridor between the gold merchants' shops. Slowly they realized there was a sound of the padding of feet far above them along the edge of the south wall. Far off in the distance beyond the wall was another rumbling sound of movement. They looked up and saw many people lining the railing, silently looking out over the top of the wall.

Ishmael cupped his hand to his mouth and yelled loudly. "What's happening? What do you see?"

An old man slowly turned and leaned over the edge. "Romans!" he called back. "They're moving in."

"The hour has come." Yochanan shook his head. "The pestilence is at hand."

"What'll we do?"

"Let us finish lunch. Who knows when we will eat again."

"I don't think I'm hungry anymore."

"Then we'll go to the Temple compound. We shall look from the pinnacle of the Temple before I see what the high priest wants. Surely that's the highest place from which to watch this parade of death."

As they hurried through the streets, Ben Zakkai reflected on the irony that combatants now stood shoulder to shoulder watching the ubiquitous Romans. *Apparently they discovered who the real enemy is. If they could have only realized what unity might have meant!*

Once the Temple Mount was in sight, the contradiction in their division was even more painfully apparent to Ben Zakkai. What better symbol of Jewish potential when united? King Solomon had first built on a place hardly sufficient to hold even the Holy House. Across the centuries, Jews had filled in the valley with dirt, building up the banks until the Temple Mount seemed very large. Huge stones had extended the natural sides of the hill, creating one of the wonders of the world. Nothing was impossible if they were only harnessed together!

At the southeast edge of the high Temple wall, Ishmael pushed his way through the crowd, opening a path for Yochanan. People grumbled and shoved back until they saw the sage walking behind the Arab. Grudgingly they parted for the teacher to peer from the highest corner in the city at the extraordinary march proceeding down the valley beneath the city walls. An endless line of Roman soldiers marched down from the Mount of Olives.

The old man next to Ben Zakkai leaned over and spoke in a hushed, almost reverent voice. "Some report that Titus marched with two legions during the night from Emmaus and camped on Mt. Scopus. The tenth legion has come up from Jericho and is camping on the Mount of Olives. Terrifying!"

Yochanan nodded his head but said nothing. He watched the columns of soldiers march ever forward with steady precision. Carts filled with baggage lumbered alongside the legionnaires while the wind blew clouds of dust down the sides of the canyon walls between the city and the Mount of Olives. As the auxiliary units disappeared down the Kidron Valley, the men with their long, pointed spears filed past. The even ranks and steady pace bore ample witness to Roman discipline. Next, the men and horses slowly pulled the engines of war down the steep hill. The catapults and slings rumbled away, crushing the underbrush and rocks beneath their heavy wheels. The devices of death were quite capable of creating their own roads. Behind the rolling contrivances were lines of horsemen riding with the legion's ensigns, standards, and, of course, the Roman Eagle.

"Is there any end to it?" the old man asked Yochanan.

Ben Zakkai only shook his head and turned away. For years he had anticipated the specter. Never had he had one moment's doubt about the capacity of the Romans to annihilate the city. Like a ghostly image from his worst nightmare, the endless lines of soldiers touched a nerve in his soul and he shuddered. Yochanan pushed back through the crowd and walked through the cloisters toward the high priest's compound.

Ishmael stayed close to his side, but when they approached the partition into the second court of the Temple, he stopped. Above the pillars stood the stone sign declaring the law of purity. Chiseled in both Greek and Latin letters, the warning forbade foreigner to pass into the Temple proper. Ishmael simply sat down by the marble columns to wait for his friend's return.

The bright spring sunlight flashed on the gold-covered buildings, nearly blinding Ben Zakkai. He cupped his hand over his face and pushed on toward the side entrance of a building near the Temple. Once in front of the white-gold door, he banged the gold knocker. Immediately a servant ushered him into the high priest's quarters.

Six men in the white linen robes of the priesthood sat around a large mahogany table in the center of the room. Each rose politely when Ben Zakkai entered. "Shalom to our friend and good brother. Sit here beside me," Elezar Ben Simon, the high priest, called out and pointed to a chair.

Most unusual politeness, Yochanan thought. *The Sadducee must be in more trouble than I thought.* He bowed formally to the group.

"Are the Romans still marching?" Ananias Ben Masmatheus more complained than asked. The old man's irritation couldn't mask the fear in his eyes.

"Endlessly." Yochanan smiled ironically as he sat down. "The line must extend clear to Athens."

"Let us review the situation for you." Elezar folded his hands on the table and looked straight ahead. "Our spies estimate that Titus may have as many as sixty thousand men and obviously he brings the latest weapons. At best we have twenty-five thousand fighters left and our soldiers are divided into three camps. The Romans are famous for their discipline and unity. We all know what we have become infamous for!"

Looks of consternation and dismay went around the table. Yochanan looked carefully into each of the priest's faces. Their usual arrogance and air of superiority was gone. The mighty men of the Levites were humbled and terrified.

"We hold the Antonia fortress and the Temple Mount," Elezar continued. "As you well know, Simon Ben Giora runs the Upper City. John of Gishcala and his cohorts, the Idumeans, hold everything else they can wrestle from Simon's control. We are locked in a power struggle among these three factions while the Romans calmly proceed to surround us with every expectation that if nothing else they can starve us out."

"I have no legions to command," Yochanan said wryly. "Of what value could I, a lowly Pharisee, be in this august gathering?"

"We need you!" Elezar blurted out. "We need the backing of the Great Sanhedrin. We are the only two groups in this city who care about our faith! The rest vie for power, territory . . . or worse, they imagine they can bargain with our lives."

"And they are a pack of fools!" Ananias pounded the table. "None of these anarchists has any idea of the capacity of the Romans to ultimately level this city. Ben Giora's men seem to be in love with the very idea of dying in a bloody war. They will take us with them to their graves!"

"You come at a late hour to counsel with me." Yochanan sat back in his chair with seeming indifference.

"We sent Yosef Ben Mathias to you two years ago," Elezar corrected him gently. "Even then we deeply respected your position, your person . . . your party."

"Yes." Ben Zakkai pulled at his beard. "I have communicated many times with the general. And what do you hear of my old friend Josephus these days?"

The six men rolled their eyes and looked embarrassed. No one spoke.

"I suppose your general has become quite the traitor," Yochanan observed. "Why do you think a valiant man of war struck such a bargain?"

"I do not think of him as a traitor," Elezar answered slowly. "Yosef was always a realist. I still honor his name."

"Well," Ben Zakkai's voice brightened, "maybe we can talk. No, I do not turn my back on old friends as many of your class have done. I think Yosef has a far greater concern than merely to preserve his life and position."

Elezar leaned over the table. "Yosef knew that our institutions and way of life were at stake. If Jerusalem falls, we will lose everything that is central to our faith. For that reason, and that reason alone, you must help us, Yochanan Ben Zakkai."

"And what am I to do?"

"Unite the religious community!" Elezar shook his fists. "Pull the Sanhedrin behind us. Help us establish a united front against Simon and John."

"May I remind you that the citizens opened the gates to Simon Ben Giora and called on him to restore order." Yochanan threw up his hands. "They had already lost confidence in your capacity to govern."

"But that was before this constant fighting began with Simon and John over food and supplies." An old man on the end reached out to Ben Zakkai. "The people see the folly of their decision now. The sobering sight of Romans encircling the city will send them to bed tonight with different thoughts. They will listen with new ears." He pointed his finger in Yochanan's face. "They will listen to *you*."

Ben Zakkai folded his arms across his chest and leaned back in his chair. "My friends, the sand has almost fallen through the hourglass. The followers of the false messiah Yeshua left us long ago. The only ruling principle left is the unholy alliance between self-preservation and deception."

Elezar rapped firmly on the table. "What will we have left if the Romans burn the Temple? What would remain if they destroyed our sacrificial system? Think about it, Ben Zakkai. Can we risk such a possibility?"

"No," Yochanan chose his words more slowly and carefully. "*You* cannot afford such a catastrophe." Elezar's constant use of *we* rattled in his head. The high priest did not mean to include him in that *we* . . . nor any other Pharisees either. "We" meant Sadducees, priests, Elezar Ben Simon's establishment. *We* was a most exclusive word around this table. The priest had said *we* one too many times making everything very, very clear.

"Indeed," Yochanan found it increasingly difficult to speak and think at the same time, "*you* stand to loose a great deal."

Suddenly Yochanan's mind raced ahead as if he were another person standing behind the one speaking. His mouth continued to speak words while a strange new vision of the future crowded his mind. He couldn't describe what was flooding his consciousness with images and new forms. "However limited my resources are, I guarantee you that I will do everything possible to save our sacred ways. Yes, everything." The words kept coming, although they were completely disconnected from what he was thinking. "I must go now, but rest assured

I will go to work immediately." He pushed back from the table and started toward the door.

"But . . . but," Elezar called after him, "what do you have in mind? When will we hear from you again?"

"As soon as I have something to tell you," he answered without looking back. *Yes,* he thought to himself, *they are the ones who have everything to fear, to lose.*

Ben Zakkai hurried out toward an exit that was one of the nine gold and silver gates leading out of the inner court. Each gate had two golden doors more than thirty cubits tall, which was wondrous to behold. Yet the splendor of the idea that now gripped his mind exceeded the magnificence around him. A new mission energized every particle of his being. Just before he reached the portal where Yochanan knew Ishmael was waiting, he turned back to look once more on the splendor of the Holy House.

Twelve great steps led up to the Temple proper. The first gate into the place where the name of God dwelt had no door. The perpetual openness represented universal visibility of heaven from this place of access to the divine. Inside the huge edifice were two parts. Above the inner divide were golden vines with clusters of grapes as tall as a man but most wonderful of all was the drape that concealed the Holy of Holies. Woven into the Babylonian curtain, embroidered with blue, scarlet, and purple, was a mystical image of the universe. What Jew would not be overwhelmed at the mere sight of the veil opening into the Holy of Holies?

Ben Zakkai looked for a long time, etching every detail in his memory. As overpowering as the sight was, the structure was still of this world where moth, worm, and rust rule. His hope must be tied to something more enduring. In that moment he suddenly realized that he had come full circle.

With an almost frightening clarity, Yochanan Ben Zakkai, the outer shell of Simeon Ben Aaron, knew he had come to agreement with the false messiah. Yeshua had attacked the centrality and indispensability of the Temple as necessary for a holy life. He, too, found the Sadducees' air of superiority and privilege to be a plague on the people, recognizing how the priests used their office as a separation from the common people. Yeshua had preached against the same arrogance that Yochanan despised. Though Ben Zakkai had condemned Yeshua's teaching, the Nazarene was right. The Sadducees' concentration on buildings, rituals, the trappings of worship was actually a barrier to genuine righteousness. Yochanan now saw that he shared Yeshua's contempt for this priestly system of administration.

His avalanche of insight made Ben Zakkai dizzy and slightly disoriented. *How could I possibly be arriving at the same conclusion as this Nazarene I so deeply deplored? Yeshua concluded that Jews could get along quite well without the Temple and now I come to the very same conclusion. What am I thinking?* He walked backward, picking up the pace with each step.

The vision Yochanan could not yet articulate sent hope surging through his veins. Without looking back, Ben Zakkai ran through the pillars, leaving Ishmael sitting on the stone pavement. The Arab was on his feet immediately trying to catch his master. It was as if the old man's youth was renewed, like an eagle mounting upon new wings.

XIX

The dawn of the fourteenth of Nisan* broke over Jerusalem. Preparation for Passover began at once. Only one major skirmish with the Romans had occurred to date and the Jews had prevailed. Several unorganized war parties rushed out of the city to attack the tenth legion. Their chaotic, fragmented raid not only caught the enemy by surprise, but also circumvented the Romans' usual organizational plans. The disorderly assault without rule or reason confused the legionnaires. When observers on the city walls recognized the Romans were in retreat, the good news spread like wild fire. Waves of Jews sallied out of the city gates, turning the retreat into a rout and pushing the legion out of its own camp. Faced with disaster, Titus was forced to take the field. Their momentary victory provided new optimism for the entire city.

Yochanan walked alone toward the Temple Mount, remembering the many other Passovers when he had sat around the table with his brothers. The memories soon became bittersweet and he made his mind fasten on the present moment.

"Shalom, good teacher!" An old friend waved to him when he turned up the familiar alley that on other days would have taken him to Jarius's house.

*March to April

Yochanan saluted respectfully, taking note of the old man's chipper air. On all sides people wished each other a good Passover. He pushed on in the opposite direction, up the Valley of the Tyropoeon toward the Temple Mount.

A little victory goes a long way, he thought, walking through the narrow winding streets lined with little shops. *A little unity goes even further. Still the accidental good fortune of one day will not win a war. The siege has barely begun. Optimism will soon be tempered by a dose of hard reality.*

And yet Ben Zakkai no longer was gripped by the despair that had imprisoned him for so many months. Old dreams had been replaced by a new vision. While he could not yet put the grand scheme into words, new dimensions pushed malignant feelings aside. He no longer had a family to celebrate this Passover with, but he was going somewhere.

"Sorry." A young man pressed too close trying to get on the Krytus Bridge into the Temple area.

"So many people," Ben Zakkai answered cordially. Nothing could be done except to let the surge of the crowd carry him upward. He could see the Dyer's Quarters down below the bridge. Woolen garments were washed, bleached, and hung out to dry among the buildings. Vats for dyeing and wooden stands for whitening cloth with sulfur were scattered along the street. Farther down the slopes were the houses of the poor. Even the least of these prepared for the holy day beginning at sunset.

The pace of the crowd ground to a halt. Even the threat of imminent Roman attack had not stopped the annual pilgrimage from across the world. More than a million people poured into the city, and they all seemed to want to be on the bridge at the same moment.

I am pleased Elezar Ben Simon agreed to open the inner courts of the Temple for worship on this day, Yochanan thought when the line started to move again. *The step will help restore authority to all religious leadership and signal new self-confidence to the people.*

Just before he entered the gate to the stairs that led to the raised area, Ben Zakkai looked down one last time. To his right was Herod's Hippodrome, built after the pattern of the Roman circus. The chariot races had been the delight of every Jew and Roman alike.

The crowd pulled him along past the porticoes on toward the inner gates. Suddenly men began shouting and the crowd swayed wildly. In one violent lurch, Yochanan was thrown to the ground. Dirt flew up and pain shot through his good eye. Yochanan blindly crawled in the direction of a tree along the portico. People tripped over him and he felt the sharp pain of a heel grinding into the calf of his leg. He could hear people falling in every direction. For several moments he thought he would be crushed beneath the weight of men piling on top of his body. Trying to catch his breath, he had time for the tears to clear his eye.

The crowd unpiled as quickly as it had fallen together. Able to sit up, Ben Zakkai found the tree and scrambled for the protection of the trunk. Across the open courtyard men were casting off cloaks. In defiance of all that was holy, they had concealed both armor and swords. A full-scale battle erupted everywhere at once. Worshippers ran in all directions like panic-stricken animals. The attackers swung without discretion, killing indiscriminately.

Yochanan couldn't see anyone he knew. Fearfully he pulled his tallith over his head and prayed for peace. *Oseh shalom bimromav hu'ya'aseh shalom aleinu v'al yisrael v'imru.*

"A . . . a . . . a . . . h!"

Ben Zakkai's prayer stopped instantly and he looked up.

A young man took three quick steps toward Yochanan and stopped. The youth's mouth dropped and his eyes bulged. He fell face forward into the dirt; a small spear stuck out from his back.

Ben Zakkai clutched the trunk of the tree, clinging for dear life. Everywhere he looked people were falling on the ground while renegades slashed in every direction. Blood splattered on rocks, trees, and people. He could make no sense out of the riot. The attackers might be renegade Zealots, and with either John of Gischala or Simon Ben Giora.

Three attackers flayed the people around them with iron rods. Men fell like shocks of wheat at the blade of a sickle. Bodies began piling up on all sides.

From the direction of the Antonia Fortress Temple, Ben Zakkai saw guards counterattack. Their distinctive uniforms made it easy to distinguish them from the rogues. The random killing ceased at once and the rabble turned their attention to the new phase of the battle.

"The caves!" someone clamored. "There are caves underneath the Temple! Try to get to them!"

Everyone knew about the system of tunnels and caves beneath the whole area. The honeycombed caverns offered some hope, but Ben Zakkai stayed by the tree. To run across the open courtyard would only call attention to himself. The pain in his leg made him doubt whether he could navigate the dark passages anyway.

Peering around the tree, Yochanan watched the attackers press the Temple guards back toward the inner gates. The battle moved inside the wall and out of his sight, but it was clear that Elezar Ben Simon's forces were losing badly. Yochanan resigned himself to crouching as close as he could to the base of the huge tree. The clash of swords and the roar of the battle gradually dimmed and the low moaning of the survivors overtook the sounds of strife. Except for the judicious few who had escaped to the caves or slipped back down the entry steps, everywhere he looked people were injured. Ben Zakkai was paralyzed with indecision over what to do next. So many were bleeding and dying! What should he do first?

"We have won!" echoed across the open area.

Somewhere far inside the inner Temple men cheered.

Sounds floated menacingly out to the portico. "Clear them out! Get the bodies cleared away." Voices sounded nearer with each command.

"Don't spare anyone who resists!"

"We've won a great victory!"

Ben Zakkai peeked out and watched the riff-raff with bloody swords slowly maneuver among the fallen. Once more he pulled his tallith down over his forehead and prayed the mourner's kaddish for the fallen. The words flowed under his breath. *Ye-hei shlama raba min shmaya ve-hayim aleinu v'al kol yisrael v'imru.* He hoped his prayer would cover himself.

"What do we have lurking behind this sycamore?"

Yochanan looked up into the fierce eyes of an Idumean pointing a blood-spattered sword at his throat. Ben Zakkai knew he was trapped by a mercenary of John of Gischala.

"Who did you give allegiance to?" The Idumean flicked his sword back and forth inches from his captive's face.

"Adonai," Yochanan answered without flinching. "The Holy One of Israel! Him and Him alone."

The man threw his head back and roared with laughter. "Well said, old man. Who can argue with that answer?"

Yochanan pressed back against the tree. "I came here for no other purpose than to worship."

"And we came to put an end to the soldiers of the high priests and their control over the Antonia Fortress. We did better than you today."

"You have succeeded?"

"Of course." The seedy Idumean lowered his sword and wiped the blood off on the back of a man lying dead at his feet. "Services will be delayed today." He chuckled. "John must explain to the priests who's running this place now. I suggest you turn around and go down the stairs."

Yochanan immediately began stepping around the bodies, ignoring his aching leg as he hobbled along.

"Go tell the city that John of Gischala is the new power to be reckoned with," the Idumean called after him.

Once Ben Zakkai reached the Krytus Bridge, he looked out over a completely empty trestle. The crowds had disappeared. A few people watched behind buildings but the festive atmosphere was gone and fear once more controlled the streets.

The proud Sadducees no longer dominate, he thought. *They are gone. Their power is broken. Three factions ruled,* he looked down the bleak empty streets. *And now there are two.*

The next morning Yochanan sat down with his old friend at the table in the jewelry shop. "Ishmael, we do not have much time left. The hour has come for me to act."

"What shall I do? As always, your wish is my command."

"Find the caretaker at the Great Sanhedrin and tell him to call together the assembly. I will speak to them."

"I am sure after the debacle at the Temple, they are scattered about the city in complete confusion." Ishmael scratched his head. "Probably some still hide in the caves."

Yochanan nodded. "I do not think there is a safe place left in the city. John of Gischala and Simon Ben Giora will be fighting in every back street to gain final control.

We can no longer assume Simon controls the Upper City. Everything is up for grabs.''

''I will be careful.''

''My next task for you is more complicated. I want you to find a way for us to get out of the city.''

''What?'' Ishmael's eyes widened.

''Obviously Simon has blocked all the usual exits, but there has to be some other way to escape.''

''My friend!'' Ishmael leaned over the table. ''The Romans stand guard on the other side. We couldn't get past them!''

''I'd rather take my chances with them than what's going on in this city.''

''But, but . . .'' the Arab shook his head searching for the right words. ''You told Mariam that leaving was abandoning the people, the sacred ways?''

''In her case, yes. But now we have come to another place. Only by leaving can I save the sacred ways.''

''I don't understand.''

''All in good time, my comrade. All in good time. Now go and see if you can gather the assembly by the end of the first hour tomorrow. And this time, try not to jump off any buildings into the potter's wares.'' Yochanan laughed and slapped his friend on the back. ''We have too much to do to get either one of us killed. Our God is not through with us yet!''

The Arab's narrowing eyes filled with consternation. He pulled at his beard, shaking his head slightly. ''You're all right?''

''I've not lost my mind, Ishmael. Far from it! To the contrary, I think I've found my way again.''

Marcus Quintus Cunctator rode leisurely with Josephus at his side. Titus and two generals were only a few cubits in front of them on magnificent Arabian steeds.

The horses carefully picked their ways along the rocky hillside looking south toward the city. Just below them was the Psephinus Tower, standing tall above the corner of the third wall. Behind Marcus Quintus a contingent of twenty mounted soldiers kept guard against surprise attackers.

Titus stopped his horse and motioned for the two men to join him. Although only thirty years of age, the commanding general had developed the authority that was the hallmark of his father. Titus was broad-shouldered, with thick, sinewy arms. His skin had the rough, leathery texture of a leader who fights in the fields with his men.

Titus pointed to the wall looming before them. "I think that is our best point of attack. The Himmon and Kidron Valleys are far too steep to mount an attack. Cunctator, what is your opinion?"

Marcus Quintus turned in his saddle and pointed to the Women's Gate. He shielded his eyes from the noon sunlight. "That's the only entry. Herod Agrippa completed this new wall four years ago around the Bezetha, the new city. The area inside is sparsely populated. Breaching these walls will be much easier than at any other place."

Titus glared arrogantly at the Jewish general. "Well, Josephus, what observations do you have?"

"You cannot easily set up catapults in either of the two valleys," Josephus answered. "Missiles wouldn't go over the walls from such a distance."

"What would you suggest?" Titus stuck his finger in Josephus's face.

"I cannot help you defeat my people," the Jew answered solemnly. "But if I can save lives, I serve both sides well."

"My father would find that answer amusing," the young man smirked. "You walk a tightrope well, Josephus. But we honor your intentions. Tell me, Cunctator, what else do your studies tell you?"

Marcus pointed to the thick forest behind them. "I would cut the trees for firewood. Once we are inside, we should burn the area. After the area is cleared, we can make a better assault on the Antonia by attacking through the sheep pool and market areas. The adversaries possibly will come to their senses when they realize our power to annihilate. Killing could cease and a great deal of bloodshed would be stopped. We might be able to bring a painless end to the campaign."

"Well, well, we are to march on the Women's Gate!" Titus turned to the generals around him in mock horror. "Afraid of the clash, Cunctator?"

Marcus Quintus's face reddened. "I was thinking of sparing our men needless danger and striking for an easy victory."

"I don't want an easy victory," Titus barked. "I want a *total* victory. I want to serve this city to my father on a platter! Rome shall witness the glory of the entire Vespasian family before I am through with this place."

"Wouldn't an unconditional surrender serve your purposes just as well?" Josephus smiled politely.

Titus glared and spit on the ground. "I would prefer to burn the whole area to the ground, but I would accept quick capitulation."

"Then might I attempt to negotiate with my countrymen?"

Titus looked back and forth between Marcus and the Jew for a moment. He turned toward the only gate in the third wall. "Perhaps, they don't call it the Women's Gate for nothing! It's the appropriate place to find out if the Jews have any sense left. Go up there, Josephus, and offer your countrymen the opportunity to save their lives. Tell them to lay down their arms! Stop at once and Rome will be generous."

Titus turned his horse around and called to a soldier

in the rear. "Ride to the gate and tell them an emissary comes from Titus with terms. Do it quickly." The soldier immediately raced toward the wall.

"I welcome the opportunity to be your servant." Josephus headed his horse toward the gate. "Might I ask the primus pilus to accompany me?"

"By all means," Titus answered. "And I will send another guard to make sure your old comrades inside the walls aren't so overjoyed to see you, they shoot you down."

Titus's aides laughed as Josephus and Marcus rode slowly away. "Hurry back with a new victory for us," Titus chided.

The two men and their escorts rode slowly to give ample time for their arrival to be announced. "You are different." Josephus turned to Marcus. "Titus is here for glory and power, but not you. You seek something more noble. Titus toys with you but he respects the difference."

Marcus Quintus looked straight ahead. "I've seen something more significant than pleasure and fame. As strange as it may sound to you, I search for something eternal."

"In the midst of all of this killing, the death?"

"Perhaps because of it." Marcus Quintus looked up and down the length of the city wall. "I've had my fill of children with throats cut and women stabbed with swords. I've grown sick of their cries in my sleep. Surely we can do better."

"Strange talk from my country's conqueror," Josephus answered, "but very refreshing. And where are you going to find benevolence in the midst of Rome's arrogance of power? Where will you discover virtue in a nation built on the bodies of slaves and cemented together by their blood?"

"Ever hear of the Christus? The Christianios?"

"Of course!" Josephus nudged his horse forward.

"What Jew has not been embroiled in the debate over the Messiah? We are obsessed with the identity of the man."

"What do you think of this Jesus they proclaim?" Marcus Quintus faced the Jew squarely. "Is He your Messiah?"

Josephus laughed. "Oh, not at all. Certainly not the messiah the people looked for. If he had been, you Romans would have been pushed into the sea by now."

"But Christians tell me your people misunderstood the true meaning of the Messiah's mission and purpose. You missed your own salvation. Is that possible?"

The general's levity evaporated. "Tragically possible. Everything in our world is being shaken apart. Who am I to say who has the final truth? I will tell you this! If wc had listened to His teaching, we would not have come to these tragic divisions among ourselves."

Marcus Quintus reached inside his breastplate and pulled out the gold cross Mariam had given him. "The answers I seek are locked up in the mystery of this death." The Roman held the cross out to Josephus. "They tell me he died in order for us to have life."

Josephus shook his head. "I don't know . . . I just don't know."

"I have seen the power and courage of these Believers. I am alive because of their prayers." Marcus Quintus pulled his horse to a stop. Not far ahead their man was calling to the guards at the gate, explaining envoys were bringing terms. "If I could leave this place with what I found in the Believers' lives, I would consider myself a rich man indeed. Titus can have his parade past the Forum Romanum and through the Capitolium with the crowds cheering him on. I want to look deep within my soul and know that I have found peace."

XX

The afternoon shadows covered the ten men standing around the assembly room inside the Great Sanhedrin, listening to Yochanan Ben Zakkai. Chairs were scattered and turned at odd angles. Dust covered the tables. The high priest's throne had been empty for a long time. Even Haman, the caretaker, lost interest in his responsibilities and did nothing to maintain the great room where so many critical and historic decisions had been made over the centuries.

"The seventh day of Iyar* will be remembered always," Yochanan's voice rumbled with solemnity. "The Romans will surely never let the world forget the day they penetrated the first wall of the city. Friends, we gather today under dire circumstances."

The enormous mahogany doors burst open and light exploded in the dim room. The setting sun framed a man's silhouette.

"Please forgive me for my tardiness and not being here when you called the gathering last week." The young man hurried down the center aisle of the Sanhedrin. "I was hiding in a cave beneath the Temple." Perez doubled over heaving as he tried to breathe.

"I'm here, too!" Aristeus the scribe of the Sanhedrin came in next.

*April to May

"You're all right?" Zorah stepped forward and reached out to Perez.

"I thought they were chasing me." Perez could barely speak.

"Who?"

"Them!" Perez threw up his hands. "Whoever *them* might be this morning . . . thieves, soldiers, Sicarii, thugs. But I guess I was wrong." He sat down in a chair.

"What's happened in the last week?" Aristeus pressed. "I hear nothing but rumor and confusion."

"A week ago Titus sent Yosef Ben Mathias to the Women's Gate of the First wall with a proposal for surrender," Yochanan answered.

"Ben Mathias? *Our* general?" Perez gasped.

"Yosef?" Aristeus sputtered spitefully.

"Some idiot on the wall ordered an attack on Yosef and the soldiers riding with him," Yochanan continued. "Several Romans were hit with arrows. Jewish spears put an end to any possible overtures for peace."

"Fools!" Zabor shook his finger in the air. His terribly bent back forced the old man to tilt his head to speak. "The Zealots threaten to cut the throat of anyone who even hints of surrender. They are afraid the people will capitulate rather than resist."

"Of course!" Malchor added. "We are already on the verge of starving to death. Now the people who welcomed Simon Ben Giora would more gladly invite Titus and his legions through the city gates."

"And how does the battle go?" Perez tugged at Ben Zakkai's sleeve. "Are we enduring the siege?"

"Three wooden towers were erected above the first wall," Ben Zakkai continued factually. "From those heights the Romans are able to pick off our soldiers on the ramparts. They stormed the Women's Gate and started burning the new area of the city. They are in an excellent position to storm the Second Wall as well as strike at the Antonia Fortress."

"What shall we do?" Zabor dropped his head to his chest and doubled even further. "What did you discuss last week?"

Yochanan sat down on the small desk in front of him. He rubbed the black patch around his empty eye socket as if the vacant space still hurt him. "The Sadducees are gone. Their power is destroyed," he said sadly. "No, I cannot rejoice over the demise of our adversaries, for surely they had a place in the scheme of things. But John of Gischala's conquest of the Temple put an end to any authority the Sadducees had left. My friends, we are all that remains of the religious order."

His words echoed off the paneled room. The chamber that had been the sight of so many violent arguments sounded hollow and empty. Yochanan looked at their stunned faces. No one even suspected the humiliation he had experienced in this very hall over three decades earlier, forcing him to disappear from the city. Those old leaders were dead, gone like shriveled brown leaves in winter. Only he remained. In the absence of his old accusers, Simeon Ben Aaron was still vindicated. And yet the one-eyed man knew his victory was equally incomplete, diminished, and stunted. "We are the true remnant," Ben Zakkai concluded.

"What shall we do?" Young Malchor stepped forward. "We await your guidance, Rabbi."

Suddenly Yochanan came to life and pounded the table. "We don't need them! . . . Sadducees . . . priests . . . high priests! We existed without the priests and the Temple once before. The Babylonian exile only prepared us for this hour. We will do it again! The Sadducees did nothing anyway but corrupt the truth and lessen personal holiness. We will not let the errors of the past stop us from recasting the future. We shall reclaim what is ours exactly as Ezra and Nehemiah did!"

"How?" old Zorah puzzled. "How can such be?"

"Listen to me!" Yochanan's voice dropped, forcing the

group to draw closer. "The city will soon fall and the Temple will burn."

"No! NO! NO!" echoed across the room.

"The Holy One would never allow it!" Zabor rung his hands.

"Of course, He will!" Yochanan snapped back. "Do not let prejudice blind you! Adonai did not stop the Babylonians and He has done nothing but aid the Romans. Not to recognize these facts is to be as big a fool as are the followers of Ben Giora and John of Gischala!"

Men shook their heads and pulled at their beards. Old men buried their faces and wept.

"Never," Aristeus mumbled, "I could never leave."

"Stop it!" A young Pharisee interrupted the dirge. "Listen to the master of the Torah." Malchor demanded. "He has seen light."

Yochanan beckoned Malchor forward. For the first time the old man smiled broadly. "Ah, you shall be a source of strength and hope to me. Stay close to me, my young friend, for the future is with such as you."

"What must we do?" Malchor begged.

Yochanan rubbed his black eye patch again and squinted his good eye in pain. "We must flee the city. I want us to escape and regather in the village of Yevnah. We will start over again and recast our faith without Sadducees and the Temple."

No one spoke. Most shook their heads uncomprehendingly. Only Malchor nodded approval.

"How can we do such a thing?" Perez leaned forward. "I would not even know where to begin," his voice trailed away.

"I do!" Yochanan pounded the table again. "I know exactly where to start!"

"But no one can escape." Zorah shook his head. "Ben Giora has blocked every gate. No one can leave through any of the great city gates."

Malchor's eyes flashed. "Oh yes! A few of us could

get through a side passage at the Tower of Hippicus. Not many know there is an obscure gate on the east side. Dressed like the soldiers of Ben Giora, we can easily get inside the tower. Once night has fallen we will slip out into the no man's land and get through the Roman lines."

Yochanan laughed aloud. "You are a man after my own heart. We shall prevail, Malchor."

"But you could never escape!" Perez pointed his finger at Yochanan's face. "Everyone in this city knows the one-eyed sage. You could never conceal yourself adequately."

Yochanan smiled. "I want everyone in this room to leave with Malchor. It is your only hope. Do not worry. I will join you in Yevnah."

"Yevnah?" the old man puzzled.

"Long ago a dear friend told me this village was the right place to start over again. Do not worry. I have my own devices. I will join you in Yevnah and we will begin our work once more."

The rabbis looked at each other, more in consternation than disagreement. A few wandered aimlessly among the tables as if seeking an omen and hoping that some unconsidered alternative might arise from the floor or descend from the high ceiling. Yochanan waited patiently in his seat while no new sign appeared.

"The time has come to close this place," Yochanan finally arose to his feet. "Like the Temple itself, the Great Sanhedrin has been one of the foundations of this whole society. But it will never meet again. The final hour of reckoning has come. Let us pray the ancient Aaronic blessing and depart."

Each man pulled his tallith over his head and lowered his head. With one voice they prayed, "May the Lord bless you and keep you. The Lord make His face shine upon you and be gracious to you. The Lord lift up His countenance on you, and give you peace. And let us say Amen."

The last word heard in the old hallowed chamber was

a second resilient "AMEN!" The master of the Torah resolutely led his followers out.

Yochanan Ben Zakkai barely stepped out the large doors when Ishmael rushed toward him. The noise of battle was nearly deafening. "Master!" the Arab shouted in his ear. "We must get out of here quickly. The Romans are moving toward the second wall."

"What is their strategy?" Yochanan pulled his friend back into the shadows of the building. People ran down the street in every direction. "How do they attack?"

"Surprisingly, the Romans are not burning the houses. Neither are they killing everyone. Once again they have offered terms of peace."

"And has Ben Giora answered?"

"Even the mention of the word *surrender* brings death."

"An old Roman plan!" Yochanan pulled at his beard. "Titus offers the people the opportunity to kill each other before he comes in to pick up the pieces. We meet our demise through our own civil wars."

"What will happen next?" the Arab pressed.

"Presently the Romans will withdraw and allow our own confusion to do its most efficient work. After chaos has further deteriorated our resistance, Titus will come surging back in. We have very little time left. Listen carefully to what I tell you to do."

Ishmael cupped his hand to his ear.

"Go and find a coffin and send it to the shop. Buy a burial shroud and the cloths."

"What?" The Arab stepped back in disbelief.

"You must also arrange for eight professional mourners for tomorrow. We must be ready to bury as soon as the Romans withdraw. I think we will need to parade our coffin down the street as early as possible."

"What is all of this about?"

"We have someone of considerable importance that we must bury. Now be off with you. It will not be easy to find anyone who still has a simple pine box left. Death does a brisk business these days. Hurry!"

The Arab kept looking over his shoulder in bewilderment as he trotted toward the square where such matters were handled. Yochanan waved him on each time he looked back. Once Ishmael disappeared around a corner, the old man started back in the opposite way toward the shop. He stopped at the last bend in the street and took one final look at the ornate ancient building that had always been the judicial center of Jerusalem. The great doors of the Sanhedrin were ajar as if the tumult had cracked them open. No one was left to secure the latch. A knot tightened in Yochanan's throat. "How many more of these final scenes must I witness!" he cried aloud.

But no one answered. No one heard. Terrified men and women scurried past, oblivious to all but their own fear. The desperate quest for survival took precedence. People ran in every direction without clear destination.

Yochanan walked close to the buildings as he wound his way back to the shop. When he crossed the food vendors' plaza, the stalls were empty. The merchants had disappeared long ago, their vegetables and fruits dried up from lack of supply and frantic demand. Even the dogs had disappeared from the streets. Where the smell of bread once lingered in the air, now the smell of death seeped from the stone walls.

Once inside his jewelry shop with the door secured, Yochanan tried to push the wooden display case aside. Every ounce of his strength was required to move the heavy counter across the dirt floor. Slowly the wood legs scraped forward. Finally a depression in the floor was in sight. Quickly, the old man dug out the dirt with a metal bar until he worked a metal chest loose. Carefully, he lifted the heavy box out of the hole and opened the lid. Scraps of gold were scattered over gold coins. Here and there were bent necklaces and broken chains. Yochanan closed the lid and put the box behind the pallet on which he slept. He placed a knife on top and covered everything with an old robe. Once secured, he lay down on the pallet to wait Ishmael's return.

XXI

After the workmen delivered the coffin in front of the Ben Aaron jewelry shop, they pushed the pine box inside. Ben Zakkai stayed concealed in the back shadows until only Ishmael was left.

"What are you hearing in the streets, Ishmael?"

"They've put Josephus's father in prison," he huffed as he pushed the crate forward. "Afraid for security, I guess." He stood up stiffly. "Josephus returned to the south wall offering terms of surrender. Then someone hit him with a rock. The report went around that he had been killed." Ishmael stopped and took the lid from the wooden box. "But the whole business turned out to be a rumor. Josephus is still riding around the walls offering terms of peace, and Ben Giora is terrified that the people will revolt. The Romans offer free passage to anyone who escapes from inside the city but, of course, there's no way out."

"Except one."

Ishmael scratched his head. "No one gets out of here alive."

"Precisely. Only the dead are leaving."

The Arab looked at the coffin and back at his old friend. "I don't understand."

"Unfortunately Yochanan Ben Zakkai was struck by just such a rock that sailed over the opposite side of the wall. In keeping with Jewish custom, he must be buried in the tomb of his family beyond the Ephraim Gate. Just

218

as Mariam left the city, so he must go to the place of the tombs." Ishmael shook his head uncomprehendingly.

"In a few moments we will prepare the one-eyed rabbi for his departure from this world. In the morning, you and the professional mourners will go through the streets proclaiming the tragedy as you move toward the burial caves."

"But both John of Gischala and Simon Ben Giora have been throwing bodies off the walls. Piles of bodies are on the side of the Kidron and the Himmon valleys."

"And is that the treatment this city would afford the Master of the Torah? I think not. We will process down the city with the plain coffin as is the normal custom of our people. Woe to the man who interferes with that procession."

Ishmael stood with his hands on his hips, blinking his eyes and shaking his head. Ben Zakkai immediately began to work on the bottom of the coffin. He quickly spread a thin pallet over the bottom. "Help me." He pointed to a thick blanket stretched over his bed. "Careful. The cloth is lined with many pockets and is very heavy."

When Ishmael picked up his end, the entire bundle sagged and hardly moved. "What's in this?" He heaved again. "Feels like gold."

"Exactly." Ben Zakkai swung his end of the blanket over the top of the coffin and lowered it down on the pallet. "Spread this out carefully so the weight is evenly distributed."

Once the blanket was in place, Ben Zakkai picked up the burial shroud that was twice as long as a person's height. He tucked one end at the bottom and then laid the cloth over the pallet and up the far side.

"Stop it!" In uncustomary defiance, Ishmael stomped his foot on the ground. "I want to know what in the world you think you are doing. This is nothing but madness!"

"We have just put more gold in the bottom of this crate than anyone knew was left in any merchant's shop in all Jerusalem. The amount should be far more than adequate to care for us the rest of our lives in Yevnah."

"Gold!" Ishmael pulled at his hair. "People kill for even a glint of the color. Our people are swallowing it, jumping over the walls hoping to survive the fall and recover the treasure when it passes through. We couldn't begin to remove such a stash from the city!"

"Unless it was covered by the body of a dead man that no one would dare touch." Yochanan smiled condescendingly. "Come now, Ishmael, it is time to prepare me for my burial. You will wrap the shroud over me and tie the napkins in place just as if I am to be placed on the stone slab in the Ben Aaron family's mausoleum. What more appropriate place to bury the trusted family friend and business associate?"

The Arab looked down into the empty coffin. "What if they insist on looking inside?"

"We will rub enough ashes on my face to take the color out of my skin. I want you to find a dead baby or a piece of a leg. Wrap it up and bring it here for my coffin. Death is everywhere in this city. The odor of death is strong enough throughout the city to satisfy the suspicious."

The Arab's unusually dark skin suddenly lightened. He put his hand to his throat and heaved deeply.

"Cover the flesh in a blanket and put it in the bottom. I will keep my head at the top and pray that my two-day fast has sufficiently cleared my stomach."

Ishmael sunk down in a chair. "I'm not sure I can go through with all of this."

"You must! I can't be seen on the streets. Remember, I am dead. I must be nailed in this box as soon as you return. No one must even have the slightest opportunity to discover this ruse. Not only our future, but also the future of our people depends on our success."

"But how will I ever persuade the gate keepers to let me

and the mourners through? They would suspect that we would escape once we crossed the threshold of the city."

"Can the men of Ben Giora be bribed?" Yochanan smiled cunningly.

"Of course," the Arab snapped, "but if they thought there was gold in that box, they'd shred it on the spot."

"Then they must be bribed with a gem. Perhaps, a priceless black pearl." Yochanan reached up and pulled the black eye patch from his face. The usually sunken eye lid strangely bulged. With one finger he rolled the lid upward and with the other hand he gently stuck his index finger inside and popped out the pearl Stephan had long ago sent from Rome.

Ishmael's mouth dropped. He stared at the perfectly round, iridescent pearl in his master's hand.

"If it is necessary, you will buy our way out of the city. I think this prize will be more than enough. One pearl cannot be divided among several men. You will find some man more than ready to make sure we are ushered through the Ephraim Gate."

The Arab picked up the pearl and held it before the flame of the little clay lamp. "Magnificent!" He put the gem back in his master's hand. "I will be back as quickly as I can with the smell of death."

The day had just started when the mournful dirge began. Six professional mourners hoisted the coffin on their shoulders and started their incessant wailing. Two women walked in front screaming and tearing at their clothing.

Because it was the custom not to address the bereaved, no one would question Ishmael as the cortege wound through the familiar market streets. Simply seeing Ishmael following the procession would be sufficient evidence that Yochanan Ben Zakkai was dead. Ishmael also was quite aware that his old friend wanted to leave the jewel shop without looking back. Too much life had been spent within those walls. The final pain would be too great.

The recollection of Yochanan's ashen color made Ishmael shudder. When he secured the linen shroud around Ben Zakkai's face and tied the napkin, the Arab was sure no one would take more than a peek. The deteriorating remains Ishmael found in a pile of bodies and stuffed at the opposite end of the coffin was ample insurance.

The rabbis made a distinction between the *onen* and the *avel*, the sorrowing one and the fading one. The former lamented on the day of the funeral and the latter mourned continually in the days that followed. The city would recognize that Ishmael was both *onen* and *avel*. With torn inner garments, Ishmael walked slowly behind the coffin with his head down.

As the mourners trudged through the street wailing, Ishmael reflected carefully to make sure no stone was left unturned. *The scarcity of food ensures that no one will expect to prepare a funeral meal. No, not returning to the shop will not raise suspicion. The Romans will soon swarm over the south wall anyway and then the building will be gone forever. The little shop can no longer be anyone's.*

For the first time in decades Ishmael let himself remember Al Aqahah in the deserts of Saudi Arabia, only a short distance from the life-giving waters of the Gulf of Aqaba. The faces of his mother and father had long since evaporated. He recalled how Simeon Ben Aaron found him, a starving boy, wandering the back streets of Elat. *Simeon has been father and mother, aunt and uncle, friend and companion. Perhaps, I replaced his nephews, but he was my family. He saved my life; I saved his. This one last time I must make sure that nothing jeopardizes my comrade.*

Thoughts of a thousand kindnesses floated through Ishmael's mind, with memories of watching the young Simeon Ben Aaron look every night out into the empty desert. Ishmael pictured the good-bye after Mariam and

Zeda returned. He had no trouble fabricating tears. His companion had always been the loneliest man the Arab ever knew.

"Is this not the Arab servant of Ben Zakkai?" some voice asked from the crowd.

"The master of the Torah is dead!" a woman gasped.

"The light has completely gone out of Israel!" a Pharisee wailed when they turned the corner.

Not far from the house of Jarius, the funeral party crossed the first or north wall and began the final trek toward the Ephraim Gate. The early spring days were quite warm. Ishmael urged the mourners to walk faster, lest the sun do its work too well. When they approached the plaza in front of the Ephraim Gate, the sounds of battle and the movement of troops outside was painfully loud.

To his left Ishmael could see the three great towers Herod built. The largest Phasael Tower was for the despot's brother, the Hippicus Tower for a friend, and the Mariamne Tower for his beloved wife whom he had murdered. The sight seemed strangely appropriate as a final view of the inside of the city before Ishmael pushed out into the Bezetha, the new city where the Ben Aaron family tombs were now encased within King Agrippa's new third wall.

"Halt!" a burly guard pointed his spear at the procession. "No one crosses the gate." The man's robes were tattered and splattered with blood. He wore makeshift leather armor and a Roman helmet scavenged from the field of battle.

"We pay honor to the dead," the woman in front beat on her breast.

"We drop the dead over the walls," the soldier pushed her aside. "No one leaves this city without the permission of Simon Ben Giora. That's final." He stamped on the pavement with the end of a spear shaft.

"Simon knows me well." Ishmael stepped from behind the casket. "We have done business many times."

"I don't care who you are," the guard sneered. "No one gets out."

The other two guards beside the small door at the side of the large gate laughed. Both men were equally shabby and unusually dirty. The smell of smoke drifted in from behind the gate.

"The Romans are burning houses over there," the guard snarled. "They'd probably just roast your carcass if you crossed, and that wouldn't be fitting for a good Jew, now would it?"

"These are the remains of Yochanan Ben Zakkai," Ishmael announced at the top of his voice. "Respected master of the Torah! He has a special burial plot in the caves near the sight of the great resurrection. Who would dare deny him the dignity due this leader of the Great Sanhedrin?"

"I would." The guard put his face into the Arab's. "I know nothing of this business of the rabbi."

Ishmael leaned even closer to the man. In contrast he spoke very quietly. "If honor does not prevail, would a priceless gem suffice?"

The burly guard blinked.

"I have one . . . and only one . . . offering, but it could change the course of your whole life. This man's proper burial is very important to me."

"What do you offer?" the guard's voice dropped to a whisper.

"I'll not show you unless you guarantee passage."

"If the sight is worthy, you are through."

Ishmael pulled a small leather pouch from beneath the sash around his waist. He slowly opened the top and let the guard peer in at the black pearl, cushioned by a piece of white linen. "A king's ransom," the Arab cooed.

"When it crosses my hand, you are through the gate," the guard snapped.

"Lead us past the sentinels," the Arab's eyes narrowed. "When we stand on the no man's land, the prize is yours."

The guard spun around and waved the other two men aside. "Get the dead out of here," he sputtered. "I'm starting to get nauseated."

"But . . ." one of the men reached out.

The sentinel slapped his comrades aside. "I'm in charge here. Follow me!" he beckoned the caravan onward and immediately Ishmael and the pall bearers stepped through the small portal inside the Ephraim Gate. As he passed the guard, the Arab dropped the small leather pouch in the dirty hand.

Once the mourners were beyond the shadows of the high gate, their wailing began again. The six men trudged on with the coffin on their shoulders and the women flayed the air with their arms. To Ishmael's left loomed the hill of execution known as Golgotha. Beyond the chalk-white rock were the new houses and buildings that had sprung up in the last thirty years. Herod Agrippa's new city wall made a sprawling backdrop for the smoke curling upward from burning houses. Ishmael could see the large hole Titus had knocked in the distant wall, allowing his soldiers quick access to the city.

Not far ahead of the procession, Roman soldiers seemed completely indifferent to the passing commotion. The enemy continued to pay little attention as the little band found their way to the burial caves. Once the procession passed through the metal gate into the Ben Aaron family's grounds and the coffin was set down, the mood instantly changed.

"This is all we promised," the woman with the loudest voice demanded. "Pay up and we're gone."

"No one agreed to roll the rock back or put the body inside," a pall bearer snarled. "That'll cost plenty extra."

"No one is paid a shekel until the top is pulled loose from the top of the coffin," Ishmael crossed his arms over his chest. His hand rested easily over the knife tucked in his belt. "That *was* the agreement!"

"Get it done!" the other woman motioned the men toward the box. "We won't have much time to get out of here."

Grudgingly the men began prying back each of the top slats. A staggering smell leapt from the box.

"Done!" a pall bearer pushed his hand into Ishmael's face. "No more!"

Ishmael pressed a gold coin in each palm. "I promised you would get out of the city. Now run for it before Simon Ben Giora sends out a search party."

Without looking back the men and women ran toward the Roman soldiers.

"They are gone," Ishmael sounded very relieved.

At once the shroud rippled. A wrinkled hand emerged from the side and reached up for the edge of the coffin. "Get me out of here!" Yochanan Ben Zakkai gasped for air.

The Arab pulled the binding from his friend's neck and reached in to help him to his feet.

"I thought I would gag one hundred times over," Ben Zakkai sputtered. "No matter." Ben Zakkai shuddered. "I will take a bath every day for a year!" He rubbed the ashes off his face.

"We must not waste time," the Arab warned. He reached down to the bottom and lifted the pallet. "Let me get the belt with the gold wrapped around my chest and we will be off."

In the distance, drums began a rhythmic slow cadence. "The Romans are moving troops and siege equipment into place." Yochanan cupped his hand over his eyes. "The assault on the south wall will start soon."

Ishmael pulled the makeshift money belt tightly around his chest and tied it in place with leather tongs.

"I will never be able to return here." Ben Zakkai walked toward the chiseled stone door in front of the family mausoleum. Sealed inside were his father and mother, his brother and his brother's wife; a lifetime of dreams, hopes, traditions, expectations . . . buried . . . gone . . . never to return . . . dead.

Yochanan touched the round boulder so firmly blocking the opening and felt the hard cold edge. Ben Zakkai pressed his face against the unyielding granite door and wept.

XXII

By early summer, life in Jerusalem deteriorated even beyond Ben Zakkai's worst projections. Daily the Romans showered the city with arrows, darts, and rocks. The pressures of continual fighting and starvation ground together like two great mill stones pulverizing human life to dust. Death was the omnipresent reality.

Piles of cadavers lay in heaps across the city. Some families attempted to care for their own, but often there was no one left to help. Some attempt was made to count the bodies being cast out of the city. At least six hundred thousand corpses were thrown out of the city gates. Often the bodies of the poor were piled and left in vacant rooms of large houses. A continual stench settled over the city.

But courage was not lost. Jewish soldiers fought on in the ominous atmosphere of devastation. The beauty of the city had long since disappeared. Gardens, trees, and shrubs dwindled as the increasing heat of summer continued to dry and shrivel the living. Many survivors driven to depths of despair searched through the sewers and the old dung heaps searching for anything that might be used for food.

John of Gischala feared losing control of his tenuous grip on the Temple compound and knew that Simon Ben Giora was closing in on him. In order to buy time and influence, John melted down the sacred utensils of worship in the Temple. Cauldrons and cups were turned into silver ingots to barter for what John could no longer take by force. Even sacred wine was passed out like common drink to numb the rabble's awareness of the inevitable.

Titus was keenly aware of the plight of his adversary. The few Jews who escaped from the city were generally caught, interrogated, and released. The Romans knew all about the chaos on the other side of the walls. Near the end of the day, the Roman supreme commander assembled his personal staff in his tent on Mount Scopus. Josephus was included in the group of twenty strategists.

Titus stood defiantly, his arms across his chest. "I commanded Marcus Quintus Cunctator to bring a detailed study of the situation within the first and second walls of the city. I want to know how we can make the quickest possible end to this siege. Common sense seems to have no place with these Jews." The general glowered at Josephus. "Why will your people not surrender?"

The Jewish leader looked straight ahead. He was taller than most Romans, but less stocky. His white linen, Judean robe was a sharp contrast to the armor of the soldiers. "Our people are proud," he said unapologetically. "You are attacking our Holy City . . . a place for which we are willingly ready to die."

Titus interrupted. "But twice I have offered them reasonable terms and my personal assurances of protection if they will only desist."

"The Zealots will not allow compromise!" Josephus raised his hands in hopeless resignation. "No responsible person is in charge. Long ago reason was numbered among the casualties."

Titus cracked his knuckles. "I do not wish to be remembered as a butcher of the weak and helpless. Come now, Josephus. Give me a vision, some dream as you did my father."

"I see nothing but charred ruins and a city burned to the ground. I wish I might tell you otherwise but I cannot."

Titus glared at the Jew. "I expected more from you," he sounded contemptuous. "What can you tell us, Cunctator? You'd best do better than your friend."

Marcus Quintus unrolled a scroll on the table. "We know a great deal about this city and have very accurate records. I believe that one principal point of attack will bring us the quickest success. We already know that any approach by the Kidron and Himmon Valleys is extremely difficult. However, we have much better access to the whole city by attacking the Antonia Fortress from within the walls of the new city."

"Why?" Titus sat down in his field chair and stared skeptically at the primus pilus. "The fortress is a major stronghold."

"We built the place," the primus pilus answered. "We are the ones who turned the building into a guard tower to oversee the Temple area. I have plans that go back before the period of Pontius Pilate, detailing every inch of the fortification. I believe I know how we can undermine one corner of the tower."

"H . . . m . . . m . . . m." Titus pulled the scroll in front of him. "Why not attack the south wall instead?"

"That's exactly what Simon Ben Giora expects and his men are firmly lodged along the wall. The truth is the soldiers who still hold the Temple area are the weakest unit in the city. If we make a concentrated attack on this point, we reduce their capacity to use larger numbers of soldiers against us."

Titus turned to Josephus. "And the Temple is the heart of your Holy City?"

Josephus nodded solemnly.

"Cut out the heart and the body ceases to have a

reason to resist," Titus smirked. "Come now, Josephus. Go and dream something for me. Surely you can give me a timetable. Pray to this God of yours who has delivered your people into my hands. In the meantime, Marcus Quintus will prepare an exact battle plan for taking the Antonia. In the beginning I only wanted a quick total victory, but that is no longer possible. Just get this nasty business finished."

Marcus Quintus Cunctator was so preoccupied with studying the plans of the Antonia Fortress, he did not hear the flap of his tent open. The light of morning suddenly fell across his work table, making the oil lamps appear very dim.

"Working all night?" Josephus asked.

Marcus rubbed his eyes and looked around wearily. "Slept some," he yawned. "Been checking and double checking how the foundation of the fortress was laid out."

"I brought you some fruit." Josephus laid a small basket on the table. "And perhaps a little food for thought."

Marcus studied the Jew carefully. He had slowly accepted Josephus as a true friend and knew that nothing happened by accident with this exceedingly bright man. At times the cleverness of the priest-general was even frightening.

"Perhaps, a chunk of bread might encourage you." Josephus pulled a hard-crusted disc from the basket and tore the loaf in two pieces. "Titus should be impressed with your diligence."

"And what happened to you since we stood in Titus's headquarters yesterday?" Marcus's red eyes followed the Jew across the tent. "I suspect you've been equally occupied."

Josephus sat down and stared into the oil lamp flickering on the table. "During the night, I saw a great light burst over the Temple. In my dream the area was first illuminated and then total darkness fell over the city. The ground quaked. Suddenly the eastern gate of the inner court of the Temple began to move. The brass door is so heavy that twenty men have difficulty shutting it. But in my dream the great gate moved by itself, opening the way to the enemies of the holy Temple. At the conclusion of the dream, I knew the end was close at hand."

"And on what day?"

"I have no vision or dream but offer a calculation."

Marcus pushed the scrolls aside and pulled his stool closer. "Speak up, man. One word from you is worth ten annals of history and twenty scrolls of correspondence."

Josephus leaned back in the leather chair and slowly stroked his beard. "Six hundred and sixty years ago the prophet Daniel foresaw this hour. I believe he saw it coming twice. The first fulfillment was the defilement of the Temple by Antiochus the Fourth, which resulted in the rebellion of the Hasmoneans. The hour has returned again."

Marcus picked up the piece of bread and bit off a large hunk. He chewed hard, staring at his friend. "Well?" he gestured with the loaf. "Tell me more."

"As I view this moment, our tribulations with Rome began essentially seven years ago. Vespasian entered this war about three-and-one-half years ago."

"Yes, yes," Marcus sounded irritable. "So what?"

"The prophets often spoke of a year as being a day. If my calculations are correct and I have understood the prophet, I would suggest that the seventeenth of Panemus on the Roman calendar will be a very significant day of attack. Predictions will be fulfilled on that day."

"Panemus?"

"The month corresponds with Tammuz* in our calen-

*June to July

dar. In another two months, I believe in the month of Ab,† daily sacrifices in the Temple will cease. I would expect defilement and the fall to follow immediately."

Marcus Quintus scribbled the date on a piece of parchment and began to calculate. "You are suggesting that in about two weeks, we should be able to successfully invade the inner city."

Weariness settled over the Jew's face. Light no longer sparkled in his eyes. The general shook his head with the certainty of one who is painfully correct.

"Amazing! You confirm my hunch about how long it could take to topple the corner of the fortress. Titus will think that I am a genius!"

Josephus looked blankly at the flame in the oil lamp. After a few moments he said slowly, "The fall of the Temple will come exactly seven hundred years after the Temple was completely destroyed the first time by the Babylonians."

"All of this is in your sacred writings?" Marcus Quintus puzzled. "How have you and you alone come to such conclusions?"

"I suspect a few others have understood. Perhaps, only one other. I hope he has fled the city by now."

"But why have the people not listened and—"

"Ears have nothing to do with the capacity to hear," Josephus cut him off. "The heart is where one understands. Deception and confusion begin in the hardness of our own intentions. God has merely allowed our nation to inherit the consequences of our own moral deafness.'

"Deafness? I don't understand. How can you believe in a god who causes you to fall, to fail? Who reprimands you like a parent disciplines a child? What good is a god who causes defeat when you bring the proper sacrifices and offerings?"

†July to August

"We believe . . . because . . . He is the only One. There is none beside Him."

"But to let you lose? To allow His own Temple to burn?"

"In what seems to be weakness, God still reigns supreme over the most audacious claims of any pantheon Rome, Greece, or Babylon ever dreamed up. Even defeat can be His instrument of future vindication."

Marcus's eyes narrowed. "On what do you base such an idea?" He leaned forward. "How have you come to this strange conclusion?"

"One of our greatest prophets foresaw the last fall of the sacred Temple. He believed that through our national humiliation, the Holy One of Israel revealed a unique strategy for our people and their future. The Divine One demonstrated the very greatness of His power by using our weakness as his primary instrument. Israel was to be his suffering servant in the world. The redemption of creation itself would finally come through our adversity. As priests to the universe, in our affliction we are bearing the sin for which the world should be rightly judged."

"How long ago was such an idea written?" Marcus's voice filled with amazement.

"Over five hundred years."

"Amazing! Josephus, look at this symbol!" Marcus pulled a chain from around his neck. "The Christians gave me this gold cross. They taught me the death of the Christus embodied the mystery of the love that would someday liberate the world. My friends believe Jesus was God's suffering servant. I was taught this love conquers by giving . . . not taking."

The Jew looked at the gold cross and chain carefully, studying the exquisite detail. "Ah, the workmanship is familiar. Yeshua, the suffering servant?" he mumbled. "I wouldn't have thought of such a thing . . ."

"Are you telling me that Israel has always been part of a plan God had to use suffering to overcome evil?

Do you realize the implications of what you are saying? Nothing can subdue a people who use even defeat as a means of future conquest. This cross offers the same secret of victory under any and every circumstance."

"Redemption is to come through our people," Josephus answered thoughtfully, "through the nation."

"But did not the death of the man Jesus accomplish this exact same thing?"

For the first time in the months that Marcus Quintus had known him, Josephus looked genuinely mystified. He did not answer.

Marcus Quintus took the necklace back and lowered the chain around his head, letting the cross fall beneath his tunic. "You have given me great assistance today, my friend. When I present my plan to Titus, I will credit you with the timetable." The weary Roman stood up and stretched. "You promised to give me food for thought. Josephus, you have done much more; you have fed my soul."

XXIII

Yevnah lay approximately two day's journey west of Jerusalem, down on the coastal, sandy plain, which finally rolled out to the Mediterranean. Between the gentle hills were good fields for tilling and grazing. The fertile land was free of the mountainous, rocky outcroppings, which seemed to grow nothing but stone. Vineyards flourished and flowers lined the streets.

The little village was far enough south of Caesarea-by-the-Sea and sufficiently distant from the Holy City to remain undisturbed and peaceful. Yevnah was spared the horrors of pestilence and war.

The dry heat of summer had already turned the streets to powder. Dust made the eyes red, the nose itch, and the feet cake with sweat and dirt. Only the main street of the village offered the reprieve of a stone-laid avenue through the middle of the town.

"If Perez, Malchor, and the others escaped, where would we find them, Master?" Ishmael stopped at the edge of Yevnah and shielded his eyes from the sun.

Yochanan Ben Zakkai cast a long gaze through the little town. "I think we might inquire in the local synagogue. I believe we will find our friends waiting somewhere nearby."

"Shouldn't be hard to find the building." Ishmael walked on. "Usually they are in the middle of the village."

People watched the pair slowly trudge past the simple

236

food market and down the drowsy street. Finally Ben
Zakkai sunk down on a flat piece of a stone column.
"I'm truly an old man." He rubbed his good eye. "And
you're not a boy, my friend. I don't know how you've
carried that load of gold with you."

Ishmael laughed.

A young boy in a brown robe walking past stopped
abruptly. The lad turned back and stared at the black
patch over Yochanan's eye. He took two steps backward
and began running in the direction from which he had
been coming.

"Do I really look that frightening?" Ben Zakkai asked
in mock consternation.

"Probably don't get that many visitors here these
days." Ishmael shrugged. "We both look shabby. Fortunately when you left the outer robe, some of the smell
of the coffin stayed behind."

Yochanan shuddered and pushed himself up. "That's
it. Now I have to move on. Can't be much further ahead.
Let's go."

The pair went on only a few furlongs when they saw
the boy come out of a small flat house and point toward
them. Immediately two men joined him.

"Our rabbi is here!" the smaller of the two men
clapped his hands and shouted up the street.

"I believe it's Perez and Haman the caretaker!" Ishmael
pulled at Ben Zakkai's dusty robe. "We've found them."

Other men came out of the brown stucco dwelling and
rushed toward the travelers.

"Praise the Holy One of Israel!" Perez ran forward
with his hands extended. "You escaped!"

"They're here!" the other man yelled back toward the
house. "Prepare the wine, the water!"

The group surged forward. "We've found the master
of the Torah!" they chattered together. "The Romans
didn't catch him. You escaped! Praise the Lord!"

The men surrounded the weary pair, hugging each

one, kissing them on the cheeks, shaking hands. "Come in and refresh yourselves. Sit down! Let us wash your feet!" Each friend offered some additional service.

Inside the mud-brick house, the coolness of morning still lingered. Barely had the two friends sat down than their feet were placed in a basin of water, washed, and dried; then cool wine was set in front of them. At least a dozen men hovered around the table.

Young Malchor beamed. "When night came, we rushed out of the side gate of the tower and were gone before Ben Giora's soldiers even realized our intent. The Roman soldiers virtually ignored us as we walked out of the city. How did you get out of the gates?"

Yochanan waved the question away. "Another day. I need a little distance from the memory and purification before I can speak of the matter." He raised his eyebrows and shook his head.

"We brought a new member for our group." Perez beckoned a young man to stand. "Gamaliel is a direct descendent of Hillel. His father, Simon Ben Gamaliel, was one of the leaders of the original revolt against Rome."

"Ah!" Ben Zakkai sized up the bright-eyed youth. "The House of Hillel was always suspect by Rome. There could be no higher recommendation."

The raven-haired youth profoundly bowed to the rabbi.

"I believe your father also taught Saul of Tarsus," Ben Zakkai spoke from the corner of his mouth. "The man the Believers call Paul."

Gamaliel blinked uncomprehendingly.

Yochanan took a long drink of the cold wine and set the cup on the table. The room was completely silent as the group eagerly waited. The one-eyed rabbi looked at each man carefully and soberly. Finally he asked, "Where can we meet?"

"There is a pigeon house near the vineyard in back."

Malchor pointed toward the rear door. "The owner welcomes us to gather there."

"And I have found an attic where we can study in a house next to the synagogue," Perez added.

"Ah!" Yochanan nodded approvingly. "We have an attic for the cold winter days and an airy shed for the summer. The Holy One is providing." The old man stood up slowly and lifted his hands toward the ceiling. *"Baruch atah Adonai!* Tomorrow we begin again!"

Ben Zakkai's disciples leaped to their feet immediately applauding and dancing around the room. "Yavneh!" someone cried. "A place to start again!"

The next morning the band of survivors gathered in the small pigeon house behind the vineyard. The little mud hut covered with a flat wooden roof had many openings in the wall. The floors had been scrupulously cleaned and even the ceiling swept in anticipation of the assembly. Outside the promise of summer was evident. New winding vines were growing profusely and clusters of small green grapes already hung from the spindly canes. A gentle, warm breeze invigorated the remnant. The space was small, forcing the dozen men to huddle around the master of the Torah.

The morning prayers blended into the mourners' kaddish. With talliths over their heads, they prayed with one voice. *"Yit gadal ve yit kadash shmei raba, b'alma divra khir'utei ve yamilikn mal khutei be hayei khon uve'yomei khon uve hayei dikhol beit yisrael ba agala u vizman kariv v'imru amen."*

Obviously their prayer for the sovereignty of God to be accepted by all nations could not be fulfilled in their lifetime. Nevertheless, their voices became even louder when they petitioned for the Holy One to be praised forever. *"Ye-heir shema raba meve rakh l'alam ul'almei 'al-maya."*

At the final "Amen," the men straightened up slowly. The heaviness of the prayers tempered their zest for the adventure of starting again. Morning sunlight beamed in through the little portals around the ceiling and the large windows in each of the walls. The golden rays fell across the talliths covering the head and shoulders of each man. Yochanan Ben Zakkai's white hair and beard were radiant in the soft light.

"Let us begin with the words of the prophet Isaiah." The old man tilted his head back and began speaking as if he were reading from an invisible scroll just in front of his eyes. "How beautiful upon the mountains are the feet of the messenger who announces peace, who brings good news, who announces salvation, who says to Zion, 'Your God reigns.'"

"Amen! Amen!"

"Our task is clear," Ben Zakkai spoke rapidly. "The Great Sanhedrin is gone, the Temple will soon be destroyed, and the city devastated. In fact, I expect on the tenth day of Ab, our worst fear will be fulfilled for I am sure the judgment of the Holy One will come on the same day the Temple was last destroyed."

"A . . . a . . . a . . . h," the group moaned. "O . . . o . . . o . . . h. No . . . No."

"Our task is to replace the old Sanhedrin. We must, here, in this place, reconstitute the authority that will guide our people into a new day. We must become again the spiritual center of the nation. The hereditary priesthood and the Sadducees have disappeared. Pharisaic rabbis will be the only remnant Adonai uses as His instrument for rebuilding the future. Once the Temple is gone, the synagogue will be the only institution left to lead our people. We must rebuild in every town. Synagogue and rabbi are to be the brick and mortar."

"Yes, yes." The group pressed forward.

"I always opposed the madness of fighting Rome." Ben Zakkai wrinkled his face disdainfully. "Our politicians were fools, busily playing politics and trying to grab power. In their mad dash, these power seekers lost all sight of the reason for their existence. Never forget what Isaiah wrote in the great scroll!" Once again Ben Zakkai began to read the invisible lines. "Thus says the Lord: Heaven is My throne, and the earth is My footstool. Where is the house that you would build Me? And where is the place of My rest? . . . But on this one will I will look; on him who is poor and of a contrite spirit, And who trembles at My word."

"The word?" Zorah probed.

"The Torah!" Ben Zakkai thundered "The commandments of God! The decrees of the Almighty must become the fortress that surrounds the hearts, minds, and souls of our people! We shall expand our understanding of God's guidance. Commentaries will be made, applying the law to every area of our existence. Our security can never again be in a political system, a government, a national state. Our permanence must be in the commandments of God."

"But, perhaps, the Messiah will yet come!" Malchor interrupted. "We may yet be spared—"

Ben Zakkai abruptly stuck his hand up before the young man's face, stopping his words. "If you are planting trees, and someone tells you the Messiah has come, put the sapling in first, then go and welcome the Messiah."

The chastened youth shrunk back.

"Let us forget the sword as well," Ben Zakkai said firmly. "The day of attack and counteract is now passed. The time has come for the pen to rule. Zealots and warriors must be replaced by students and scholars."

"But there are many writings," Gamaliel objected. "Different rabbis recognize varying texts, scrolls, and a wide range of prophets."

"And now the sect called Christians claim to be people of the covenant," an old man added. "They are producing their own writings and claiming parts of ours."

"Yes, yes," others protested.

Again Ben Zakkai held up his hand and waited for silence. "We must define the law from Torah carefully. Boundaries must be set and the text fixed. Soon we must issue a ruling on what is the proper canon of holy Scripture."

"But sacrifices will no longer be possible," Perez agonized. "Our lives, our religion, our practice has been built around the sacrifices in the Temple! How can we go on after this place is destroyed?"

"Good deeds will replace sacrifice," Yochanan answered dogmatically. "Atonement will come through our actions. We must interpret festivals such as Passover and Yom Kippur in this new light."

"A calendar should be fixed!" Malchor's eyes flashed with renewed excitement. "Our people will need a new guide to the festival days and times! We can clarify the days and weeks for prayers and fasting."

"Yes," Ben Zakkai nodded solemnly, "this work must be done here in Yavneh. We have been a powerful people." Yochanan sagged back in his chair. "At one time Jews constituted at least one tenth of the whole Roman Empire. Nearly half of the citizens of Alexandria are our people. In a world of illiterates, every one of us reads quite well. All we lacked was unified leadership. Now the hour of disaster has placed this responsibility on our shoulders alone. When the conflict with Rome is over, we will be a greatly diminished people, but our race will endure if we take our new task with the uttermost seriousness."

"Rabbi?" Gamaliel raised his hand respectfully and waited for acknowledgment. "Why should anyone listen to us? How will we gain the ear of the survivors? We are but a poor band of disciples huddled with their master among the ashes of the past."

"We shall use the authority of our captors." The old man winked his good eye. "I have a plan to ask the Romans themselves to certify us as the academy they recognize as valid for our people."

The dumbfounded assembly silently stared at their confident leader. No one seemed to be able to ask the next logical question.

"How can this be?" Yochanan finally inquired for them. "Let me give you something to remember. 'Do not hurry to tear down the altars of the Gentiles least you be forced to rebuild them with your own hands.' We must use what we have to work with regardless of the shape it takes."

"I don't understand." Perez stated in bewilderment. "How could we possibly gain access to anyone in authority?"

"I have an old friend who will, perhaps, be the last Sadducee to do a favor for the Pharisees. I think he will find it easy to put our request before General Titus himself."

"Who could possibly do such a thing?" Malchor threw up his hands.

"Yosef Ben Mathias," Ben Zakkai answered without emotion. "My friend, Josephus."

XXIV

At noon Titus struck. His charge straight through the marketplace completely caught Ben Giora's soldiers off guard. The Romans penetrated the Upper City with extraordinary success. They quickly mounted the inner wall. Titus and his aides ran down the length of the entire wall, watching his best soldiers slaying their opponents on both sides of the inner city's dividing barrier.

"The diversion worked well," Titus said to Marcus Quintus. "The Jews are watching the undermining of the Antonia Fortress today. When we retreat, they'll move every man they can find over to guard this section of the city. Just what we want them to do."

Marcus Quintus held his shield close to his chest. "We'd better not stay on top long. We make too obvious a target."

Titus swung his sword wildly over his head, urging his soldiers onward. "Cut a wide swath," he called to the men below him. "Let them remember that we held the entire south wall on both sides. Our success ought to sober up the population!" The commander turned to the man a short distance behind him. "You're all right?"

"Certainly." Josephus pulled his large helmet off. The right side of his head was heavily bandaged and his cheek swollen. "The wound has not slowed me down."

"We want to make sure the whole city knows the rock that hit you last week did no significant damage." Titus

244

starred across the top of the city. "Let them see every possible sign that surrender is far more intelligent than further resistance."

"Fear, not ignorance, holds them in check," the Jew answered. "Only Simeon Ben Giora's terrorism keeps the city from surrender."

"Fools!" Titus looked down on the scene on the other side of the great wall. "Bring up some prisoners!" Soldiers battled near a flat-roofed building that was burning.

"Ever been down?" Titus pointed to the street below.

"That's the street of the gold merchants, the jewelry makers," Josephus answered. "One of my most respected friends once owned the burning shop."

Three legionnaires brought two ragged Jewish men forward. "Got two of 'em for you." The soldiers goaded the terrified young men with the points of their swords.

"Look here!" Titus jerked one of the men forward. "Take a careful look. Here is Josephus, alive and well! Your lives are being given back to you so you can spread the word through the city."

The prisoner's robe was torn and blood stained. He had to push his disheveled hair back to see clearly. A nasty gash marked the side of his face; his lip quivered and his eyes looked like a caged animal's.

"Tell the people to desist at once," Josephus's voice was hard. "Rome will yet deal equitably with them."

Immediately the frightened man's eyes dropped and he clutched at a wound on his shoulder.

"Do not be afraid to speak." Josephus put his arm on his countryman's shoulder. "No one will hurt you."

Slowly the shaking Jew looked up apprehensively at the former general. "They kill anyone who even appears to defect," the man spoke hesitantly. "Ananuus, Simon's most barbarous guard, just slew the high priest Mathias and his son because he suspected their motives. Each boy was killed in front of his father. They also killed

Aristeus, the scribe of the Sanhedrin. They left their bodies on the ground as a warning."

"How bad is life in the city?" Josephus pressed.

"We're starving." The man put his hand on his stomach. "People torture each other to get any information on where a scrap or morsel might be hidden. Cornmeal is eaten before it's even baked, in case someone snatched the loaf from the fire. Children cling to pieces of food only to have it yanked from their mouths as they fall to the floor. Grass and weeds are gladly eaten if any can be found."

"My own father . . . ," Josephus asked slowly. "Would you know of him?"

"Imprisoned him," the man mumbled. "No one is allowed to talk or go near him."

Titus suddenly jerked the terrified Jew around. "Go through the city and proclaim my generosity," he shouted in the man's face. "I will leave the city as it is if they surrender now, but if you persist I swear nothing will be left but burned stones. Do you understand?"

The two men's heads bobbed up and down. "Tell them to stand against this criminal Ben Giora's intimidation or they will face my sword for sure!"

The prisoners kept bowing to the Roman commander.

"Get them out of here," Titus yelled at the legionnaires. "And make sure they get back into the city safely."

"We cannot stay here much longer," Josephus warned. "We must retrace our steps through narrow, winding streets and we will become easy prey once Ben Giora's men regroup."

"Yes, yes." Titus impatiently stomped toward the steps back down the north side of the great wall. Suddenly he stopped and peered down into the street of the gold merchants. "Look!" he pointed to a group of men attacking their fellow citizens. "They're killing each other!"

An aide pointed with his sword toward a savage

brawl. "The merchants swallowed bits of gold when our attack on the wall started. Those thugs are cutting the shop owner's stomach open, hoping to get at the gold."

Titus screamed, "We'll be blamed for the savagery. The common people will never surrender." He turned to an aide. "Dispatch some men to go down and kill those swine. At least we'll make it obvious that Romans won't stand for such barbarism. Make the order clear! I want no plundering of the city as we retreat. Leave the best impression we can."

"I would make one more plea to my countrymen." Josephus stood squarely in front of Titus. "If we are to make the most of this moment, I should at least go to the far end of the wall and attempt to shout to the leaders on the other side."

"Surround him carefully." Titus whipped his sword in a circling motion. "I'll take the life of the man who lets any harm come to this Jew." Titus frowned at Josephus. "Hurry. We will go on ahead." Titus hurried down the stone stairs.

Ten soldiers hustled around Josephus while he ran toward the opposite end of the wall to stand within shouting distance of the Temple Mount. The legionnaires formed a protective covering with their shields, the length of the Jew's body.

"Listen to me, you miserable creatures!" Josephus shouted across the Krytus Bridge toward the western wall. "I am Yosef Ben Mathias, priest, general of Galilee, your countryman. Have you ceased to believe in the God of our fathers Abraham, Isaac, and Jacob? Since when has the Holy One of Israel not avenged the unjust treatment of His own?"

Josephus's deep resonant voice vibrated against the stone wall and echoed down the Tyropoeon Valley. Even with the sounds of battle going on behind him, a silence settled along the edge of the western wall. Along the porticoes men seemed to be listening intensely.

"Why are you so desperate? Why do your children starve and your women crawl through the streets scratching for garbage? Can you not see the truth? Your enemy is not Rome. Have you forgotten the words of our own prophets, Isaiah and Jeremiah? You fight against the Holy One, Israel! Repent or His judgments on you will only increase. Why should you fear the likes of such despicable men as Simon Ben Giora and John of Gischala? You had best cringe in terror before the wrath of the Almighty! The hour is late but you can still save the city and the Temple. Resist and all will be lost!"

Josephus paused. There was no jeering or retaliation An eerie silence lingered. The hush carried its own poignant response.

"God maintained our cause when we were just and righteous. Defeat was always synonymous with national sin! Stop now lest the Lord use Rome as He once did Babylon. You have become more stupid than the very stones on which you stand. If not for yourself, can you not take pity on your women and children? What reason can I possibly have to say these things except to save your lives? Regardless of what is gossiped in the streets, what personal gain can I have by reminding you of the truth? Even now you hold my own family captive for no reason other than that I am despised. Hear this! I will gladly give you my own body as a sacrifice if such an offer will bring you to your senses. Spill my own blood if it can procure your preservation. Think carefully about what I say, for only you can make the decisions that will save this city."

"We can wait no longer," a soldier behind Josephus pulled at his armor. "The counterattack has already begun in the narrow alleys. We must withdraw quickly."

Josephus backed away from the edge; his face contorted in pain. As he and the soldiers ran toward the stone staircase, arrows flew in every direction. The easily invaded streets were now filling with bodies, both Jewish and Roman.

A week later Josephus watched Titus pace back and forth in front of his command tent while the legions marched into review formation in the valley below the supreme commander. *Walks just like an arrogant Roman,* he thought. *Titus struts like a true Caesar.*

Rather than the plain armor of battle, the son of Caesar wore a breastplate decorated with copper and brass eagles and flying horses. Beneath his arm he carried a dress helmet with a red horsehair plume down the center. Sword and scabbard hung from his waist. Titus still wore his dirty sagum over his shoulders. The woolen cape was the genuine symbol of a solider of the field. Although the greasy woolen texture was nearly waterproof and smelled terrible, the battered condition certified battle.

And yet Titus is as good a soldier as any man I've ever known, Josephus thought. *Young, but impressive.*

Titus kept glaring at Josephus and Marcus Quintus Cunctator. Josephus tried to maintain his natural stoic countenance.

"You assured me we could break through the foundations of the Antonia in a matter of weeks!" The young general confronted Marcus Quintus. "We are no closer to taking the Temple compound than when I led the charge into the city a week ago!"

"Sir." Marcus Quintus stood at military attention. "We did break through the foundation wall in exactly the period of time that I indicated. There simply was no way to know that John of Gischala had built a new secondary wall behind the fortification. None of the scrolls or plans indicated . . ."

"You are not meeting my timetable!" Titus slammed his helmet to the ground. "I cannot afford miscalculations. I want immediate results. Do you understand?"

Josephus carefully watched the young man nearly two decades his junior. *The most powerful army in the world is under the command of this tempestuous youth. And yet I*

*admire his brash courage. Compensates for his lack of experience
and wisdom.*

"Sir," Marcus Quintus continued, "the entire wall has
now fallen down."

"More by accident than design," the general shot
back. "The only good thing is that the improvised wall
should be easier to scale than the original. But we must
have more complete access to the Antonia. We will never
take the Temple itself until we do!"

"I have already assigned men to complete a tunnel
into the center of the fortress." Marcus's face flushed as
he explained. "Our diggings on the original wall made
a natural extension from which we continue our efforts.
It is quite possible that we might also be able to bypass
the fortress and come up inside the Temple area."

Titus suddenly turned his attention toward Josephus.
The unusually muscular quality of the lean athletic
leader was evident in his thick neck and tight jaw. His
eyes narrowed. "And I believe *you* had a prediction?"

Josephus silently returned the stare.

"Well?"

"Yes," Josephus said slowly. "I said that on the seventeenth day of Panemus which is our month of Tammuz
daily sacrifices would cease. Many reasons could create
such a disaster."

"Like our invasion?" Titus snapped.

"More like the death of the priests," Josephus answered. "Possibly no one is left to offer the sacrifices."

"What good do your predictions do if they are always
qualified!" Titus threw up his hands in disgust.

"But he said the ninth of Ab in the Jewish calendar,"
Marcus Quintus interjected, "would be the date of the
fall of the Temple."

"And you'd better be right about the time of the end!"
Titus turned away and looked down at the troops assem-
bling in proper order before him. Row after row of men
filed in behind their standards and the centurions who

led the units of one hundred. "I want that tunnel to come up inside the fortress as quickly as possible. I want men working night and day until we are inside. That's a final order!"

Marcus struck his breastplate with his fist.

Titus glared at Josephus. "When we get to the city, make one last attempt to reason with these fools. I do not want the gods to heap blame on me for the destruction of your Temple. I want every man and deity to know that I tried to avoid transgressing holy ground. If the Jews stop fighting, I will gladly spare this place, but if the battle continues everything will surely burn. Tell them these are my final terms."

Josephus bowed in humble acknowledgment. *The Lord will surely judge my people double for their obstinance.*

Titus picked up his helmet and dusted it off. Throwing the sagum over his shoulder, he stepped up on a small mound. Trumpeters blasted a call to assembly and the ranks snapped to rigid attention. Titus struck an imperial pose with his feet defiantly parted and his hand on his hips. He slowly raised his sword in the air. Instantly the legions burst into cheering and applause. The hillside around Mount Scopus rumbled with the adulation for the supreme commander.

"My fellow soldiers," Titus shouted to the troops beneath him. "The hour has come for us to make a final sweep of the city. We must move quickly and valiantly. I have called you to this place to remind you what a glorious thing it is to die bravely." His words rang far out over the valley as Titus waited for the effect to settle.

"When the Antonia Fortress falls, we take the city! The Jews completely understand this fact and know the final hour of conflict is at hand. Yes, they will fight fiercely. But Rome will not forget those who distinguish themselves at this moment. I will make the world aware of the glory of your valor."

Once again the troops shouted and began beating their swords against their shields.

"Men of virtue! Know when your souls are severed from your bodies in valiant battle. You are received immediately by the ether, the purest of all elements, and joined to the company of the courageous who live among the stars of the sky. We become good demons and posterity remembers us as heroes! On the other hand, those whose bodies waste away with age stand in danger of their souls also shriveling and shrinking into that subterranean night where all is lost. Since fate decrees that we must die, the sword is a far better instrument than any disease. To such opportunity, I add this promise. To the first man who mounts the walls of the Temple, I will blush for shame if I do not make that man envied by the rewards I bestow on him. To those who escape in this battle, I will give command over their equals. Let us not forget that the greatest rewards of all accrue for those who die in the fray!"

A black soldier named Sabinus leaped forward from the ranks. The Syrian was known to Josephus because of his reputation for valor and his unusual color in the Roman legions. The lean, thin solider raised his sword straight up in the air and he rushed forward. "I readily surrender myself for you, O Caesar!" The black solider shouted to his commander. "I will be the first to ascend the fortress wall. If I fall quickly, let none mistake that I go forward with every expectation of dying and that I have voluntarily chosen death for your sake."

The legions broke into wild applause. Josephus watched the legions swarm around the bold black man. The usual discipline of the soldiers gave way to their enthusiasm for the attack. Titus turned away with a smile.

XXV

———

Marcus Quintus stood on the edge of the north wall, watching the attack begin. Titus had chosen daybreak to gain as much sunlight as possible for a sustained attack on the inner Temple compound. Sabinus, the Syrian, led the attack on the fortress wall. Followed by eleven other soldiers, the Syrian ran through the rubble of the first wall and mounted the jutting stones of the second line of defense improvised by John of Gischala.

Immediately the Jews began shooting darts and arrows from the top of the wall. Sabinus and his cohorts held their shields above their heads as they climbed steadily upward. Legionnaires from every side surged forward behind their bold advance. Most of the arrows bounced off the shields but several men fell back when the darts hit them in the neck or face. When the legionnaires were almost halfway to the top, the defenders began pushing boulders over the edge. Roman soldiers at the bottom tried to cover themselves with their shields but the rocks were so large that no protection was adequate.

Marcus watched in astonishment when the Syrian reached the top and immediately began slashing the guards along the edge. Jews quickly fell on all sides. Although four or five of his fellow attackers were knocked off the wall by rocks, others quickly gained the

253

top next to Sabinus. The Jews were forced back from their privileged position of defense. Across the entire length of the wall, legionnaires were slowly scaling the heights. Suddenly the Syrian fell forward, apparently tripping over rocks. Immediately the Jews focused their darts on his prostrate body. By the time Sabinus recovered, his body was covered with the deadly little arrows. Although he tried to fight off the attackers, the slip had already proven fatal. However, when the Jews rushed forward to trample Sabinus's body, Julian, a centurion from Bithynia, cleared the top of the wall and charged toward the attackers. The soles of Julian's shoes were filled with sharp nails to help create traction on the rocks. He lunged into the Jews surrounding his fallen comrade and cut two of them down with one swath. Julian threw his weight behind his shield and knocked another Jew down. The centurion's next thrust caught the man in front of him squarely in the chest. Without stopping, the Roman pushed on, leaving Sabinus's body behind him.

Marcus Quintus waited until more reinforcements were mounting the top of the wall before giving the signal to his troops, waiting to enter the tunnel underneath the Antonia Fortress. "You are sure the final breakthrough will only take a matter of minutes?" he asked his aide.

"We are just beneath the Temple's stones," the soldier assured him. "I am sure that we have cut around the corner of the Antonia and will come up inside the corner of the Court of the Gentiles as soon as we drop the roadway."

"I trust you are correct," Marcus Quintus answered cynically. "No errors will be tolerated. Titus is to be informed of every phase of the battle. Give the order for our men to attack with all haste. Make sure the command is relayed back to Titus." Marcus tightened the helmet on his head and made sure the metal flaps covered the sides of his face. Automatically he felt for his sword at his side. Wrapping his sagum around his arms, he prepared to leave the wall and direct the attack that within minutes should open the Temple to the Romans.

Marcus could see the ladders placed beneath the western wall of the Temple Mount. Battering rams lumbered slowly toward the exterior support wall. Lines of soldiers stood poised ready to mount an assault on the porticoes lining the western wall. Other Roman soldiers kept pouring over the wall around the Antonia. Finally Marcus Quintus studied his own men as they clambored into the tunnel. Each part of the strategy was unfolding with precision. He shook his head sadly and rushed toward the entrance.

Even in the depths of the tunnel Marcus could hear the roar of the battle overhead. The rumble of movement and the cries of attack penetrated the black passages while his men quietly marched forward. By the time Marcus reached the other end, the pavement stones had been dropped into the tunnel, allowing a quick entry for the first troops. The exiting Romans immediately circled the hole, protecting those following them. As more legionnaires popped out the ring of protection expanded. Marcus Quintus climbed out into the center of the circle and the thick of the fray. Hand-to-hand combat was so fierce that the clash of swords against shields was deafening.

We must secure our position, Marcus reasoned. *If the Jews force us back down the tunnel, it may be impossible to ever get up again. Even if we must fight in a circle all night, we cannot let them overpower us.*

Abruptly a soldier fell backward with a spear rammed through his body. Marcus Quintus leaped to plug the hole in their defense but another foot soldier rushed past the primus pilus, forcing his shield into the breach in the line.

A smell of smoke caught Marcus's attention. He

looked back toward the high towers of the Antonia Fortress, peering through the constantly changing pattern of openings between his men's shields. Near the far columns a burly man with wild black hair was waving men toward the porticoes on the north side that joined the Antonia. When the man bellowed his commands, he exposed the side of his toothless mouth.

Simon Ben Giora! Marcus Quintus recognized the leader. *If we could just get him! Ben Giora must have been forced to join forces with John of Gischala.* He yelled into the tunnel, "Tell Titus we have established ourselves. Send me archers! I need bowmen as quickly as we can get them up here."

Marcus watched in amazement as Ben Giora's men rushed forward with torches and began burning their own porticoes adjoining the Fortress. The Jews ran underneath the stone columns holding their torches to the wooden ceiling above them. In the dry heat of summer, the roof of the portico instantly burst into flames. Quickly the fire spread toward the fortress, licking up the sides of the granite walls. As the smoldering timbers fell down, the Jews began breaking the support columns apart, completely disconnecting the covering from the Antonia.

"They are going to make us fight for every cubit of this place," the primus pilus said grimly to a soldier next to him. "This will be one bloody fight. Tell our men to hold their ground. We cannot retreat."

Marcus shaded his eyes, casting a glance overhead. The intense heat of late summer burned mercilessly down on the endless struggle. He swallowed hard. The salty sweat running down the back of his neck only made him more aware of how dry his mouth had become. "Get water up here!" he called down into the tunnel. "I want relief for the front line! Fresh soldiers move into place!"

New legionnaires worked their way into the thick of

the fray, allowing their comrades to slip back and refresh themselves. Marcus drank quickly as the water came up. *We have clearly established ourselves. Troops should be coming up the western wall at any moment and the Jews will be forced to fight on three fronts.* At that moment he realized the enemy had come to the same conclusion.

Ben Giora's men were also running beneath the cloisters on the western wall, spreading dried straw and hay along the walkway. Other soldiers were pouring pitch and bitumen over the highly flammable grass. As soon as the Roman assault ladders appeared above the roof line the Jews torched the straw. By the time Roman soldiers covered the roof line, the cloisters were an inferno. Legionnaires plunged through the burning roof into the tar and were immediately devoured by unquenchable flames.

A few soldiers were able to avoid the burning roof planks, but they were soon trapped on the marble lintels decorating the cloisters. At once the Jews began taunting the soldiers with offers of security if they would surrender. Marcus recognized Longus, a soldier well-known for his valor. The Roman was hopelessly caught on the narrow ledge with no way back to the ladders.

Longus lifted his sword into the air and cried, "For the glory of Rome and Caesar!" With one quick thrust, he plunged his sword into the opening beneath his armor. With the sword protruding from his abdomen, he tumbled forward to the pavement at the feet of the astonished Jews.

At that moment the sound of the pounding of the battering rams against the western wall began. Each blow shook the entire area. Soon the machines hammered away in a steady rhythm, creating the sensation of an approaching earthquake. Like a repetitious note, the battering became an ongoing staccato beneath the chorus of swords striking shields. Voices screamed in defiance while men died in great agony. A symphony of pain arose above the Mount of God and settled over the city like a pall. Smoke from the burning porticoes and cloisters rose like an enormous funeral pyre.

Everywhere Marcus Quintus looked men were covered with blood. Bodies were pulled back to make room for new combat. Injured Roman soldiers were hustled down the dark tunnel for medical attention, but the battle did not diminish in intensity or fury. Sweat and soot lined Marcus's face with ugly black streaks and grimy splotches. Whatever toll the furious intensity of the sun added was not evident in the relentless battle.

Marcus Quintus calculated the movement of the sun, knowing that another legion had now begun work undermining the northern gate of the Temple. The Jews could do nothing to stop the steady Roman advance toward the silver-covered doors that led into the Temple proper. Marcus knew it was time to return to Titus and make a full report. His men would hold the line.

Titus stood in full battle attire before his temporary headquarters in the new city. The thick sagum was gone. Beads of perspiration stood out on his forehead and his sinewy arms were wet. While guards circled the general and his staff of five aides, he watched the smoke curl up from porticoes. Marcus stood at attention waiting to be recognized.

"Cunctator," the commander barked. "How do we stand?"

"We are in the place called the Court of the Gentiles. They will not be able to drive us out."

"H . . . m . . . m, good. What about the fires?"

"They are burning every possible connecting link to the inside of the Temple compound. Suicide. Sheer stupidity."

"A stiff-necked lot!" Titus raised his eyebrow and

spoke from the corner of his mouth. "I believe that was Josephus's description of our people." The general turned to one of the soldiers. "Bring them in now. I want you to hear these reports, Cunctator. The end has to be near."

The guard brought two grisly looking Jewish soldiers from the back of the house. The men were scarred, dirty, and battered.

"Tell me again who you are," Titus demanded.

"Archelaus, son of Magadatus," the shorter of the two men answered. He was extremely dark-skinned and bedraggled.

"Ananuus from Emmaus," the other added. His eyes were deep set and twitched like a cornered animal. The ugly man had thick lips and his front teeth were gone. "I am the chief guard to Simon Ben Giora."

"What is it you seek?" Titus folded his arms across his chest.

"We are friends of Rome," Ananuus smiled ingratiatingly. "We offer our services to defeat Simon Ben Giora."

"And you are his chief guard?" Titus mockingly raised his eyebrows. "His friend, too."

"We heard of the offer of clemency." Archelaus began to bow. "If we help you assassinate Ben Giora, we thought Rome would have a special place for us."

"Special place?" Titus pursed his lips and smiled at his aides. "And why did you not come forth weeks ago when we could have prevented all of this bloodshed?"

Both men looked at each other, momentarily stunned.

"I think your people have reached the place where even fools can see the obvious." Titus's countenance abruptly changed. "And you are certainly fools. Do you think we've not already tasted enough Jewish tricks to recognize the likes of you?"

"But . . . but," Ananuus protested, "I am a confidant of the general Ben Giora himself."

"I think we've heard of this man." Titus turned to Marcus Quintus.

"Yes." Marcus glowered at the pair. "Assassins all right. Ananuus was in charge of killing the high priests who wanted to defect to our side. He also murdered the scribe of the Great Sanhedrin. They are treachery personified."

Titus stroked his clean-shaven cheeks and rubbed his chin. "The likes of the two of you give the human race a bad name. We can defeat your people without assistance. Both sides of this conflict will be well served by your demise." Titus turned to the guard. "Execute them at once!"

"Wait . . . ," Ananuus held out his hands.

"Mercy!" Archelaus dropped to his knees.

"Lop off their heads!" Titus clapped his hands and pointed toward the back of the house. "Quickly."

The guards dragged the two protesting men away.

"Any other reports?" Titus turned to the men around him.

An aide beckoned for other guards to bring a beggar out. Equally dirty and tattered, the man was frail with sunken cheeks. His eye sockets were hollow and gray. The elderly man's arms hung limply at his side.

"I think you should hear this report." The aide roughly pushed the old man forward. "Let 'em hear what you saw in the city. Tell the commander how things are."

"Your name?" Titus snapped.

"Phineas," he mumbled. His eyes were glazed as if his mind were out of focus. "Phineas of Jerusalem."

"Conditions difficult?" Titus asked arrogantly.

Slowly Phineas looked up but his eyes didn't quite make contact. He seemed to be seeing something lodged in his mind. "Famine . . . starvation . . . ruin." He shook his head. "Horrible things happen to people when . . ."

"Feed him." Titus motioned to the guard. "Feed the

beggar and send him back into the city to share the story of our generosity as well."

The soldier led the dazed man away.

Titus ground his teeth. "The attack is not to stop until the Temple is burned to the ground and every soldier of Simon Ben Giora is dead or in chains. Show no mercy to those who resist us!"

XXVI

Yevnah simmered in the heat of late summer. Yochanan Ben Zakkai and his band of scholars gathered to debate, every day except the Sabbath. Their more than occasionally loud arguments were the only significant disruption in the otherwise sleepy village.

The Sabbath now past, the rabbis began again. By the end of the morning the entire group was irritated. Perspiration dotted their foreheads. The smell of the ancient abode of pigeons increased with the temperature. Mingled with the human scent permeating every stitch of clothing, the smell and smallness of the pigeon house only added to the agitation. In spite of the odor, the men were hungry.

"I say all synagogues must be purged!" Malchor continued to demand. "We must have nothing to do with followers of false messiahs, particularly Yeshua Ben Yosef. Many of the Christian sect still frequent synagogues."

"The time has come for a moratorium on talk of messiahs." Yochanan Ben Zakkai shook his fist angrily. "The trouble all started with—" he abruptly stopped.

"But if the messiah had defeated the Romans," Gamaliel immediately took advantage of the pause, "then the so-called extremists would have been justified in their hopes for a messianic intervention."

The old man cringed and tightly squinted his good eye.

"But the messiah didn't come," Perez spoke quickly. "That's the only point that is relevant. Speculation got us nowhere."

"But . . ." Gamaliel raised his hand in objection.

"No!" Ben Zakkai barked. "You listen. Have you grasped nothing that I have been explaining about the prophet Jeremiah's message? Armed rebellion has never accomplished anything. Adonai's deliverance will come in His own time. It is foolishness to suggest our own military solutions. The Holy One of Israel will vindicate us when our cause is righteous. If such is not the case, we cannot escape His wrath. Rome prevailed because the Gentiles were the tools of God's judgment. That's the end of it!" The old man pounded on the table with his fist. "The time has come for us to learn to pray for the peace of every nation where our people reside. Forget the talk of messiahs rising up with swords and armies!"

Gamaliel sunk back into his chair and looked down at the dirt floor.

"If such is the case," Malchor asked timidly, "doesn't collaboration with Rome become acceptable?"

Yochanan Ben Zakkai's good eye suddenly opened and he smiled for the first time. "Yes, such follows." He held up his finger instructively. "The issue is not collaboration but the acceptable limits of collaboration. One must avoid the extremes of being either a traitor or a fool. Such is the lesson we have learned from the Zealots, Sicarii, and the likes of Simon Ben Giora."

"Another example, please?" An old man in the back asked respectfully. "Has anyone properly understood the boundaries of collaboration?"

"Yosef Ben Mathias," Ben Zakkai answered immediately. "Josephus was maligned in the back streets of Jerusalem and yet his efforts to save his people were tireless. Josephus is not to be counted as coward or traitor for his attempts to work with the Almighty's judgment upon our nation."

Gamaliel squirmed uncomfortably in his chair and looked out the open window.

"And that is why you petitioned Rome to recognize us as an academy and a court to be overseers for the religion of our people?" Perez asked.

"Exactly!"

The group nodded agreement.

"It is not even permissible to anticipate reconstruction of the Temple?" Gamaliel asked more in disgust than inquiry.

A trickle of sweat ran down Yochanan's cheek. The old man slowly wiped the side of his head with his hand and sighed. "If the Holy One wants a temple, He will raise it up about the ashes, but I do not expect to see such in my lifetime, your lifetime, or your children's children's lifetime." He pronounced each word very carefully. "The . . . Temple . . . is gone . . . gone. The priests are gone forever. The Sadducees will not return; the Zealots are dead; and, thank God, the fanatic Sicarii are dead!"

Ben Zakkai held up his hands to the heavens and then dropped them. "The Essenes are gone and the Samaritans are virtually gone. Unfortunately only the Christian sect seems to have survived. We must reconstruct on the basis of what is left, not what might be. Do you understand? Only the rabbis remain."

"Please," Gamaliel sounded apologetic and defensive, "Your conclusion suggests that we will be forced to live in a world dominated by Gentiles."

"We have no alternative," Ben Zakkai spoke firmly. "But, paradoxically, we must also turn our back on their culture and teach our children to avoid their ways. We must huddle together as islands of righteousness in a defiled world. However, let us not be naive or simplistic. Their world is not entirely corrupt. There are some righteous Gentiles."

"How would we recognize them?" Gamaliel asked cynically.

"I believe the laws of Noah are the solution," Ben Zakkai concluded. "If the Gentiles keep the minimal requirements given to Noah and avoid idolatry, they are acceptable in the sight of the Holy One."

"Noah's six laws!" Perez explained.

"Seven laws," Gamaliel corrected him.

"Six!" Malchor insisted.

"Seven!" Gamaliel persisted.

"Gentlemen! Gentlemen!" an old man in the back waved his hands. "I believe the time has come to eat. Let us dine and rest. Perhaps our differences will settle with the food."

Yochanan stood and lifted his arms in the familiar stance of prayer. "*Birkat ha minim.*" He prayed a benediction to destroy all heretics.

The rabbis filed out through the vineyard, arguing as they walked toward the inn in the middle of Yevnah. Once inside the packed dining room, servants provided basins for foot and hand washing. Because of crowding, the rabbis sat together around one long table rather than reclining as was usual for formal meals. They only ate food appropriate for mourning. The bread, hard boiled eggs, and lentils were quickly set before them in clay bowls. After the blessing, they ate in silence as they sought personal reprieve from their constant debates. Other men came and went eating the regular kosher food, fruits, and vegetables. Little was said to the solitary cluster of scholars lost in their personal preoccupations.

The owner of the inn had just brought in a bowl of honey and dates for sweetening the food when the front door flew open. A battered and disheveled stranger looked wildly about the room, his face was sunken and arms were shriveled. The dirty, forlorned man was obviously starving. Leaning forward on a crutch made from a tree branch, his long outer haluk hung limply from his shoulders. The dark brown cloak was torn and shredded around the edges. Underneath, his white linen kolbur was so soiled it looked gray. Dark blotches of blood had dried in ugly brown stains. The man slumped against the doorway to keep from falling.

Talking ceased as all eyes turned toward the door. "It's over," the stranger croaked. "The Temple is no more. Adonai has abandoned his people." The raspy voice faded and the man tumbled forward.

Perez leaped forward. Immediately the other rabbis followed. The man's brown, matted beard was pushed aside to feel for the pulse in his neck.

Ben Zakkai gently lifted a gold chain concealed by the dirty beard and scraggly hair. "This man is no beggar," he said quietly. "Feel the quality of his kolbur."

Other men from across the room quickly helped lift the traveler to a chair. The innkeeper put a cold towel on his forehead. Slowly the man opened his eyes, staring blankly at the ceiling. Only after a little wine was poured into his mouth did coherence begin to return.

"Haven't eaten in weeks," he mumbled. "I thought I'd never get out."

"Where did you come from?" Perez asked gently.

"Jerusalem," he sighed. "The Holy City . . . everything is gone."

"You saw the end?" the innkeeper asked.

"I was there." The stranger's eyes gradually focused. "I saw the Temple burn. The city is being torn to the ground."

"When?" one of the townspeople pressed forward. "When did the city fall?"

"Give the man breathing room." Yochanan Ben Zakkai pushed the crowd back. "Open the door. Get more ventilation in here." Ben Zakkai sat down commandingly in front of the pale stranger. "Speak slowly. You are among friends. Do you need something to eat before you begin?"

The Fall of Jerusalem

"Oh yes." The frail fingers closed around Ben Zakkai's arm. "A little bread would be wonderful."

Ben Zakkai snapped his fingers. "A small piece. If he eats too quickly or too much he'll be sick. Someone prepare a light meat broth."

The man seized the piece of bread.

"Easy, friend," Ben Zakkai comforted him. "Not too much for now. Tell us. Who are you?"

"Judas." He reached out for more food. "Judas Ben Merto. I have been a merchant . . . cloth . . . for years."

Perez handed him another small piece of bread. "What did you see?"

"I am a pious man," he began slowly. "I went up to the Temple one last time. Even with the battle . . . I thought to worship in the holy place one last time. I got caught in the struggle and couldn't escape." He rubbed his temples slowly for a few minutes. "The battering rams continued day and night, but they did not crack the western wall. Somehow we . . . the Jews . . . started a fire that spread to the Temple. The Romans began to burn the outer gates and the molten silver spread the fire everywhere. Everything! The cloisters, the great doors, the Temple began to burn! We were covered by fire everywhere!" Judas Ben Merto sank back in his chair.

"Do you remember the day, the month?" Ben Zakkai asked.

"The tenth day. The tenth of Ab."

Ben Zakkai looked intensely at each of his disciples. "And what was my prediction? The very same day the Babylonians burned the Temple!"

"As the fire became more intense, our men rushed against the Roman soldiers encamped in the Court of the Gentiles. The press of our forces and the panic was so great that I thought we would overwhelm the legion, but reinforcements came from the Antonia Fortress and the slaughter began. Bodies piled up everywhere. Many of our people were so weak they could no longer fight. The Romans cut their throats immediately. Bodies were heaped along the steps up to the altar, around the altar, and on top of it. Blood flowed like rain water. The Romans went crazy cutting us down like ripe wheat waiting for the harvest."

"You escaped?" Gamaliel probed.

"I'm no soldier." Judas shook his head. "Fortunately I don't even look like a possibility. People ran past me. I hid behind a column and watched. An arrow hit the calf of my leg. Went right through but didn't hit the bone. I pulled the shaft out. Finally, I slipped in among a pile of bodies and didn't move until long after the battle was over. Even after the fight stopped I could hear the people in the city wailing in mourning for the demise of the Holy House."

"Everything burned?" Ben Zakkai asked.

"The Romans raided the Treasury House. Carried off the gold, money, priests' robes . . . everything. Then they burned the building as well. Yes, everything was torn to the ground. When the defeat was complete, the Romans brought their ensigns into the Temple. They set them up by the eastern gate and offered sacrifices to their standards on our holy altar."

"The abomination of desolation!" Ben Zakkai exploded. "Just as I foresaw! The prophecy of Daniel fulfilled twice!"

"A few of the priests were caught in the caves beneath the Temple. When they were hauled before Titus, the commander berated the priests for resisting his pleas to surrender and for burning their own Temple. He decreed they should die with the Temple. I think the entire priesthood is gone."

"Was anything saved from the Temple?" an old man lamented.

"Yeshua Ben Thebuthus, a son of one of the priests,

bargained for his life. Titus gave clemency in return for the treasures.

"Ben Thebuthus gave the Romans the great candlesticks, the gold cisterns, and the vials. He brought out of the repository the veils and the garments covered with precious stones. The cinnamon and cassia with the other spices mixed to make the incense offering were seized by the Romans. They tore down the great veil that divided off the holy of holies and took it away. The pride of Israel is in the hands of our enemies."

"And the people?" a rabbi asked hesitantly.

"There is still some fighting in the Upper City but everything is almost finished. The rumor is the Romans saved the best of our young men to take to Rome for the triumphal parade. Others will be sent to the mines in Egypt or be used as gladiators. Generally, the aged and the sick were killed."

"But you are here?" Yochanan asked suspiciously.

"I lay on the Temple's stones for two days. At the darkest hour of night I slowly dragged myself toward the steps that led out of the Temple compound. By the grace of the Almighty, no one paid attention to me. I hid in the Lower City and then stole away in the night. Only Adonai knows how I reached this place."

"Do you know what became of Simon Ben Giora and John of Gischala?" Yochanan continued.

The stranger only shook his head and shrugged in consternation.

"Dead?" Yochanan probed.

"I just don't know.."

"And the Master Scroll? The canon?" Ben Zakkai pulled at his beard. "The supreme scroll in the Temple from which we measure all readings of the Torah? What happened?"

"I don't know either," the traveler's eyes clouded and he looked at the floor. "Gone, I'm sure. Probably burned."

The rabbis gasped. Several men's knees buckled. Yochanan Ben Zakkai buried his face in his hands.

"The Romans will not stop until the entire city is torn down," Judas concluded. "All hope is gone."

The villagers stared in shock at the forlorn, broken traveler. No one seemed capable of speaking. Finally the one-eyed sage rose to his feet. "It is time for us to go back to work." Ben Zakkai beckoned his disciples to follow. He walked across the room and slowly opened the door. He looked very tired and old. "Come, friends, we have much work to do."

XXVII

YEVNAH. SPRING A.D. 71

The morning sunlight bathed Yochanan's wrinkled, tired face. He dozed in and out, reclining against the side of his house in Yevnah. Dreams, memories, and images intermingled in a tapestry of reflections. The invigorating spring breezes made him feel like a boy again. Recollection returned of chasing his older brothers, Zeda and Jarius, through the winding alleys of Jerusalem. Once again he thought of himself as Simeon, the youngest of the Ben Aarons.

The pleasant glow dissolved into the dim of lost consciousness and sleep. The little jewelry shop reappeared in his dream. The building was new and in good repair, the display table filled with wonderful creations. He was on one side of the room trying to walk over to Jarius working with his back to Simeon. No matter how hard Simeon tried, he couldn't get close enough to touch Jarius. The dream dissolved painfully, leaving him feeling empty.

Simeon Ben Aaron was gone and only Yochanan Ben Zakkai remained . . . alone . . . solitary . . . singular . . . depleted . . lonely. Everything looked blurred. He rubbed his good eye and blinked several times. Before him stood a lovely young creature, small and slight. Her raven hair hung down the middle of her back. Only the Master Sculptor could have molded such an exquisite face with its petite nose and perfect mouth. Radiant olive

271

skin framed her sparkling black eyes. "Uncle?" the small voice asked.

Ben Zakkai blinked again and squinted. No, the hair was streaked and nearly gray. The face lined and the black eyes more deeply set. The slender grace of flowing line and perfect proportion was all there, but the forehead far more wrinkled.

"Uncle? You're still asleep?"

"Mariam!" Yochanan shook his head to clear his mind. "I'm afraid I stayed up much too long at the Passover last night. A little too much wine, perhaps." He stretched his arms.

"I'm sorry to disturb you, but Zeda and I must start back to Pella soon. Ishmael is helping him load the donkey with our baggage. The journey is so long. I'm just glad we could be together one more time."

The old man shook his head wearily. "A great blessing for me. I'm glad for this last minute alone." He beckoned for his niece to sit down next to him. "Does Zeda still seek the Ben Ephraim family?"

"Yes," Mariam sighed. "He has not given up hope. The Ben Aaron family is a persistent lot. We are tenacious in our commitments, our affections . . . and our beliefs."

Yochanan nodded solemnly.

"The last time we were together we spoke of lost dreams. Uncle, have you recovered hope?"

The old man pulled at his beard and chewed on his lip. "Yes," he said slowly, "we are finding our way to a new place where hope is possible once more. The Holy One of Israel has graciously given me a task to help our people survive."

"Are we still numbered among *your* people?" Mariam asked.

"We are family," Ben Zakkai shrugged.

"Are we?" Mariam smiled thinly. "I sense your colleagues are very uncomfortable around us. They avoid speaking when you are not present."

Ben Zakkai scratched the dust with the toe of his old worn sandal. "The old world is gone. Everything has been rearranged by the Romans, the war, your new belief—even by the Lord Himself. The path is not easy to find."

"And these men have become your family," Mariam observed. "You have reconstructed your world in this place."

"I had no other choice," Yochanan concluded. "And have you done any differently?"

Mariam shook her head, trying to keep her composure and smile. "I suppose it was inevitable that we would have to take different paths in the road. I care not what they call us . . . Believers, Christians, heretics . . . you will always be my Uncle Simeon."

"We must try to keep touching."

Mariam squeezed his hand. "Do you still hold on to the old ways? The old beliefs?"

"Somewhat. Of course, we still believe in the final resurrection of the dead and the eternal covenant with Israel. We emphasize justice and the efficacy of repentance, but the Temple and the sacrifices are gone. In the place of making offerings, we substitute righteous deeds. On Yom Kippur we replace oblations with righting relationships and doing good deeds." He turned to his niece. "And you? Have your convictions changed?"

"No," Mariam tried not to sound defensive. "We still believe Yeshua is the Messiah. But we have reinstituted the meaning of the sacrifices in the Temple. We believe the offering of Yeshua on the cross was a once and for all sacrifice for sin. Yeshua is our great high priest. When we receive His cup, atonement is once again made for us."

Yochanan sighed deeply and shook his head. He

wrung his hands and looked away. "Incomprehensible," he muttered.

"We take the old ways very seriously," Mariam tried to explain. "The Torah is sacred scripture. Of course, we keep all the kosher laws."

"Rabbi! Rabbi!" a boy shouted. The innkeeper's son ran toward Ben Zakkai's house. "Important men are here to speak with you," he called. "Please come to the inn!"

"I wonder who." Ben Zakkai slowly rose to his feet. "Let us go see."

The old man felt relieved. Their conversation had been interrupted at just the right moment. He wanted Mariam and Zeda to leave without confrontation. He held Mariam's arm as they hurried after the young boy. "Perhaps someone has come with more information on conditions in Jerusalem."

When they entered, Yochanan's good eye couldn't adjust at first to the dim light inside the inn. For a moment he was blind.

"My good friend!" a familiar voice boomed. "You are alive and well!"

A large shape loomed before Ben Zakkai. "Yes?" He reached out groping for a hand to shake. "It's me! Josephus!"

"You've survived!" Yochanan threw his arms around the strong shoulders. "Thank the Almighty you are here! Alive and well!"

"Ah, the Master of the Torah." Josephus stepped back. "You never age."

Ben Zakkai laughed, his sight adjusting to the room. "You were always clever with words. Welcome to our humble surroundings in Yevnah."

"Marcus Quintus Cunctator!" Mariam exclaimed.

Only then did Yochanan look around the room. A Roman soldier sat at a table in front of him. The local men had left. The innkeeper stood apprehensively in the rear.

"Mariam!" The soldier stood up. "Mariam Ben Aaron!"

"You know each other?" Josephus gawked.

"This woman and her son saved my life!" Marcus Quintus bowed profoundly at the waist and extended his arms to Mariam. "They have instructed me in the ways of the Christus."

Ben Zakkai looked on, dumbfounded as his niece gently kissed the soldier on the cheek.

"Peace to you, Marcus Quintus," Mariam beamed. "God has graciously granted us another meeting."

"You are here together?" Ben Zakkai looked back and forth from the Roman to Josephus.

"Indeed." Josephus pointed to the table and gestured for them to sit down. "We traveled here just to talk to the new rabbi who is preserving our heritage. To see *you*, Ben Zakkai."

"Why?"

"To tell you that your rabbis are now recognized by Rome as the duly constituted authority for religious matters in this land!" Josephus slapped Ben Zakkai on the back. "Titus himself smiles on you, and Caesar recognizes you with favor. Yochanan, you have outlived them all. Rome has granted you special status."

"Praise the Holy One!" Ben Zakkai held his hands up. "You did receive my special communiqué."

"My friend Marcus Quintus and I eat at the table of Titus." Josephus continued. "The request was easy to fulfill. I simply explained who you are and that you had the good sense to leave the city."

"Someone must restore order," Marcus Quintus continued. "I brought a letter from the emperor certifying you as our recognized envoy in religious matters. The court you hold here will be considered religious law.

Similar scrolls will be sent around the country, indicating you have replaced the Great Sanhedrin."

Yochanan pounded his fist against his palm and beamed. "I am deeply gratified. Thank you. Thank you, Josephus. You have been a true friend."

"No," the Jewish general boomed across the small room. "You have been the true friend. I am well aware that when all Israel turned away from me, Yochanan Ben Zakkai stood fast and understood. What I have done for you is a small matter compared to the gratitude I carry in my heart for your steadfastness."

"And you?" Mariam asked hesitantly. "Marcus Quintus? Do you still believe in the things we taught you?"

The Roman reached to his neck and pulled out a gold cross from beneath his leather breastplate. "I still have many questions to ask, but I stand in this way. What I have seen in the last few months has left no doubt in my mind. The way of love is the only hope in this world of madness."

"Is it over?" Mariam probed. "Is the war over now?"

"Not quite," the soldier continued. "Herodium and Machaerus are still centers of resistance. We are pressing the battle on toward Masada, but the great city has fallen. We will soon rebuild it to our specifications." Marcus shook his head sadly. "The fate of this land is sealed. Only death reigns supreme in your Holy City."

"Do you have any idea how many died?" Ben Zakkai asked haltingly.

"By the end of the siege, their soldiers were very angry, often irrational, and indiscriminate in their killing." Josephus's voice flattened as if all emotion had long since been squashed. "The rabble were slaughtered but so were many of the sick and elderly. Young men were herded inside the walls of the Court of the Women on the Temple Mount. At least eleven thousand starved to death during their imprisonment." He reported, "After the fall of the Temple over two thousand people committed suicide. I estimate at least one million three hundred thousand were killed in this war."

Yochanan sunk down in his chair. "What about insurrectionist, the Zealots . . . John of Gischala and Simon Ben Giora?"

Marcus Quintus answered, "Most of the leaders fell in the caves beneath the Temple. They took a great deal of treasure with them, but you can't eat gold. John was finally starved out and surrendered. Simon put up a better fight but was finally taken alive."

"What will become of them? Mariam asked.

"John of Gischala will die in prison," Marcus continued. "Ben Giora will be taken to Rome to march through the streets in Titus's triumph, after which the old tyrant will be put to death in the forum. Unfortunately many of your youth will become gladiators in places like Caesarea-by-the-Sea and across the empire. No small number will end up in the Colosseum in Rome."

"Marcus," Mariam spoke cautiously, "we once spoke to you about the Ben Ephraim family, my son's betrothed. Did you . . . I mean was there any word or . . ."

"I'm sorry." Marcus Quintus shook his head. "I asked many times but no one remembered the name, the family. I deeply regret that I couldn't help your son."

Marcus slowly removed his helmet and put the red-plumed headgear on the table. "I came here because I was in trouble with the emperor and had a chance to redeem myself in this war. I have. I go back a hero. Nero is dead and my friends rule the empire. I suppose I should believe in the ultimate victory of Rome in all things." He looked at the table and rapped gently with his knuckles.

No one spoke.

"But I also came here in search of truth. I came here to find out about this one called the Prince of Peace." The soldier's eyes clouded. "When I think of the loss of this innocent girl your son loved and the other million that died, my heart hangs heavy in my breast. I want no more killing. I find no joy in watching slaves kill each other for sport. Unless the Roman world finds a messiah, the injustice and tyranny of wickedness will go on without end. I *must* believe in your Christus if I am ever to find harmony and tranquility. I go back to share His story with any who will listen."

Ben Zakkai shook his head in disbelief. "A messiah for Romans?"

"For all of our conquests, Rome is sick at heart," the soldier answered. "You struggle with the ignominy of defeat and we with the excesses of victory, but the need is the same. We both crave someone to do for us what we cannot do for ourselves. Is that not what your Messiah means? If truly there is only one God and He gave you this promise, how can it not also be for the rest of the world?"

The old rabbi pulled at his beard and stared at the Roman soldier. Only a low guttural moan slipped out.

"The world turns on another axis now, Yochanan," Josephus added. "Once we thought the center of the universe was in Jerusalem. Rome is the center of all things now. If I am to be of any value to our people, I must go to Rome. Things are different . . . forever."

"Help our people?" Yochanan grimaced. "I don't see how?"

"Bitter hostility will follow this war. Jews will make good scapegoats for Roman anger. I must explain who we are before the wrath of the world is continually dumped on our descendants."

"Who could ever have believed our paths would lead in such opposite directions?" Ben Zakkai threw his hands up in the air. "The ways of the Holy One are unfathomable. They will bury me in Yevnah and you in Rome, both exiled from our beloved city. Josephus, we are men of intelligence but neither mind nor will has been able to bend this road we have walked down."

"Only God controls the weather and the future," Josephus concluded. "Unfortunately we must be on our way north to the port at Caesarea. I will catch the next ship out for Rome. Marcus Quintus will stay awhile longer."

"Perhaps, you will come and visit us in Pella?" Mariam asked quickly.

"I had that exact thought in mind." The primus pilus smiled. "Yes, I had already made such plans. In the late summer, I think."

"Wonderful!" Mariam clapped her hands. "We will be honored to have you among us."

Marcus Quintus pulled a scroll out from beneath his sagum and laid it on the table. "This is the authorization of Caesar to continue your work. The document is signed by none other than Titus himself. Treasure the decree. As long as you have this signatory no one will trouble you." The Roman stood up. "I'm sorry but we must hurry on."

Yochanan looked intensely at his old friend. "I will not see you again in this life, Yosef Ben Mathias. Like everything else solid and stable in my world, you are about to vanish in the air. I've never learned to accept the pain of the inevitable."

Josephus threw his arms around his old friend and hugged him tightly. "Let history note that the last true Sadducee and Pharisee parted friends. We will both do our best for our people. What more can any man offer?"

Yochanan returned the hug and turned away. He did not look as the two men rode away. Mariam quietly watched from the window.

"Ah, Zeda and Ishmael are coming now with the donkey," she finally broke the silence. "I'm afraid we, too, must be on our way."

"Regrettably," he answered without looking up. "How is it that the very things that bring so much delight can leave such profound anguish? Families are the source of our highest joy and deepest pain. When we split apart a piece of our soul is lost."

"Uncle . . ." Mariam reached out her hand but couldn't quite touch his. "We have such a hard time living together, but we can't live without each other. We both are seeking the way of the Lord but we have ended up on opposite sides of the street. It seems we both can't be right, but neither can we both be wrong."

"The mystery of incompleteness," Yochanan slowly turned around. "Neither of us is a finished work. We are still creations of gold waiting for the final touch of the Master Artisan. We both wait for a messiah."

Mariam shook her head. "Yes, we must remember that neither of us is the enemy. In this hostile world we need each other."

Ben Zakkai smiled. "Yes, we both remain people of the covenant."